A TRUTH

THAT WHISPERS

LIES

Copyright © 2025 by Joyce Harrington

ISBN eBook: 979-8-218-82473-0
ISBN Print: 979-8-218-74272-0

Published by Wild Dandelion Books

First edition October 2025.

Book design by Laura Boyle.

A TRUTH THAT WHISPERS LIES

A WILD DANDELION STORY

JOYCE HARRINGTON

To all the wild dandelions.

PART 1

ONE

MANY PEOPLE IN my community knew me. Few, however, liked me.

Perhaps I should say "genuinely" liked me. For the most part, I was known as Nicolette—my government name. My mom was told she couldn't have children, so naming me "Victory to the People" was her testament to women's ability to create beauty in the midst of sorrow. The name implied I stood for something powerful or meaningful, but with each passing year, that impossible expectation deflated.

Why couldn't Mama have named me "Jane" or something equally bland that blended in with the crowd? No one expected a Jane to have soaring ambitions. She faded into the background like a foggy landscape behind the hills, neatly tucked away and protected by the bolder, brighter shades surrounding her. If given the choice, I'd have faded into the background. I'd also have chosen to be called Nikki, not that most residents of the Bright Lakes Residential Community—my home since childhood—cared.

Maureen was an exception, and I was beyond lucky to have her as a real friend. Her laugh was mesmerizing. She didn't offer it freely, but when she did, her whole body joined the chorus. Bowed over at the waist, hands on knees, head tipped back—the rich and expansive melody was raw happiness poured out, inviting everyone's full participation. Within our religious community, her laugh was a daring invitation to steep in untapped joy.

Our friendship was a gold mine, and the proceeds from it made my soul rich. Reen and I accepted one another exactly as we were. Unlike the Pillars – the nosey matrons of our Faith - who decided to size us up during weekly Service. Reen and I would dissect every ounce of our annoyance from their brutal inspection, sharing what we wish we said in the moment then vowing to be unbothered the next time it happened.

Because it would happen again.

When it came to younger women, the Pillars had unceasing demands and harsh criticisms on wardrobe, hair, behavior… even posture. *A respectable lady should walk with a balance of elegance and modesty, not like a quarterback.* Amongst other things, an undignified laugh like Reen's wasn't socially acceptable and I wasn't exempt to their scrutiny. Being single at twenty-two yielded the same attention as a crying infant during Service. I definitely deserved a degree in fake smiling and yes ma'aming.

The time of year Reen and I anxiously awaited was upon us—May, when our carefully tended harvest of strawberries made their first appearance and the plump, candy-sweet fruit was ready for harvesting. I loved nothing more than the feel of cool, moist soil smushing through my fingers. The action of burying something in deep darkness then leaving it alone to grow roots was absolutely magical. When a tiny, once-buried seed eventually produced a robust plant full of bountiful fruit, I never failed to be amazed.

"It's all over your chin!" I squealed through bursts of laughter as juice from a freshly picked strawberry raced down Reen's cinnamon-colored neck.

The backside of Reen's deep brown hand removed runaway nectar from her chin and neck just before her unruly, honey-blonde dreadlocks joined the juicy mess. She gathered them all in one fist then secured them with a rubber band into a scruffy ponytail at the crown of her head.

"How can one berry hold that much juice?" She wiped the residue from her hand onto her stretchy pants and giggled. "I'm not complaining, but we should probably place warning labels on these after packaging them."

I shook my head, smiled, then continued picking. Ten berries inside the basket, one for me. Ten more inside the basket, another for me. I maintained that happy rhythm until my stomach had enough.

While bent over plucking another plump strawberry, heavy footsteps sounded, but I stayed focused on my work.

"Pass me that flat."

The deep, familiar timbre grabbed my attention. My head instinctively tilted upward, and my gaze landed upon the spring green eyes of my fiancé, Jason Tucker. He stood five feet eight inches but appeared much taller from my vantage. Broader too, though his physique was average. He'd left the top two buttons of his blue flannel shirt unbuttoned, and a white t-shirt underneath showed at his open collar. Old blue jeans and sturdy boots completed his outfit.

Without waiting for my reply, he moved to pick up the large cardboard flat of berries. "This is too heavy for you ladies to lift on your own. Next time, Nikki, tell me when you're getting ready to pack so I can help."

"Maybe she would if you asked nicely," Reen sweetly sang the accusation.

I wished she would stop saying stuff like that. Day or night, she was ready to argue with Jason, and he'd always be ready to make me pay for it… in private, of course.

"Good morning to you too, Maureen." He glared.

I'd take no part in their shenanigans. It was too early for that. I placed the old bushel basket on the ground then stood to face him.

"J-Jason, I didn't know you were coming by." That annoying stutter. My mouth was hell-bent on betraying me… exposing my nervousness, my immature lack of composure. "I would never bother you this early in the morning. Shouldn't you be helping your dad right now?"

His eyes shone with hurt. "Finn's helping him today, and it's slow right now." With a final glower at Reen, he continued in a flat tone. "My time is better spent helping you. What else do you need to get these berries ready to go?"

Jason was as dependable as the seasons. The son of one of our respected Elders, and a Trainee within our faith, he took responsibilities seriously. A little too seriously at times, if you asked me. No one could become a Trainee without having three letters of recommendation from other Elders and Pillars, and those wouldn't come before being thoroughly "examined" for at least two years. Examination mainly consisted of the candidate brown-nosing and running errands for those higher in rank. Women who hoped to become Matrons or Pillars and men who hoped to become Elders all went through the process. Jason and I weren't dating during his examination, but he told me it was "a necessary, enlightening, humbling experience."

They all said that, but did anyone ever provide details? Nope.

Two hours later, with aching arms and numb fingers, I pushed the last flat of freshly picked berries into the bed of Jason's pickup truck, all labeled for their final destinations. He hopped in the driver's seat, closed the door, then slid down the window.

I approached with the intention of thanking him but never got the chance.

"Nikki, it's time we discussed wedding plans. It's been five months since your mom passed, and I know it's been hard." His gaze held mine.

I fought the urge to squirm or look away.

"You don't have to sell strawberries, and you don't have to do all this by yourself."

He was wrong. I wasn't completely poor, but since I became solely responsible for our—*my* household management, I found myself relying on what was once a happy hobby to keep me financially afloat. Even strawberry pre-sales weren't enough to pay all my bills, so I'd begun tutoring kids in math and English just to make ends meet.

"Four months." I gripped his door where the window had retracted. "It's been *four* months, and I'm not by myself. I have Reen." I glanced at my friend, who was busy dusting soil off her leggings. "Besides, I love selling strawberries. It makes me feel like I'm doing something good for myself and the community."

It also kept my unstable mind from wandering down darker paths of death and loneliness, dwelling on ominous thoughts that led to nightmares and middle-of-the-night journaling. Last night, I'd been jarred awake by horrific images and was too disturbed to fall back asleep.

He placed a calloused hand on my cheek. "Let's talk tonight. I'll come by at six? We can have dinner together."

I nodded in agreement.

"I'll text you when I'm on my way." He pulled me closer toward him, fingers sliding through my hair and resting at the nape of my neck. His unspoken request was evident in the heat of his hand, the warmth of his eyes.

My answer also remained wordless. I allowed him to place his lips upon mine for a brief kiss—more like a peck—before he drove away to deliver the strawberries.

He was right, we needed to have this conversation. I needed to be myself again. To be normal and happy again.

TWO

"FIRST-OF-ALL." REEN ANNOUNCED, picking up her empty gathering baskets.

"Did you notice the moving trucks outside the Winters' house today?" Her words were just above a whisper.

My head whipped in her direction, and I squinted as if it would help me hear better. Her face was tight, and she pursed her lips.

"I guess you didn't know either. I saw it while walking here this morning." She mumbled, shaking her head at the news.

"I had no idea they were even thinking about moving, and Clarissa didn't say anything during our Wednesday tutoring session." I admitted.

The Winters had signed their daughter up for tutoring last spring, when the once-sweet girl began acting up in class and trying to skip Service. Twice she ran from the hall during our Champion's teachings. Most little girls between the ages of five and eight exhibited signs of rebellion toward our structured way of living, but they always snapped out of it around ten. Not so with Clarissa.

"I just wish it wasn't so hush-hush every time someone decided to move."

She was right. Moving out of the community wasn't taken lightly by Leadership. The Bright Lakes application and acceptance process was thorough, resulting in long waitlists, so when someone moved… Well, we just didn't talk about it. Our community was for devout members of the Bright Lord's Faith, a loving religion open to anyone with a heart to serve and follow the community guidelines.

"And, what's second of all?" I asked, joining her in clearing supplies and empty crates from the driveway.

"You know, Nikki, he's not going to wait forever."

"Smooth transition, Reen."

"I'm just making sure you understand. I've already seen Serena giving him Minnie Mouse eyes when you're not around. Don't worry. I made sure to accidentally elbow her in the side during Lunch."

"You can't go around doing stuff like that!"

"I gave a very sweet apology afterward, so it's fine." The sly smile on her face said otherwise.

"You crazy!" I chuckled and shook my head at my friend.

The girl had a death wish. Some of the things she said and did were completely against Community rules, which made me simultaneously love her boldness and fear for her reputation. Nevertheless, I could always count on her to side-eye or accidentally elbow any perceived enemy of mine. It seemed Serena Henderson— with her perfect, hour-glass shape and cat-like eyes—was on that invisible hit list.

Good thing too. I also saw the way she looked at Jason and noticed how she'd engage him in conversation every time I excused myself. When he was around, she'd start sashaying and smiling way too big. I'd avoid her when possible and be polite when it wasn't but kept a mental tally.

I never mentioned those observations or my annoyance to Jason nor Reen. I shouldn't have been surprised she'd noticed and couldn't stop wondering if he had, too.

Youthful chatter broke through my thoughts as we strolled toward my house. Children of varying ages trotted down the asphalt streets, making their daily trek to the Bright Lakes Community School. I watched as they rounded up other kids from the neighborhood, and I smiled as their colorful backpacks bumped against their backs, weighing down their tiny legs.

"Good morning, Nikki! Hey Reen!" Sheila Carmichael held her son's hand as they descended their porch stairs.

Reen squatted to wave at James while simultaneously ignoring his mother's greeting. He waved back with a wide smile, showcasing two missing teeth. So cute.

"Looks like you're packing strawberries today." Sheila observed. "You happen to have any leftovers I can purchase? With taking care of James and Anthony and all of my Examinee responsibilities, I completely forgot to put my name on the list."

Sheila—or Mrs. Carmichael, we had to call her in public—was a mere three years older than Reen and I. She married Anthony Carmichael, high school sweetheart, as soon as they turned eighteen, and now they had little James Anthony. He was five years old and such a sweet boy. The fact that we all went to high school together, didn't add any value to our relationship or on how we addressed her. The only detail of importance was that she was a married woman, and we were not.

"They're all accounted for." Reen's clipped tone usually shuts down any further discussion, but Sheila was built differently. If she wanted something, she got it.

"I'm sure it's hard for you to understand because you don't have a husband or children or a home of your own, but little James and I would be so grateful if you had even a small amount to spare. Don't you want some of Miss Nikki's strawberries, James?" She sing-songed the question with narrowed eyes thrown at Reen before kissing her son on the forehead.

"That heifer." Reen spewed under her breath then opened her mouth to say Bright Lord knew what.

"I'll see what I can do. I'm sure there'll be some left in the next batch." I shouted to drown out anything my friend was about to say that we'd inevitably have to pay for later.

Reen's infamous side-eyes abruptly made their way to me as we said goodbye to Sheila and James. I ignored her irritations as we headed toward the side entrance to my backyard.

I loved my backyard.

When Reen and I turned eighteen, my mom encouraged us to transform it from a barren dirt land into a garden play shop. That's exactly what we did. The first two years were rough. We failed at everything we tried until, through failing, we eventually learned how to do it right. It was gratitude for our community and consistent sister-friend time that initially drew me to selling strawberries instead of just eating them. Now we felt like semi-farmers.

"She always forgets"—Reen made air quotes— "to put her name on the list. People like her get on my nerves, and I'm not bending over backwards for them, Examinee or not."

"Giving Sheila an extra bundle of berries isn't a huge deal. I don't mind." But I did mind, a little. Making an exception for her wasn't fair to those who took the time to request berries by our deadline two weeks ago. It made me uncomfortable to show favoritism. On the other hand, if people found out we turned her down, we'd be called selfish and ungrateful—because she was certain to become a Matron, then a Pillar.

Reen knew just as well as I did that both of those titles gave her higher standing and more influence within the community. So, it was best just to give her the stupid strawberries.

"That's not the point." The words flew out of her mouth as she grabbed the heavy-duty lawn broom. Holding it in one hand and resting the length of its pole at the dip of her hip she stared at me, eyes on fire. "You know how that one passage in the Sacred Text says, 'It is more honorable to extend gifts to your neighbor than to extend your hands awaiting a gift from your neighbor?' Well, I'm starting to wonder when we get to choose which neighbors to extend gifts to. I honestly don't mind doing things for others. I actually enjoy giving and helping, but when it feels natural. It hardly feels generous when Leadership tries to make us feel guilty if we don't want to do everything they say. And I don't see nothing in the Text about that."

I had no idea what she was talking about, but she'd obviously been wondering about this for a while. She was too agitated, too frustrated. Was someone trying to make her do something she didn't want to do, or was she just fed up with Sheila's constant last-minute requests and condescending remarks? And since when did she quote the Text as a basis for her arguments?

She began sweeping soil away from the back door.

"Hey, is everything okay with you? With Shawn?"

Reen and Shawn King began officially courting a little more than six months ago. Perhaps her irritation was because he still hadn't proposed. Community Rules clearly stated no one could court for more than nine months. Doing so indicated the couple weren't a good match, and everyone living in Bright Lakes would know it.

"Shawn and I are good. Really good." A shy smile brightened her face, and her shoulders dropped a little. "I'm not in a rush to get married, if that's what you're thinking. And we still have time. It's some of the other things around here"—she spread out her arms, indicating the community— "that don't sit well with me anymore. I don't know. Maybe I'm being overly emotional or paranoid, but a lot of people here are kinda… mean. Spiteful even."

Did she really mean that? Sadness wafted from her in palpable waves, drenching me in sorrow for her.

Reen was one of the most caring and honest people I knew, but it didn't seem to matter. Most ladies in the community would not befriend her. She was born and raised here, and her father was the respected Elder Johnson who, curiously, had been lying low for a few years. Logic would place her at the top of anyone's invite list and among the most respected of our peers, but that wasn't the case. The women, married and single, intentionally did and said little things to exclude Reen or make life difficult for her. None of it made sense to me. What a waste of time to go out of their way just to annoy her.

This was the first Reen indicated those underhanded slights bothered her. She was the "just keep rolling" type, always smiling, being helpful, and saying whatever she damn well pleased regardless of what others said or did. I admired her for it. Now, the pain in her eyes and intensity of her words made my heart ache—partly because she was hurting but mostly because it wasn't new. After all these years, I missed it. Her loneliness.

Was it because I had become intimately acquainted with the sting of loneliness that I could now discern it within her?

When Mama's illness occurred, it hurled itself into our lives like a thunder-strike—swift and earth shattering. One day she was her normal stubborn self. The next day, she was on a ventilator. After five heart-wrenching days at the city hospital, she was gone, and suddenly, I was alone.

Alone.

A word I'd only ever used to describe short periods of time spent taking walks, working in the garden, or running errands. At that time, being alone was an independent choice I got to make, and I enjoyed those precious moments of solitude. But that damned word had transformed from a pleasant, temporary state of being into a dreaded, perpetual condition. It filled me with a sinking sensation of loss, cloaked me in a cold, suffocating fog… and there was no escape.

I placed the garden tote down and walked toward her. "I'm sorry, Friend." I placed an arm around her shoulder. "I promise to be nicer to you from now on."

She glared and playfully pushed me away from her.

We both laughed, diffusing the tension. But I knew the respite was only temporary.

ℰᏆℭᏒ

CLEANING THE BACK yard didn't take long.

Reen left to freshen up before heading to the community school. Unlike me, she had a real job teaching fifth graders. I merely volunteered at the Administration Building three days a week. Fridays were non-volunteer days, so after showering, I spent the rest of the morning cleaning the house, finishing by throwing out old food from the refrigerator and pantry. I really needed to learn how to meal prep better and stop wasting the little money I earned on overpriced microwaveable meals.

The house was eerily quiet with just me in it. Being busy kept me sane, but with everything clean and Jason bringing me dinner tonight, there wasn't much else to occupy my nerves. Mama's room loomed like a forbidden portal in the hallway—a sacred gateway that would transport me back in time to when she was slouched in bed reading or putting on her "sinners' suit" to plant new herbs in the front yard. I hadn't allowed myself to cross that threshold since the morning I selected her burial clothes.

Back then, everything happened so fast. My emotions couldn't keep up with the intensity each day brought. The worst part about her death was the lack of answers. She didn't have a pre-existing condition. There wasn't a car accident, like when Dad passed. Mama just… died.

Knowing a healthy person can die for no reason rocked my whole world. The ripples caused me to challenge all my beliefs and even those I respected couldn't escape my newfound scrutiny. I hated my new "normal." It made me feel unstable, made my unchecked thoughts seem reckless. But the change in my outlook—my thoughts and feelings and beliefs—was permanent. Much as I wanted to, I couldn't unlearn this lesson. Nothing was permanent. Nothing was guaranteed.

I stood at her closed door, determined to enter. Ignoring it another day wouldn't help me. The light-hearted, easygoing girl who didn't doubt and didn't question had been gone for too long. If I were to regain any semblance of my former self, taking this step was necessary. It began here with me facing the truth—my mother, my rock, was irrevocably dead.

Closing my eyes, I dragged in a deep inhale then released an even longer exhale. I did that a few times until resolve outweighed the tenderness of my emotions.

In the ten years we lived in this house, the walls of my mother's room remained bare except for the full-length mirror to the left of her window and a decorative tapestry above the center of her bed. It was embroidered with the Bright Lord's symbol, underneath which were stitched the words "I Am Kept"—her favorite passage from the Sacred Text. Everything in her room was simple and humble, just like her. A white bookshelf housed her many self-help books on grief, parenting, and financial literacy lined the shelves alongside numerous journals of various sizes and designs.

The scent of lavender and myrrh essential oils still lingered, milder than before but present within the walls and fabric of the pillows and down comforter upon her queen-sized bed. I slid my fingers along the dust-covered vanity adjacent to her bed. Bottles of perfume, makeup brushes, and hairpins were neatly placed in separate compartments.

I sat on her bed and studied the framed photo of us in the backyard. It was taken after my first tiny batch of strawberries successfully bore fruit. The familiar lump in my throat grew as welled-up tears fell non-stop from my eyes and I clenched my chest to stop my heart from caving in. This time, I didn't hold back the choked howl from escaping my lungs, didn't wipe away the salty tears nor snot. I'd denied myself the full release of grief for four months, and the bulging reservoir within my soul no longer had room to hold another drop.

I don't know how long I sat and cried before falling asleep, but the joyful sounds of children laughing and talking awakened me. After a yawn and a stretch, I opened the top drawer of Mama's nightstand, fumbling through her various hair scarves, prayer books, dark chocolate, and other random items until I landed on a thin purple journal. My head swiveled around the room as if someone might magically appear and catch me invading her privacy. I shook off that dumb thought and thumbed through a few pages, smiling as I read my mother's private thoughts and began seeing her in a new light.

THREE

J ASON ARRIVED PROMPTLY, as he always did, at 6:00 p.m.

His hair fell over his forehead, stopping just above bushy eyebrows, and emerald eyes shone with hesitant warmth against his pale skin. He greeted me with a bouquet of wildflowers—bright golden poppies, lavender sprigs, and a few sweetly scented geraniums in a soft shade of purple, almost lilac. Although rather average in comparison to other men in the looks department, Jason made up for any visual disadvantage with his consistent generosity.

I reached for the flowers with both hands and brought them to my nose in a deep inhale. "Ahh, I just love the smell of geraniums. Thank you. But you didn't have to."

His wan smile, framed with a day's worth of stubble, was a subtle reminder of what he expected tonight.

Unfortunately, I couldn't give it to him. Not yet.

"I knew you'd like them. Can I come in?" He lifted a big paper bag with greens and a long loaf of French bread peeking out the top.

I stepped aside to usher him in.

He made a beeline to my kitchen. Over the past year of our extended courtship, he'd been to my home many times, so there wasn't a need to show him where anything was located. I quietly observed him as he removed a large glass container of what looked like cooked pasta from the bag and placed it upon the counter. He continued putting ingredients on my counter—a freshly picked head of romaine lettuce, fresh field greens, tomato, red onion, and a block of parmesan cheese— until the bag was empty. After taking a chef's knife and carving board from the drawer, he reached for the romaine.

I loved how sure he was of himself and the sturdy way he moved about, even if it was simply chopping vegetables to make a salad. This man did everything with dutiful intention, and that always made me feel secure in his presence. Chosen.

I removed a vase from under the kitchen sink then went about trimming the stems of the flowers. Once I was happy with the arrangement, I began setting the dining table and raised my voice louder so he could hear me. "Thanks again for helping package and deliver the strawberries today. It saved us at least two hours of time." And a lot less strain on our bodies. "Did anyone have concerns when you dropped off the crates?"

"No concerns. Matron Patterson was happy you helped Lilliana with her math this week and wants to know if you can go over again on Thursday after you're done with the Admin Building. I told her I'd ask you."

Lilliana was a particularly stubborn little girl who required some special attention to motivate her into completing schoolwork. She'd recently turned eight and, much like Clarissa, had developed a strong dislike for attending Service on Wednesdays and Saturdays. I didn't mind giving her extra attention since she was such a joy to be around. Her vibrancy and tenacity reminded me of happier, carefree days, so tutoring her became more of a reason for me to play and dance silly as much as it was for Lilliana to learn math.

"Of course I will. I wish more kids were as easy to tutor as Lilliana." Before I could return to the kitchen to help him, Jason entered the dining room, plates in hand. We almost bumped into each other. He placed our meals on the table, gestured for me to sit then, like the gentleman he was, pulled out my chair.

Once we were seated, he said a short blessing, thanking the Bright Lord for our meal and, surprisingly, for me. I loved when he did that. I reached over to gently squeeze his hand. The innocent touch reminded me of our differences—or at least, one obvious difference. I was black, and he was white. A non-issue for us so we never discussed race. Our families had been connected since we were young, so the topic—if it ever required adjustments or explanations—had been settled years ago. Still, seeing our fingers intertwined was always served as a stark reminder.

He scooped a heap of the saucy pasta onto his fork then casually announced, "I want to have at least two children of our own." He met my gaze. "How many do you want?" The fork-full of pasta made it to his mouth, and he proceeded to chew the food without breaking eye contact.

I could feel the muscles in my face twitching as I attempted to force them into neutrality. Why did he always do that? Who just blurted out a serious topic without any context or build up? I needed to prepare for these things, ease into them carefully, but he never gave me the chance. Whenever he made life-changing declarations and looked at me the way he was right now, it didn't feel like genuine curiosity but a subtle demand for which there was only one acceptable response. Like a test. A test of my loyalty to him and the marriage we would have.

The stupid question caused my breath to halt as my mind skittered, searching for the right answer. We'd only lightly discussed the subject once, and I'd been uncertain. That hadn't changed.

Being an only child, I'd often wished for a younger sibling. I wanted someone to play with and talk to, but shortly after we were accepted into Bright Lakes, I met Maureen in Children's School. She saw me playing alone that first day, struggling to complete a puzzle of a dark green tree lizard. Back then, I was extraordinarily quiet and kept to myself. I didn't realize she even noticed me until I felt someone hovering, and it was her. She stared down at me and my incomplete puzzle with her big, deep brown eyes. She asked if she could join me. Ever since then, it's been the two of us and any lingering desire for a sister was fulfilled by her.

I must have been lost in thought longer than Jason liked because he repeated the question in an impatient tone.

"I think I'd like to have two children." My voice was a near whisper. "One would be lonely, but I imagine two kids could be great friends. Like Reen and me."

Yes, that is what I'd like. Maybe even three to balance things out when the two fought with each other.

"Could we have one conversation that doesn't involve Maureen?" he drawled.

My whole body flinched at the audacity of his question. "What are you even talking about?"

"You know what I'm talking about. Every time I ask you anything, you immediately bring up what Maureen would like or what Reen would think." He says, mocking my voice. "Even now, we're talking about *our* kids, Nikki. Ours! And here you are bringing Maureen into it as if you're looking for her approval to have kids."

"That's not what I'm doing." My heart sprinted so fast I couldn't look at him. I felt stupid. I'd failed the test hidden beneath his question. His real aim wasn't about having kids but about Reen, and I should have known. It's a rare day when Reen held back her thoughts, and that type of freedom went against Jason's idea of how a lady should behave.

"I only mentioned her because I'm an only child, and being friends with her helped me get over feeling so lonely." My stomach definitely had led in it, and any previous hunger disappeared, so I picked up a fork and mindlessly moved pasta around my plate.

"So, when is our wedding date? What's stopping you from committing to our plans? I've been patient enough. But the way you keep putting it off... I'm starting to wonder if you actually want this anymore."

There it was. The question I originally thought he would ask, and the thing I suspected he wanted from me tonight. A wedding date.

He grabbed the French loaf from the center of the table then ripped off the end. "People are gossiping. Even my dad is asking questions." He shoved the chunk of bread into his mouth, and his attention settled on the wall in front of him, across from the dining table. It was unlikely he was focused on the painting of the tree line behind the hills of my home, leading to Yosemite National Park. No, his stare was locked on a framed photograph from our engagement. I sported a broad smile as Jason knelt on the field, holding my outstretched hand while placing an engagement ring on my ring finger.

To say I was shocked is an understatement. We'd had the best night out downtown, at a beautiful, candlelit restaurant, then he led me to a field of wild dandelions at the edge of the community, the marker between us and the city. I rarely needed to go into the city, so seeing the field and its vast stretch of green, white, and yellow was a happy surprise despite the chilly December evening. It reminded me of childhood dreams, of twirling, outstretched arms, and of loud, long belly laughs. The sun's deep golden rays encased everything around us in a warm glow. It was the most romantic sight.

We'd blissfully courted a mere five months. My arms would sprout goosebumps at his touch, and I'd often found myself giggling at every little thing he said. He was so smart! He consistently brought me sweet little gifts, treated me like a lady, and always showed up when I needed him. He would even invite Mama to join everything we did until one day she half-jokingly asked him, "Are you courting me or my daughter?" It made me happy that he was so considerate and thought of everything.

I'd had no idea he was actually in love with me until he proposed, saying sweet words and making promises of care and unending affection. I should've known something was going on. He'd worn a charcoal gray wool coat over fitted denim pants, and his hair had been neatly gelled in place. It was unusual for him to make such an effort, even on my account, but he'd gone to so much trouble that day. When he asked me to be his wife, it was easy to say yes. What else could a girl want?

The next month, Mama was gone, and I withdrew from the world, including Jason. Things had changed. Why didn't he understand that?

"I know it's been a long time," I finally replied. "And I've also heard the gossip. I love you, Jason, but I need a little more time. We'll set a date soon. I promise. Let me get through the busy harvest time, and I'll be able to think more clearly."

Even though my stomach felt heavy and my head felt light, I reached for his hand again and braved direct eye contact. I owed him more than this. His recent bouts of anger and frustration were my fault, and the least I could do was offer a firm date to plan again. "July first. We'll sit down and discuss the date and all the details of the wedding, so tell your dad and anyone else who asks that we're fine. I just… I just miss my mom." Saying the words out loud broke something within me, and I couldn't stop the tears that followed.

How could I think of my happiness and getting married when she could no longer walk me down the aisle? How could I set a date when I could feel Jason's growing anger toward me? When I felt so unsettled within my own body and thoughts?

He gripped my hand within his and rose from his chair, pulling me up with him. Strong arms wrapped around my body, and he let me cry onto his navy-blue t-shirt. My tears turned into full sobs as he stroked the back of my head.

"I'm sorry for forcing this conversation. I can't imagine what you're going through, but I'm here for you. I promise I'll take care of you, Nikki."

He pressed soft kisses on the top of my head and rubbed circles on my back. As I settled, he tipped my chin up so my tear-streaked face met his then pressed his lips to mine. The tension from our conversation slowly melted away and was replaced with warmth. I basked in the strength of his embrace and the scent of bergamot and spice.

Our kisses became more urgent as his tongue slipped into my mouth. I obliged the intimate invitation, and our mouths danced as his hands roamed freely over the rapidly growing heat of my body. I loved Jason. He was the first man to ever pay me real attention, to take time to get to know me and actually like what he saw. He was brave enough to ask out this shy, awkward girl then listened to my hopes and dreams, even if he disagreed with them. He was always there when I needed help and was the first person who arrived at my doorstep after Mama was pronounced dead. Even if he was behaving strangely lately, I knew he loved me and would always be there for me. But I didn't completely trust him. His temper concerned me, as did his feelings about my best friend.

The cool evening breeze brushed across my legs as his calloused palms danced over my skin. I'd barely realized his hand moving up my thigh, along with my summer dress.

In a breathless pant, I separated our mouths and took a wobbly step back. "We have to stop."

Jason quickly closed the space between us. He grasped my waist, pulled me toward him, then pressed his mouth to mine. His breath heated my lips as he moaned, "Nikki, I need you."

I owed him at least one more kiss. Besides, being this close to him felt good. And still… not quite right. I tore myself from his embrace then took three steps back, creating enough space between us so he couldn't reach me so easily.

"We have to stop now before we go too far."

In a tone between a beg and a demand, Jason said, "I'm your fiancé. We'll be married soon. You just said so yourself. No one will care if we're together now, and I know you want it just as much as I do."

Is that what he really thought?

"I want to be with you when the time is right, Jason. When we won't have regrets." In a pathetic attempt to distract and calm the lust gleaming in his eyes, I angled toward the dining table. "Let's finish our dinner. You worked hard to make this for us, and it'd be a shame to let it go to waste."

He let out a deep breath and ran a hand through his hair. "I better go. I need to help my dad with a few things before it gets too late."

In a few wide steps, he was out of sight. A second later, the sound of my front door closing rang through the house.

FOUR

THE NEXT MORNING, I released the delicate ribbon of my silk bonnet then set to the daily task of unwrapping my hair, which always felt like winding a jack-in-the-box.

I never knew if the right side of my hair would lie flat or stick up at the crown of my head, even with the effort of using moisturizer and sweet almond oil. The bonnet was a gift Mama gave me two years ago that I didn't fully appreciate until she was no longer here to mumble about maintaining moisture in 4c relaxed strands. Years of poor haircare routines coupled with three months of shedding after Mama died, left me fighting to maintain shoulder-length hair.

I'd texted Jason to let him know I'll sit with him and his family during service today. It was the least I could do to make up for rejecting him at dinner. Throughout the night, my mind wandered with ways I could have made the evening go better, and short of giving in to his request, I came up empty. I hated when we argued because it often ended like last night, with him walking away.

Sitting with the Tuckers was no small deal. They were one of the most prestigious families within the community, so I chose clothes that wouldn't embarrass me or them. I selected a buttoned down, lightweight, mustard colored dress that cinched at the waist and hung loosely along the non-existent curve of my hips. Cursed with moderate-sized breasts and no hips to balance them out. An inverted triangle, I believe they called it. What good was it to have full breasts only to wear oversized clothes? "So as not to tempt our good men and showcase desperation for their attention," the firm scolding from finger-wagging Matron Smith, a pillar in the Bright Lord's Faith, resounded in my mind. If this blasphemous body resulted in limited clothing options, I'd at least wear colors that made my dark skin radiant.

Services were held on Wednesday evenings and Saturday mornings, and although the Bright Lord's Faith didn't command weekly attendance, the condemning stares and endless gossip of other Community members guaranteed a full house and timely presence. Especially if you lived within the Bright Lakes Residential Community. My mother, having been our Champion's bookkeeper, earned our tiny family a modicum of respect, including seating in the third row of chairs from the altar.

The first row was reserved for the Champion's Elders and their families. The second row was for more prestigious Community members, whose joint generational wealth purchased these hundred acres of land southeast of Fresno. The third row was for Service leadership and administration. Lay members piled in wherever they could. Although never stated out loud, nor written in any book of the Bright Lord, community members who fell out of grace with our Champion or anyone in the first couple of rows, involuntarily sat in the last two rows of chairs or didn't attend Service at all. Those who skipped were called Unfaithful and risked losing their home within Bright Lakes after multiple violations.

The mid-May sun felt like a caress upon my skin while waiting by the fifteen-foot water fountain between the service hall and the courtyard. It was a cloudless day, the kind where the sky looks like the still sea. I preferred clouds so I could entertain myself by thinking of the shapes and forms they resembled. The mist from the falling water was refreshing against the dry heat, but more-so, it was an immediate threat to the straightness of my hair. I wouldn't dare risk a frizzy hairdo while sitting next to Mrs. Tucker, so I moved to the wide steps at the entrance of the hall.

Kimberly found me first. Her bright green eyes and golden-brown hair were identical to her older brother's. If they were closer in age, they might be mistaken for twins. I could tell her parents were finally allowing her to tan, as her arms were a severe shade of red—a sure sign she'd stayed in the sun too long. Poor thing, I hoped it didn't last too long. At sixteen, Kimberly was a sweet teenager, despite what most people said at this "trying age," but the brightness of her eyes and the lightness of her countenance had recently begun shifting into a more agitated form. She always greeted me with the kindness of a little sister. Having babysat her for many years, stopping once she turned thirteen, I felt the same about her.

"Hey, Nikki. Jason said you're sitting with us today. I'm so glad. Now I don't have to pretend to enjoy the teaching all by myself." She said it as a joke, but I knew she half meant it. Ever since she was a child, Kimberly never minced her words about anything, much to the embarrassment of her mother, father, and older brother.

I secretly found her honesty refreshing.

"But I do like hearing the updates members announce at the end of service." She looked proud of herself for having something positive to say about her Service experience.

I also liked the updates. Any Faithful member could raise their hand and share how they overcame a challenge in their life, or they could ask for a special blessing.

"Your secret is safe with me, although I doubt I can call it a secret." I winked.

Jason approached, and I admit, he looked good in his navy trousers and starched white linen shirt. He stopped within a mere foot of me and smiled as he reached for my hand, lacing his fingers between mine. "You look lovely in that dress, Nicolette. I'm glad you're joining us for Service today," his mother said. "I was just telling Jason we haven't seen enough of you lately." Mrs. Tucker—Anna—had always been kind to me and made me feel like one of the family, even before her son proposed. She was a beautiful middle-aged woman with shoulder-length blonde hair cut in a layered style that bounced with each poised step she took. Today, she wore a glacial blue blouse with a ruffled hem paired with a matching skirt. She looked like a movie star.

"Hi, Mr. Tucker. Thank you, Mrs. Tucker. Jason brought me some delicious spaghetti last night, so I figured I'd repay the kindness."

Mr. Tucker looked at me like he couldn't decide if he'd never met me or had but didn't like me. He said nothing and motioned us toward the huge double doors leading into the hall.

☙❧

WALKING INTO THE Service Hall each week felt like a grand social event.

Ladies and little girls in bright colored, frilly dresses trailed demurely behind little boys and men wearing suit jackets, brimmed hats, and ties. They strutted in, chests outstretched, and heads held high.

Before the teaching portion began, most of the Bright Lakes Residential Community gathered throughout the hall or around the water fountain, chatting and mingling. The liveliness and hospitality always uplifted me. Overhearing shared news about loved ones, exchanged pleasantries, and community gossip truly made the environment feel like family. There was peace in knowing no matter what happened in my life, these people—this community—would always be there to wrap their loving arms around me.

When Mama died, their aggressive hospitality knew no bounds. Women came to my door at all hours of the day with trays of food, bottles of tinctures and teas, journals, and books on grief. One morning, a group came to clean the house, which surprised me. By that time, dishes were piled up in my kitchen sink, and the bathroom tub was more than nasty, but I didn't have the energy to care. Without any questions, they each took a room within the house to clean—except Mama's room—and by the time they left, our... *my* tiny home looked brand new. But that wasn't all. Those ladies returned once a week for three weeks straight. I'd never seen the windows so invisibly clear before.

When I was deep in mourning, no one forced me to clean the service hall as I usually did each week, nor was I expected to attend post-teaching Saturday Lunches. They gave me time, and I cherished all of them for every kindness. In every sense of the word, they made me feel like I belonged.

So long as I followed the rules, that is. An unsettling realization I was slowly awakening to.

We entered the hall as a unit, then Jason's parents and sister split off to seek out their friends, leaving the two of us alone. The hall doors in the back opened to a long center aisle dividing the seating—two columns of twenty-two neatly lined rows of burgundy-cushioned chairs. The walkway led straight to the altar, where a plexiglass podium stood. It was engraved with "The Bright Lord Welcomes You." Six feet behind it, to the right and left, stood two rows of white pews forming a quarter circle. They were reserved for holidays and special occasions, when the all-boys' choir sang hymns as a special treat.

I searched through a sea of laughter, hats, and dresses in hopes of spotting Reen and her family—her twin brothers, Timothy and Thomas, and their parents Mr. and Mrs. Johnson. A quick squeeze of my hand halted my search, redirecting my wandering eyes to Jason, who was being approached by none other than our Champion, Malachi Aprey, and his beautiful wife, Lady Maribelle. Trailing no more than five feet behind them was Jeremy, the Champion's fish-eyed assistant. The man always made me want to take two steps back.

Malachi was a towering bear of a man. I think he was in his late fifties, with tanned skin and deep-set ice-blue eyes.

"Jason, Nicolette, Bright Blessings to you both. It's so good to see you *together* this Saturday morning," the Champion greeted us. I heard loud and clear the emphasis placed on the word *together* and knew that he was saying—without saying—Jason's dad and Community members were gossiping about our delayed wedding, and he too had questions about our delay. During his teachings, his voice soothed even the fussiest of toddlers to sleep, but I always felt the crack of a whip underneath his tone. He kept his eyes focused on me, and the half smile he offered didn't soften his gaze, nor slow my heartbeat.

He turned toward Lady Maribelle. "My lovely bride and I were just discussing what a gift you two are to our community and the Bright Lord's Faith, weren't we, dear?"

Without delay, Lady Maribelle pinned me with her intense brown eyes, causing the pit of my stomach to plunge. Summoning a smile that hopefully looked genuine, I mentally prepared for her to recommend a change to my clothes, hair, makeup, attitude… or anything else she found displeasing.

"Not only are you two gifts to the community, but marriage in itself is such a blessing, *mija*." She exuberantly repeated her husband's sentiments, but her voice was laced with an accent indicative of her Mexican heritage.

Lady Maribelle was always smiling and happy. I desperately wanted to be like that, to live in a constant state of levity where I wasn't weighed down by incessant doubts and suspicions. It didn't matter that I felt insecure around her, like I was being examined under a microscope. Though she seemed positive about herself and her station, I feared to fall short of her expectations.

She took my free hand then patted it. The disparity between us was painfully obvious. Her skin was warm and smooth, her nails freshly manicured. My calloused, nubby little fingers, which were more like a tool during harvest season probably felt like sandpaper in her grasp.

"It is a gift to be treasured and a source of comfort during life's most difficult times. One not to be taken for granted lest the Bright Lord thinks us ungrateful." Lady Maribelle looked at me with compassion. Or pity. It was impossible to say.

I tried to focus on her message rather than my shortcomings. She was right, of course, marriage was a gift and a blessing. So why was I squirming and feeling the urge to run away from their prying eyes?

No, stop thinking like that!

They were genuinely concerned and only wanted what was best for me.

"The Bright Lord is gracious and merciful. Thank you for your kind well wishes, Lady Maribelle," I said.

"Nikki and I will begin our wedding plans in July, so we'll give an update soon," Jason added.

"That is great news indeed!" Our Champion's gaze drifted past me, to the left then announced to his wife, "Ah, look, the Petersons have returned from their trip." The two of them headed in that direction without further comment.

Once more alone with Jason, I scanned the crowd again, hoping to see Reen. The annoying pit in my stomach hadn't disappeared. In fact, the tension was spreading throughout my body. To make matters worse,

I could feel waves of Jason's anger wafting off him. The guy hated being embarrassed or put on the spot. Being confronted by the Champion was not going to elicit a loving reaction from him.

My hands felt clammy. I looked down and noticed my left hand was still entwined with his, so I unlaced it and tucked an invisible strand of hair behind my ear.

"I told you people were gossiping." He leaned in close enough that his breath heated my left ear as he spewed out the words in a lowered voice. "Now even the Champion is asking questions."

He was great at not hiding his frustration from me, but I'm sure to any onlookers, he would appear to be whispering sweet words. I didn't dare respond. Instead, I excused myself and quickly walked past smiling faces and polite laughter, keeping my head down and trying to make myself as small as possible. If I had superpowers, I would have made myself invisible. Instead, I entered the ladies' restroom and was relieved to see it empty. After slipping into the first stall, an extended exhale escaped my lungs, then another one. It took a minute for my pounding heart to slow its rapid drumming and another before it resumed a normal rhythm.

I was disappointing everyone. The pressure of my failures felt like a massive weight on my back and shoulders and compressed my head from both sides. I wanted to be mature enough to respond to questions and concerns with ease and grace. I truly wanted to receive the wisdom of their advice… just without the attached feeling like they were nagging me… pinning me in a corner because I didn't give the answer they wanted.

I hated feeling so deficient and combative with the people who loved me. I was tormented trying to figure out why none of this bothered me before? Before she died. I used to laugh at Community comments as regular drama, but lately their words caused an emotional tug-of-war. And I was losing.

The creaking door dragged me from my mental monologue. Someone had entered the ladies' room. I waited another minute, flushed the toilet, then exited the stall.

"I thought you'd never come out."

Reen looked amazing in a striped wrap dress, pulled together in a bow at her left hip. She stared at me like a scolding mother.

Relieved it was only her and not some other girl I'd have to fake a smile with, my nerves relaxed a bit. I walked past her to the sink. "I was looking for you earlier. I'm sitting with the Tuckers today."

"I know. I saw you walk in. Then I saw Malachi and Goody Goody with you guys, so I kept my distance. I don't need her telling me how much better I'd look if only I'd wear a little makeup." Reen replied in her go-kick-rocks tone.

"But enough about them. You looked like you were drowning over there, then you practically sprinted in here after they walked away. What's going on?"

Was I sprinting? So much for thinking I looked calm and collected. "Just the usual. They were wondering about our wedding date, and it made Jason uncomfortable."

"It looked like it made *you* uncomfortable. Are you sure you're okay?" she asked with genuine concern, and I loved her for it.

Citlali and Isabella Sanchez entered the restroom. Their timing was perfect because I didn't want to have that conversation now. After greeting the Sanchez sisters, we made a hasty exit. "We'll talk later," I promised Reen as we walked back toward the main hall. I soon took my seat between Kimberly and a somber-looking Jason, just in time for Malachi's teaching.

FIVE

MALACHI'S PRESENCE COMMANDED attention without him uttering a single word.

His massive hands rested on each side of the podium as he just stood there. Every seat in the large hall was occupied, but not a single member uttered a sound as we all awaited the teaching from our revered Champion, the Bright Lord's Chosen One. Those piercing blue eyes scanned the room, row after row, left to right, and he held his gaze at each row about five seconds before moving to the next. Though his face was a neutral mask, I had the feeling he was calculating.

After a full minute passed, he raised both his arms wide and exclaimed, "It is a blessing to be together with believers of the Bright Lord!"

A few members agreed aloud, "Yes, it is!"

He continued, "It is a blessing to know you are surrounded by those you love and who love you in return!"

This time the front row of Elders, Pillars, and other members echoed his statement and clapped their hands. Again, his gaze scanned the hall.

"I am so grateful I don't need anyone to tell me when to give thanks to the Bright Lord because I do it willingly. I do it freely. I do it as often as I can because He is worth it!"

More cheers and claps.

"If you don't know how much you are loved, we will pray for you. We will pray you one day feel and experience unwavering acceptance no matter what you do. That is the beauty and the power of entering into the Bright Lord's Faith. Unwavering love is what is offered and is experienced in many ways. One being through the bond and lifelong commitment of marriage."

The entire hall clapped and echoed our Champion's sentiment by that point, including me. I loved the wholeness of marriage and the unwavering acceptance it offered, that it was a haven to fall into and be totally supported by one person without judgement. It's why I cherished the people of this community and served them the best way I knew how. We might not all agree on how to do everything, but we had a common goal of taking care of one another in times of need and celebration.

The thought made my heart soften, and I dared to look toward Jason. I placed an unsteady hand upon his knee, and his warm, apologetic eyes lingered upon mine for a short while as he placed his large hand atop mine with a reassuring squeeze. The intimate action soothed my nerves from his earlier remarks, and I scooted a tad bit closer to him until our thighs and shoulders touched.

"Before we begin today's teaching, I want to personally congratulate Timothy Blake and Anna Beth Torrence on their upcoming wedding." Malachi gestured to the couple sitting a few rows behind us.

Everyone turned toward the couple while clapping and congratulating them. "Next month, we'll witness this faithful couple join their lives together in the Community Clubhouse, so be sure to talk to Anna Beth about the details and help make it a great celebration. The

Pillars have informed me they've finished making the marital quilt and expect many, many babies." He grinned.

"The Pillars would also like engaged ladies who have not set a wedding date to go see them immediately after Service to settle matters. Engagement is as much a commitment as marriage, and we can't keep our grooms waiting for too long."

The Champion, Elders in the front row, and a lot of members laughed. I quickly pulled my hand from Jason's knee. Burning heat shot throughout my body, my cheeks, my hands. The tiny muscles in my face tightened as I fought to maintain an impassive expression.

Was I okay with this?

Was I tripping?

Was I angry? Oh, yes, that's exactly what I felt... anger.

Jason neither looked at me nor reacted to the announcement.

I didn't hear a single word of the teaching or the member updates afterward.

SIX

MY BREATHING WAS loud, and it was getting on my nerves. I attempted to silence my breath, to slow it down, but the more focus I placed on it, the stronger my heartbeat in my agitation. The mid-sized room, which could hold about eighty people, served multiple purposes as the Pillars designated. The smell of coffee lingered, remnants from this morning's Ladies Study Hour held before today's teaching. Sounds of dishes shuffling and children laughing from the nearby courtyard slipped through one of the opened side windows as Community members prepared for Lunch.

I was grateful for that small distraction as three of the twelve Pillars sat in a row of chairs facing me, with various degrees of smiles pasted upon their studious faces. The other Pillars were undoubtedly helping navigate the minutiae of Lunch.

Matron Kirk placed her manicured fingers atop the notebook on her lap and brightened her smile. I adored Matron Kirk. Though in her mid-sixties, her face showed no signs of wrinkles. Her warm brown eyes held compassion, and she always had an inviting smile. Today, she wore her silver-streaked dark hair swept into a neat bun. She was what people called a timeless beauty. Matron Kirk had been my Children's School teacher. She smelled of jasmine and carried candy in her purse for kids like me who'd earned passing grades on their quizzes.

She would often have lunch appointments with Mama, where I'd overhear them laugh and gossip about the comings and goings of other families throughout Bright Lakes. The day Mama passed away, Matron Kirk came to the hospital and clutched my hand and held me while I wept. Her kindness was not overlooked. Pillars were not known for their deep compassion but for their stern discipline and adherence to Community rules and public image. Matron Kirk was the one exception to that rule.

"Nicolette, I'm so glad you could chat with us today." Her gaze was sympathetic. "It's been quite a while since we Pillars last condoled with you after Regina's passing. We all loved your mother very much and can see she did a remarkable job teaching you how to manage the house." Her voice was calm, and she paused long enough for me to realize it was my turn to respond.

"I think I'm adjusting to it. It's taken a little longer than I hoped, but everything is going ok."

Keep it short. Don't say too much.

"Yes, yes we're glad to hear that. Examinee Carmichael speaks favorably of how well you keep the garden. I believe you're in strawberry season now?"

"Yes, Maureen and I were packaging them yesterday, and Mrs. Carmichael just placed an order. We're happy with the harvest this year." I offered.

"Ah yes, Examinee Carmichael also mentioned Jason Tucker, your fiancé, may have come over last night and stayed for quite a while." That slow-dripped question came from Matron Butler, her gentle tone laced with daggers. She was one of the eldest Matrons, wife to the most respected Grand Elder in our Faith. The old woman's face held no smile.

Suddenly, the fragrances of their perfumes mixed with the scents of stale coffee and lunch wafting through the window. The combination made me queasy.

"Jason brought me dinner last night, but he didn't even stay long enough to eat it. We only talked. He wasn't there late."

A flash of his disappointed face leaving my house made me wince, and at the same time I was proud of myself for not letting him have what he wanted. If I'd known Sheila was prying into my business and reporting back to the Pillars this whole time, I'd never dared let him touch me the way he did last night.

Oh, Bright Lord, did she overhear me and Reen talking about her!? What else had she told them?

"Well of course you only talked," Matron Butler snapped. "At that late hour, there wouldn't be a need for anything else. Now would it, young lady?"

I averted my gaze to the oak floorboards and answered, "No, ma'am."

"Good. Now let's get this wedding date on the calendar." Matron Butler tapped a pen on her notebook. "What have you and the Tuckers agreed to?"

"Jason and I talked about it last night, and we're waiting until July to set a ceremony date. I haven't spoken to the Tuckers yet, but we will after July first."

"Oh, no, dear. July is much too far away," Matron Findhorn, the youngest of the group, stated sweetly. "That's almost two months from now just to set a date." She turned toward the other two matrons, seeking agreement. "Why delay such a joyous occasion, Nikki? You cannot seriously expect your fiancé to keep waiting this long. It's been altogether nine months since he proposed, and you've had plenty of time to mourn since your beautiful mother passed. Is there some other reason for this delay?"

Her slow and sticky-sweet voice matched the blush-pink summer dress she wore. If I didn't have a history with Tabitha Findhorn *forgetting* to invite Reen to every social event she'd held in the past ten years, I'd think the woman was a friendly Pillar. But I knew better. Her voice made my skin crawl. I wanted to get out of that room and away from their inquisition, but there was no avoiding this conversation. It'd been announced by the Champion, and if I forgave the urgency they were placing upon me, I'd reluctantly admit they had a right to know. They were the wedding planning team, after all. They cared about my relationship with Jason enough to ask me these tough questions, even if my head couldn't handle it.

Still, even if I knew why I continued postponing my own wedding, I probably wouldn't tell them.

"I just want to finish the strawberry season, is all. There's no other reason. Maureen Johnson and I will be very busy each week as new crops ripen, and I won't be able to dedicate enough time to make the wedding beautiful. Really, there's nothing else going on." The words stumbled out of my mouth, and I felt like a child explaining why she'd eaten the last cupcake.

Matron Butler coldly said, "*We* will ensure the wedding is beautiful, young lady. No need to worry yourself about that. Here's what we'll do. You and the Tuckers set the date within the next two weeks. That's more than enough time for these strawberries of yours. We won't hear of any more delays.

"As for, this friend of yours, Maureen Johnson, she's on a different path than you are, dear, so you'll need to figure out what you're going to do about that once you're married into the Tucker family. Everyone knows she's a wild thing, and I have no doubt she's contributing to your moral decay."

My moral decay? Is that what they truly thought of me? That I was decaying and Reen was responsible for it.

She continued. "As followers of the Bright Lord, we need to hold ourselves in a respectable manner worthy of his Light and Love. Do you understand?"

I blinked a few times, trying to hold back the sting building in the back of my eyes. I would not cry. Not in front of a Pillar. I respected them way too much, even if their words made my heart ache for my friend. "I'm not sure what you mean, Matron Butler. What is wrong with Maureen?"

"Elder Johnson is a respectable Elder in our Faith. His unfortunate wife is not a Pillar, and for good reason. If it were not for the contributions of Elder Johnson and his father before him, no one would tolerate the insolence and flagrant disrespect from his children." The expression on her face looked like she just smelled something rotting. "I will not sully Elder Johnson's name any more than that, but if you, Nicolette Simms, are to marry into the Tucker family, you best begin behaving and associating like one." She didn't wait for me to respond before continuing.

"Now that's settled, we'll see you back here in two weeks to begin planning the ceremony and make preparations for the bridal quilt."

Why did everyone hate Reen? They were undoubtedly instructing me to stop being friends with her in Faith to marry Jason. My head felt so light, so empty, I thought I'd fall over in my chair.

"On to the next matter." Matron Butler crossed her arms. "As it relates to your mother's house."

"What about my mother's house?" I didn't quite recognize the tone I used until Matron Butler raised her right eyebrow in disapproval. A knowing look.

Damn that look and damn that eyebrow. These were wise women, and I've always yielded to their authority, but I would draw the line here. If they thought I'd let them say anything… anything negative about my mama, they'd meet the Nikki I only showed to Reen.

"We're sorry to inform you of this now, but there wasn't a good time while you were in mourning." Matron Kirk's gentle interruption was welcomed. "Unfortunately, Community rules are quite clear on this topic, but we allowed you to stay in the home because we knew you were already engaged to Jason and would soon move out to live in the house he's acquiring for the two of you."

Quiet.

Everything around me went quiet.

No birds chirping, no sounds of Community Lunch, no footsteps down the corridor. In my selfish grief, I'd completely forgotten that, as a wife of an Elder's son—not to mention Jason being a Trainee—I would be required to move into the house he designated. Although some part of me knew this, I had not fully comprehended the fact I'd need to leave my mama's house. And my strawberry garden.

"Three months after a property owner passes away, the house returns to the community for another family to take possession of it. I'm sorry, Nicolette. As a volunteer administrator, I thought you would know this already."

My eyes focused on the shining diamond on my engagement ring. It really was beautiful. A gold, round cut, six-prong solitaire diamond. Jason said he chose it as the shape was similar to the Bright Lord's symbol.

"Due to your special circumstances, we're allowed to let you stay in the house for another two months unless your husband decides to purchase it. Only in that case could you keep the house."

I blurted in what sounded like a plea, "But Mama said the house is already paid for, so why can't I keep it? Why would it go back to the community after she died and not to me?"

Matron Butler answered, "Technically all Bright Lakes Community land, and the houses built on it, are owned by the founders and our Champion. The Administration allows Faithful Members, like your mother, to lease houses. If someone leases the house for ten consecutive years, they no longer have to pay rent, only utilities and community fees. Your mother met that condition a few months before she passed away, but it's immaterial. Once the leaseholder passes, if there's no spouse to keep the property, the home is returned to the Community for someone on the waitlist to bid upon. I'm sure this must be a lot of information for you, Nicolette, but that's why it's a blessing you and Jason are to marry. You won't have to worry about a place to live, and he is already in the process of securing a house for the two of you."

"He is such a responsible and admirable young man, Nikki," Tabitha gushed. "Many of the young ladies have said the same. Truly, you are blessed to have him."

A loud screech prevented any further comments Matron Findhorn was prepared to say, as Matron Kirk slid back her chair. After rising, she placed her notebook on the seat, smoothed non-existent wrinkles in her A-Line skirt, and clasped her hands while turning to look at the other Pillars. "Thank you, my fellow Matrons, for making this conversation go as smoothly as possible for our dear Nicolette. I do believe it's time to get over to the clubhouse before lunch officially begins. We wouldn't want to be late, would we?" She gave me a weary smile and told me to take a few moments to collect myself before joining everyone for lunch.

I stared, dumbfounded, as the three women I respected—trusted—gathered their notebooks then left me alone in the hollow room.

SEVEN

THE WALLS OF that empty room mocked me for about a minute after the Pillars left.

Too many miserable thoughts fought for dominance in my mind, but I couldn't make sense of them, so I stepped from the room and commanded my feet to move. I had a minute or two to get my face in Faith before joining everyone in the courtyard. My body, the disobedient sack of flesh, had its own plans. The lightness in my head and the sinking of my stomach made each step I took through the brightly lit corridor more unsteady than the previous.

Please, don't pass out.

Framed photographs of Champions throughout the years, Grand Elders, Pillars, and commemorative ceremonies lined the eggshell painted walls of the curved corridor leading to the courtyard. The sound of footsteps, sure and evenly paced, drew closer from the opposite direction, and I halted. I wasn't ready for anyone to see me in that condition. I couldn't even fake a smile, and if it was one of the Pillars returning to get me, I don't think my heart would survive the encounter. I quickly ducked into the closest room and, with both hands around the knob, I soundlessly closed the door.

I turned around to face the dim room and realized I'd never been in there before. In fact, the door was always locked. Sparse sunlight shone around the edges of lowered shades on two windows and my nostrils filled with the dank smell of old wood and mothballs. But there, in the center of the room, taking up more than half of the entire space, proudly stood a white grand piano. It was stunning, elegant. Old.

I stepped deeper into the abandoned room, careful to avoid the stack of dusty music stands lest my yellow dress get dirty. My gaze slid along the perimeter of the room where various instruments were organized by type.

Amazing.

String instruments, including regular-sized and small violins, were stacked on top and around one another in the far left corner, all covered in a layer of dust. Two full-sized cellos stood next to them, and beside them, a small cello. Wind instruments like clarinets and flutes peeked out of the top of an open Bankers box, and finally two trumpets sat in the far right corner. I couldn't say for certain what every item was. I didn't know much about instruments, anyway. Never played one nor saw them up close.

As I walked closer toward the piano, I could see the color was not your average white but a shade brimming with more life. It was pearl. And it seemed to be luring me toward it, daring me to touch it. I couldn't stop my fingers from sliding across the piano's face, tracing each of the shimmery gold etched letters forming the name Steinway & Sons.

"What is this place?" I breathed.

"It used to be the music classroom."

My heart leaped out of my chest at the sudden sound of a deep male voice. Instinctively correcting my posture, I pivoted toward the once-closed door.

A tall man stood on the threshold, leaning casually against the frame. Frowning.

At me?

I'd seen him before, but always from a distance, building things and carrying equipment around the Community. If I had to guess, I'd say he stood one or two inches past six feet. His short, ebony hair was curly—almost cute if not for his sharp, masculine features. His skin was like caramel. Even from where I stood, I could see the sharp curves of his cheekbones and angular jaw, which were complimented by several days' stubble. It looked good on him.

My eyes followed the path downward to his navy-blue long-sleeved shirt, cuffed midway at his forearm. His broad shoulders and equally intimidating-looking arms couldn't hide in that shirt, and I had a passing thought of how easily those arms could lift me. He looked out of place, like he belonged somewhere else. A place that required physical strength and a primal type of knowledge. And I couldn't help but acknowledge he was, unequivocally, the most attractive man I'd ever laid eyes on.

"What are you doing in here?" he asked, simultaneously throwing me out of my shameless gawking. He turned around, scanned the corridor, then closed the door, leaving the two of us alone in the dusty room. His gaze fell upon me.

I squirmed at the perusal and took an instinctive step back. No good reason popped into my brain. Not that it was any of his business, anyway.

"I didn't know there ever *was* a music class. These instruments aren't allowed here." I pointed toward the trumpets.

"The *Community*," he mocked, "doesn't allow many things, yet here you are in a room you're not supposed to be in." His face held no expression, as if he was stating a boring fact and not insulting me and everyone who lived here.

Rude! Who did this guy think he was?

"What's that supposed to mean?" I threw the question at him.

He repeated his question as if I were slow. "What are you doing in *this* room? You get lost?" He strutted toward me, the intimidation not diminished by the old rag and feather duster in his hand. "I'm pretty sure you're expected at Lunch."

I side-stepped his approach, scooting out of his way until we'd circled each other and our positions were reversed. Now that I was closer to the door, my bravery increased. Yes, technically I should be at Lunch, but I didn't owe him any explanations. The blossoming character traits of curiosity and inquiry decided now was a glorious time to experiment.

"Are *you* not going to lunch? I don't think I've seen you in Service before, but I have seen you around the Community a few times." I wasn't ready to go out to the courtyard just yet.

"Let me guess. You're one of the *engaged ladies* who had to talk to the Pillars after service, and now you're hiding in this room because they're making you do something you don't want to do."

A flush of heat sprinted to my face. At a loss for a comeback, I scoffed. Actually scoffed.

He had the nerve to smirk.

Micah. That was his name. Micah Fox... the asshole Reen told me about. Apparently, she was invited to hang out with Serena Henderson and a handful of others a few months ago. While they were talking by the fountain in the center of the courtyard, some guy abruptly turned off the fountain. The Pillar who was with them demanded he turn it back on, and when he did, water sprayed them. I was pretty sure Micah was that guy.

"I'm not hiding." I sneered. Lying through my teeth.

"Right."

Maybe if I didn't just get scolded by the Pillars, I could have brushed off his annoyed expression and condescending remarks. But my patience vanished when they exited the room, and I didn't have energy to be anything other than what I was in the moment. This guy didn't know anything about me, and yet he had the nerve to make assumptions and judgments about me. Even if I was hiding, who did he think he was trying to call me out on it?

He placed the rag and duster on the piano bench then proceeded to delicately lift the front half of the piano cover.

"You don't have to pretend with me. Go do that with the people you're *not* hiding from."

Asshole! The word almost slipped from my lips, but I held it in and shot him a disgusted look instead.

He ignored my attempt at visual intimidation, and a smile spread across his stupidly perfect face. He ignored my glare while lifting the back portion of the piano cover about a foot then securing it atop a short lever.

Logic dictated I leave, as no rules required me to participate in his rude behavior. But the inquisitive side of me wondered how he knew I was hiding and why he hadn't rushed to tell on me. Any other man, including Jason, would swiftly escort me from this room and tell a matron where he'd found me. I'd then be scolded for breaking the rules and being late to Lunch.

As he worked, each movement made his shirt tighten around his substantial biceps. As quickly as I noticed, I looked away. He didn't deserve my inward appreciation of his exceptional male form.

"Why aren't *you* going to Lunch, and why have I never seen you in service?"

"Because I don't want to attend either." His tone was matter-of-fact.

"Then how… Why are you here? In our community?" People didn't get to just *live* here without faithfully attending services. We all had to follow strict requirements, and that was one of the biggest.

He began dusting the piano keys, ensuring each was cleaned and buffed, then he sat on the bench with an elegance surprising for his size. His broad back was straight, and his neck equally poised. Without turning in my direction and in a voice with less assholeness, he finally answered, "We all have our reasons."

Before I could think of a response to that cop-out of an answer, a reverberating string of notes cascaded off the walls and leaped throughout the dusty oldness of the music room. Micah's fingers danced over the keys, and to my untrained ear, he played the piano extremely well. The suddenness of the sound shut down any negative thought I had and placed my body, my consciousness, my everything into the music. It felt as though the melody was giving shape to the visual condition of the room we were in. Filling the abandoned space with life. Sad, thoughtful, melancholic. The harmonies were exquisite. Breathtaking even.

The initial repetitions of the notes shifted into a deeper, passionate, less predictable melody, accentuated by hints of higher, brighter tones reminding me of shimmering raindrops on a solitary evening walk. The music's vibrations swam throughout my body, my veins, my blood, immersing me as I used the closed door to bear my weight. Rational thought escaped me. I couldn't muster the energy to hold them. I could only *feel* and yield my emotions to each chord, each note. The music washed over my entire being, guiding me in whatever direction the next note conducted.

Tears welled, fell. I made no attempt to wipe them away. That required a level of effort I couldn't manage. It took all my strength to breathe through the melody as it once again shifted into rapid succession. I was like an athlete breathing through another weighted rep. The music ran… no, arrowed through my coiled thoughts, fixing them in their disordered positions. As mental acuity failed, I was left to the mercy of my rising emotions—and there were many.

Discomfort from the Pillars' demands. Sorrow they were repossessing my home. Grief for Mama's untimely passing. Anger at Jason's pressure. Indignation for the things said and thought about Reen. I had to allow each emotion its due before it would pass, suffering their strength, enduring them only by believing something better waited beyond their reach. I surrendered all of it to the magical melody played by this strange man. The muscles in my legs could no longer hold my sagging weight against the door. Gravity won as I slowly slipped down to the floor. I no longer cared about dirtying my dress or how foolish I looked. I only knew this music and its relentless power to unmake me.

EIGHT

THE LONG SILENCE that ensued after the final keystroke felt like tranquility.

My head and eyes were heavy, too much to look up, but I knew Micah still sat on the piano bench. I slumped on the floor, no doubt looking like a hot mess, but for once in my life I didn't care that someone else witnessed it. For better or worse, I was wrapped in a cocoon of self-acceptance. Neither my head nor heart had the capacity for anything other than unfiltered truth, so I whispered, "That was the most beautiful thing I've ever heard."

The bench screeched as Micah sprung from his seat as if he hadn't realized I was still there. He probably thought I'd left after his last comment. Brown leather boots appeared in my line of sight. The heaviness of my head prevented me from looking higher than the bottom half of his denim-clad legs. He extended his hand down toward me, so I clasped it. In one easy swoop, he lifted me from the ground then waited for my wobbly legs to support my weight.

"People will talk if they see you on the ground like that." His voice was low, hoarse. He looked at me like he hadn't seen me before.

"People talk even when I'm standing up. Or sitting in a chair." I didn't have the energy to be witty or caring. And I didn't have the energy to explain myself to an Unfaithful guy I'd just met.

I glanced around the room. What time was it? I needed to get out of there.

My hands took to the task of dusting dirt from my dress and wiping tear streaks from my puffy face, no doubt further smudging the carefully applied makeup in the process.

"I'm going home." No use showing up to Lunch when I looked and felt so terrible.

"It's good to see you outside the house again, Nikki, and I'm sorry about your mom."

I turned back around.

"You know about my mom?"

"Of course. Everyone around here does." He slid a hand through his short curls. "I organized the team to do the repairs on your house that day. I'm sure you don't remember. Your mom had only passed away a few weeks before, and it seemed like my uncle didn't give you any notice we were coming over."

My mouth hung open as my mind tried to process what he said. I didn't recall seeing *him* that day. But then again, I didn't recall what any of those men looked like. A few weeks after Mama's passing, our Champion and five other men unexpectedly appeared at my doorstep, tools in hand just as the sun was rising. When I opened the door, he had announced, "A gift of free home repairs in honor of Regina," by way of greeting then left without another word.

"Wait a minute." I asked slowly, "Who is your uncle?"

"Malachi."

Not *Our Champion*. Just *Malachi*. The mention of his name intensified the knot in my stomach and my tension-fueled headache. I must have looked as surprised as I felt.

"My name's Micah Fox, but my mom is Malachi's sister." He returned to the piano then retrieved his rag and feather duster. "Anyway, I'm glad you liked the ballad."

I stared at Micah for a full thirty seconds. He gently closed the piano's cover then proceeded to dust the magical instrument with care.

"What are *you* doing in this room? And where did you learn to play the piano like that?"

He just looked at me, pausing for a long moment before answering. "No one—other than me, it seems—comes in here since they banned music years ago. But their rules can't stamp out my love of music, and they haven't stopped me from playing. The room's semi-sound proof." He pointed to the walls.

I didn't notice it earlier, but the walls were covered in a soft, foam-like material. I supposed it absorbed most of the sound.

"So, during Lunch, no one can hear me play. Unless they're close by."

Finally, a real answer. He was hiding too.

"Everything's a blur from the first month after she died. Sorry I didn't recognize you." My head hurt, and I was tired of talking, so I left without waiting for him to reply.

NINE

P ANIC CUTS DEEP *into every nerve in my body.*
*We're running out of time. My raised arms shake as spasms shoot
through my biceps and triceps. I'd pushed beyond what they normally
endured. Regardless of what happens, I will catch this last little girl. A broken
twig in the distance has my head whipping to the left.* "Please, Bright Lord,
don't let them find us. Not yet!"

This was the fifth little girl, around seven or eight years old and the oldest
one here.

"Hurry! You have to jump now, sweetheart. I promise I'll catch you."

Her trembling hands ball together against her chest as she searches for
another option.

"Now, honey. Please!" I whisper-shout.

She squeezes her eyes shut and lifts her knees, throwing herself off the ledge
of the rotted-out treehouse. Screams burst from her little lungs as she plunges
into my outstretched arms.

The full weight of her crashes into my chest, knocking the wind out of me. I stumble back. The heel of my shoe meets a rock, and I fall backward while cradling her in my arms. I land directly on my tailbone. Pain sears up my spine, but I have no time to think about it, no time to allow myself to feel the burning radiate through my body. We must go.

I set her on the ground in the dark field, scramble to my feet, then grab her sweaty palm. We dash through the field toward the driveway, where Reen and four other girls wait for us. Their mouths move in soundless shouts. Arms beckon in desperate circles, demanding we hurry.

A meaty hand grasps my shoulder. A brute tug drags me down.

"No!" A burly man, his face shadowed, snatches my wrist then pulls me back toward the treehouse.

The little girl freezes and stares at me, her face white and eyes wide.

"Run! Go!" She has to save herself! "Go! Go!"

Two other men appear. One places a rag over the girl's nose and mouth then scoops her into his arms.

The sound of screeching tires in the distance draws my attention, but I can't move. A rag-filled hand covers my face, then darkness falls.

𝕤𝕠𝕔𝕣

JARRED OUT OF a nightmare, I sprung from bed, greeted by the darkness of my room. Gasping, I fought to pull air into my lungs.

My body was slick with sweat. My cotton pajamas stuck to my back. No blood, just perspiration. I slid my hands toward my tailbone to assess injuries sustained in the struggle. A winded sigh escaped my throat when, after a head-to-toe examination, my body felt free of pain and no bruises were detected.

It really was only a dream. But it felt so real.

The clock on my nightstand showed it was 3:33 a.m.

Rubbing my eyes, I pulled the lamp chain atop my nightstand, and a soft glow illuminated the room. I retrieved a black leather-bound journal from the top drawer. I'd begun journaling my dreams a few years ago when I couldn't shake off the disturbing images. I've had nightmares ever since I was a child, but they increased after Mama died.

Journaling was cathartic. While remaining only in my mind, the nightmares circulated and left me feeling trapped but writing them down gave me control over them. Seeing the black words scrawled on a white page somehow weakened their power. A little swish of my eraser, and boom, I could transform the ending into something beautiful instead of frightening.

Mama believed the Bright Lord gave us dreams as spiritual messages and we should pay attention to them, even the scary ones. Because of her, I did my best to write out as much as I could remember of last night's dream. The little girls, the treehouse, the orchard, Reen in the pickup… everything but the men's faces. They were all blurred beyond recognition. It wasn't the first time I'd had that dream, but it was the first time I didn't make it to the truck. The first time I was taken. The first I didn't escape.

The thought made me shiver.

"Time to get up!" I said into the darkness.

The two windows in our cozy kitchen faced south, allowing the sun to constantly bathe the room in bright light. Beyond the backyard, past the rows of strawberry plants, the foothills lay about one hundred yards in the distance. Sweet earthy scents filled my nostrils as I slid the windows open and breathed in a deep, satisfying inhale.

Squawking birds conversed with one another as Fresno's heat warmed my face. I loved that our long summers began in early May and extended through September, sometimes October. The valley could easily reach triple digits in July or August, but May was my favorite. Steady eighties with the occasional ninety made it perfect for long morning and evening strolls, picnics, or swimming. Most importantly, it was great for strawberries. Tastier strawberries, that is.

The land was fertile, yielding multiple harvests of varied fruits and vegetables all year long. Fresno was known as the agricultural capital of the world, and with good reason. Almost anything could grow here. In acknowledgement of that fact, every member living in Bright Lakes was required to have gardens in the front yard and maintain them to "a respectable standard." It wasn't a problem for me or Mama. She adored gardening flowers indigenous to the area, so tending to them, along with herbs, was more a happy hobby than a chore.

She left the back yard for me to do whatever I chose. A few months after we first moved here, we'd visited the farmer's market, and it was my first time tasting a vine-ripened, fresh strawberry. That one experience was all I needed to make up my mind. I decided to grow strawberries and have been happily doing so ever since.

The quarter acre now displayed beautifully raised garden beds, vertical planting towers, and neatly planted rows, each nurturing a different variety of the luscious berry. This past October, we re-planted the runners—long, horizontal shoots that grew from established strawberry plants—and expected a large harvest this year. The addition would ensure plenty of fruit to sell throughout the summer and hopefully into early fall.

I placed the tea kettle on the gas stove, lit the pilot with a match, then scooped two teaspoons of dried lavender buds into my mortar. As I crushed them and dried dandelion roots with my pestle, sweet, floral scents flooded my nostrils. My shoulders dropped from my efforts.

The Pillars' proclamations resurfaced, reminding me of all I needed to do and the urgency with which I needed to do it. Their words consumed my thoughts.

Everyone knows she's a wild thing.

We can give you two more months.

Examinee Carmichael said Jason was at your home late.

She's contributing to your moral decay.

The hissing whistle from the kettle jolted me, and I dropped the pestle into the mortar, the bowl now filled with tiny herbaceous fragments. I put the tea kettle on an empty burner then retrieved a tiny mesh bag and mug. Chimes of the doorbell called for my attention, but I took the time to set my tea to steeping before seeing who had come uninvited.

TEN

"**I** KNOW YOU'RE in there!"

I sauntered past the dining room and through the sun-lit living room as pesky knocking continued at the front door.

"Hey, girl." I offered a tired smile to Reen as I opened the door.

"I see you're still wearing your sinner-suit out in public." Raising an eyebrow at her, as she'd become notorious for walking from her house to mine wearing stretchy pants, especially during harvest season—a direct violation of the Ladies Styling Guidelines for community members. We were permitted to wear pants inside our homes and for outdoor chores, but never while walking around the neighborhood or in any public setting beyond our houses.

"Don't you 'hey girl' me. I've been ringing this bell way too long." She scowled and stepped inside, heading straight towards the kitchen. "And I'm not wearing a dress just to walk five blocks, only to change clothes when I get here."

I couldn't do anything but shake my head. The girl was a rebel through and through. "I was making tea and got lost in thought. Want some?"

"What you thinking about?" She answered by casually placing the teakettle back on the burner. "And why didn't I see you at Lunch after Service? And what happened with your talk with the Pillars?"

She went to work placing the remaining tea fragments inside the other mesh bag, making herself at home as she always did.

I sat on the blue-cushioned bench of our breakfast nook and rubbed my temples. "Exactly. Too many things in too short a time. I don't even know where to begin."

She poured the boiling water into her teacup. "That bad?"

I pinched the rim of the tea bag and pulled it out just above the water line then dipped it back into the mug as I searched for the words to sum up what happened. "I'll start with the worst part. I have to leave this house by the end of July."

Reen's eyes widened, and her neck extended forward. "What? What for?" She picked up her teacup and sat on the other side of the bench, so we faced one another.

I relayed what each matron said about the house and Jason, and Examinee Carmichael… Sheila, but I couldn't bring myself to repeat the hateful comments Matron Butler said about her. When I tried to rush past certain parts, Reen demanded I slow down and tell her all the details, including Matron Findhorn's allusion to Jason being sought after by other ladies in the community.

"I knew Sheila was a rat," Reen spat. "And I figured they'd try to make you hurry to marry Jason. I'm surprised they're not making you marry him tomorrow. But this business with the house is unbelievable! You know, it's just like this *community* to impose such a rule. Did they never think people would have children?"

I cringed. She was practically screaming, but my reaction was to my misfortunes rather than her tone.

She stretched her hand over the table and covered mine with it. "I'm so sorry, friend. I can't imagine how you must've felt sitting there in front of the three of them. Have you decided anything or know what you want to do?"

Her eyes held so much compassion it made the stinging at the back of my eyes return, but I squeezed them tightly and determined I would not cry again. My gaze absently drifted to my teacup. "Well, I was already going to marry Jason, so I'm not completely upset about that except it felt overly aggressive. I guess I have been a little selfish by postponing it this far. Thinking only of me…"

"You're not being selfish!" She pounded her fist on the table.

"Your mom literally just died. And it was sudden! After one day, speech was stolen from her. Next thing you know, she was in a coma. It's only been four months. No one is thinking of a wedding immediately after a funeral."

"Well, as far as the Pillars—and apparently the whole community—are concerned, I've been grieving long enough and Jason is a good catch, so I better get it together ASAP." Saying the words out loud sent a tingling sensation through my legs. I felt overheated, antsy. I stood to pace the short length of my kitchen.

"Tomorrow I'll talk to Jason, and we'll select a few dates to share with his parents by next week. That'll give me time to take care of the next delivery batch of strawberries before meeting with the Pillars again in two weeks." I stopped pacing. Saying my plans aloud made them feel possible, even though I was being arm wrestled into it.

Reen looked pointedly at me. "You know you don't have to worry about the strawberries, right?"

I nodded.

"Okay, so what are we going to do about the house? I'm here for whatever you need with that." Determination and sadness clouded her eyes.

"I honestly don't know. It's such bad timing, and all I can think of is it's too fast. I haven't even packed Mama's room. A few days ago, was the first I'd entered since she passed, and it was awful."

"Okay, so we'll start there."

We'll start there. We'll go into her room together.

I nodded and released an exhale.

Reen stood from the breakfast nook bench and gave a curt nod as if preparing for battle. "Right now."

Holding my gaze, she took my hand then led me a few paces beyond the kitchen to my mother's closed bedroom door. With infinite patience, she waited for me to open it.

I took a deep breath. The luxury of procrastination was gone, so I turned the knob.

Inside, we were greeted by a warm summer breeze. I'd left the window open a few days ago. The loaded bookshelf in the corner next to the window held a flat screen television atop it, and beside that was the door leading to her walk-in closet. With a smile, I remembered her reaction when we first moved in. She was so excited about her closet. It was the happiest I'd seen her in a long time. Dad died two years prior in a car accident, and we lived in a cramped one-bedroom apartment before being accepted to reside in the community. It was a dream come true, and the walk-in closet was tangible proof of that for Mama. It was an extravagance just for her.

Moving into the Bright Lakes Community gave my mom a new start after a devastating loss. She'd stopped believing in people after the drunk driver took her husband's—my dad's—life. The Bright Lord saved her. Saved us. All day, she pored over the Sacred Text looking for hope. The most loving people she met of the Bright Lord's Fresno Order all lived within the Bright Lakes Residential Community, and Mama was determined to get in so she could be closer to them. I think they helped fill a void that my dad left.

"It just doesn't feel right to go through her things like this," I said. "I don't even have boxes or totes."

"We can get some when you're ready."

I nodded.

"What would you like me to do, Friend?" Reen looked about the room with a pained expression I'd not seen since the funeral.

"Would you be okay going through her books? Perhaps gathering those on the bookshelf and making a few stacks?"

"Of course."

"There's also a few books in her nightstands. You can add those to the stack."

She nodded and got to work while I turned toward the closet.

Mama's belts and purses slung over one large hook making a loud clacking sound as I opened the door. Squaring my shoulders, I turned on the light. Two bars hung to my left. The top one was full of blouses and long-sleeved shirts, organized by color from dark to light. Beneath them, half the bar held skirts of various lengths and designs, also arranged by hue. On the right side of her closet was a single bar allowing storage of longer garments. It contained dresses organized by sleeve length, short to long. Behind them were her blazers, jackets, and cardigans. I immediately spotted her favorite.

The knot in my throat returned as I fought back tears. My hand trembled as I lifted the hem of her teal blazer to my face. I closed my eyes and inhaled the fading residue of her perfume, a rose scented cologne she restocked every year. I took the blazer off the hanger and slid my arms into its sleeves. The shoulders drooped, and the cuffs fell way past my hands, but I didn't care. This was the closest I could get to a hug from her. The closest I could get to her, period.

I scanned the shelves above the bars, stacked with hats, shoe boxes, and old magazines and newspapers.

"Hey Nikki? Can you come here for a minute?" Reen's tone held a hint of concern.

I hurried to her. "Wow, you've done a lot more than I have."

All the books from the bookshelf were neatly stacked on the carpeted floor along with six journals in a separate stack. Reen sat cross-legged on the floor beside the bed, a journal in her hand—the same purple one I skimmed through the other day. She had opened it to a page near the back. If it were anyone other than Reen, I would've been pissed at her for opening my mom's journal, but Reen was as much a second daughter to my mom as she was a sister to me.

I sat on the bed and looked down at her.

"Read this entry right here and tell me what you think it means." She handed me the opened journal.

Dec 15

I told Samantha what I found behind Malachi's desk. It didn't shock her as much as I thought it would. Why not? She asked me to keep it quiet until she has a chance to talk to the other Pillars. Bright Lord, what am I supposed to do in the meantime? One of those photos was of Nicolette right after we moved here. My sweet baby.

Tension knotted the muscles in my neck. I read the entry again. Out loud this time, then thumbed to the previous entry.

Dec 13

I still can't sleep. I'll meet with Samantha on Tuesday. I pray she has some answers. Regardless, an investigation has to happen! I know what I saw was real. There's no way that hidden flap would be there if they weren't trying to hide something. Does anyone else know about this?

"Have you read the earlier entries?" I could barely hear myself speak and looked at Reen to see if she'd heard me.

She shook her head. "What does it say?"

I couldn't read it aloud, so I lowered myself to the floor beside her then held the book so she could read with me.

I flung the journal to the previous page and read aloud.

"*Dec 10*

"*I can't believe what I just saw. My hands are trembling even writing this. Bright Lord, what am I to do?*

My eyes darted to the previous page. Nothing there that stood out. On to the next page, skimmed through the text. Nothing unusual.

I continued flipping through the pages. "What the hell is she talking about?"

We read through all six of the other journals but came up with nothing suspicious.

"I'm going to speak to Matron Kirk privately," I decided.

"You better."

ELEVEN

Jason and I walked together to the farmer's market located just outside of the Bright Lakes Community.

It was an easy distance, about a quarter mile east, and unlike the residential community was open to the general public. As we rounded the corner of the pedestrian entrance, happy memories flooded my mind from when Mama used to bring me as a child. Lightness bubbled up within me from the familiar sights, sounds, and smells. A chatty group of women in yoga pants pushed babies in strollers, well-dressed men dashed by clutching bags of goodies, fellow community members waved as we strolled by, and young children with their caretakers toddled throughout the expansive grassy area, heads turning in every direction as they tried to take in all the sights.

To make it easier on shoppers, each vendor was assigned a specific color of canopy based on their wares. Only Faithful members of the Bright Lord's Faith, whether they lived within or outside of the residential Community, were permitted to sell their produce, products, and services. The market resembled an outdoor shopping center, not merely selling and buying of produce from farmers, as the name implied. Toys, trinkets, earrings, handmade clothing, chopped wood, homemade goodies, and many other fun items were available for purchase every day except Wednesday and Saturday.

The enticing aroma of cinnamon, sweet fried pastries and juicy, grilled meats made my belly growl. After a fitful night with little sleep, I'd hit the snooze button three times before finally dragging my butt out of bed, forcing me to rush to get dressed before Jason arrived. I gave a wide-eyed, toothy smile and tugged him toward Mrs. Weaver's stall. She waved as we approached, the lines on her round face deepening with her bright smile.

The plump grandmother of twelve lived outside of the community but faithfully attended weekly services and lunch. I'd been visiting the Farmers Market for fifteen years, and she was a fixture, sharing stories about her growing family while selling delicious, made-on-site hand pies stuffed with seasonal fruit fillings. The deep smile lines on her round face were framed by thick, curly strands of silvery white hair tied in a half-up, half-down style showing years of love and good eating.

"Hi, Mrs. Weaver. How are those grandkids of yours doing lately?" I asked.

"Ah, you know…" She placed her hands on each hip and smiled, "bruises, scrapes, vomit, birthday parties, and long weekends. I can't tell you how hard it is to keep up with so many birthdays." She shook her head, silvery curls dancing with her effort. "What can I get for you two this morning?"

Jason's palm rested at the small of my back as he placed our order. She made quick work of stuffing homemade dough with a sweet and spicy fruit filling while she rattled on about Johnathan, her six-year-old grandson and his identity crisis of believing he was the real Iron Man. By the time she sealed the edges of the dough and dropped both hand-sized pastries into a vat of sizzling oil, I was salivating. With a liberal dusting of cinnamon sugar, she passed the pies to Jason, and we were off to find seating. We found a round cafe table with two small chairs near the coffee stand a short distance from other patrons and the main walkway.

Jason passed me a pie. Though ravenous, I took the time to close my eyes, taking in a deep whiff of the cinnamon, nutmeg, and peachy deliciousness. "Bright Lord, that smells amazing." I leaned back in the cafe chair, careful not to apply too much weight, lest I fell out, and held the pie to my nose while Jason sat down across from me.

"I haven't had one of these in at least six months. The last time we came here together, actually."

I immediately regretted mentioning it. That was a day I wanted to forget.

"Yeah. Shame it's so hot I can't take a bite right now," Jason agreed. "But I'm glad we both have time to come this morning, given everything that's going on."

During our walk to the market, I told Jason everything the Pillars said, particularly the part about me needing to move out of my house. The upsetting news didn't seem entirely surprising to him, so I asked if he'd known.

"That's partly why I've been asking you to choose a date for our wedding. I had to become familiar with all Community Guidelines during my Examination, so I knew this was coming." His following apology made me feel worse. Perhaps if our roles were reversed, I could have understood his omission and arrived at the same conclusion as him.

"Gladys didn't have any issue with me going in to volunteer later today after I told her the reason I'd be late." My eyes involuntarily rolled.

Jason clearly noticed but graciously ignored it. "That's good."

A few steps away, a woman who looked like she could be my age was scolding a toddler wearing a soft purple dress and two pigtails. Apparently, the little cutie had taken candy from the "Sweets N Things" vendor shop around the corner. The wails from the girl's pouty mouth was adorable as tears flooded down her flaming red cheeks.

"She looks like a man in those clothes." Jason glared at the woman.

I'd been so taken with the girl I'd failed to notice the mother. Her hair was in a simple ponytail, and she wore straight-legged jeans topped with a fitted blue t-shirt— normal clothes for women who didn't live within the Bright Lakes Residential Community. The truth was, the Sacred Text didn't explicitly say what women could and could not wear, but those of us who wanted to be called Faithful Members chose to live by elevated standards. While I preferred wearing dresses—it was easier than choosing an "outfit"—I didn't expect women from other faiths to behave and dress just like me. I didn't think negatively of them.

Clearly Jason did.

He shook his head. "And she's not doing a great job parenting that kid either." He added for good measure.

He'd made similar remarks before, but this time his judgement made my body tense, and I immediately corrected my posture. He'd become more verbal with his negative thoughts lately, and it made me a little uncomfortable.

I averted my eyes to the still-hot peach pie in my hands. "So, I was thinking, since I have to be out of the house by the end of July, it should work out if we marry the Saturday before that. July twenty-third. What do you think?"

When I looked up to face him, my attention was drawn to the man behind him. His back was to me as he secured a rope on his vendor canopy—bright green for hats, bags and clothing. The back of his smoke grey t-shirt was damp with sweat in the shape of a V, trailing from mid- to lower-back. Though I couldn't see his face, there was no mistaking his short, curly, ebony hair and tall, solid stature. I'd been so busy packing Mama's room, managing the strawberry crops, and preparing for this very conversation with Jason, I hadn't had time to think of that strange day in the music room. I hadn't even told Reen! But seeing him now... a kernel of heat stirred in my lower belly and quickly rose up to my face. My breath caught within my lungs. All of my senses zeroed in on Micah Fox.

Jason's mouth moved, but I couldn't hear his words and didn't care what he was saying—until his eyes narrowed and his face reddened.

"What are you looking at?" Jason twisted his body around. After finding nothing of interest, he turned to face me with a questioning glare.

If I weren't Black, the heat in my face would tell all my business right now. "Nothing. I just zoned out for a bit. I'm sorry, can you repeat what you were saying?"

I could still see Micah's movements through my peripheral vision. He was speaking to another man, perhaps the vendor of the tent he was setting up. His presence was distracting—demanding, even—but I forced myself to look directly at Jason.

"I was saying that date is fine." He straightened his spine, sitting taller. "That gives me enough time to complete the housing transactions, so we won't need to live with my parents at all. We could move straight into our own house."

"Our own house," I mouthed in a near-whisper. The words echoed through my mind, and I tried to imagine living with Jason. Studious Jason. Structured Jason. Diligent Jason. Yes, these are the qualities I loved about him. The security and consistency I admired and desired within my own life. So why was my stomach turning in knots as those qualities rang like a gong in the hollows of my mind? Why did I suddenly want to put a little distance between our chairs?

I couldn't think quickly enough to say the right words he'd want to hear, so I placed my hand on his knee and made myself smile. "You think of everything, Jason. Thank you for taking care of all of this for us."

"I'd do anything for you, Nikki. I hope you know that by now."

"I do, Jason. I do." But would he really do anything for me? Would he let me sink to the dirty floor and cry my eyes out because too much was happening in my life?

Like Micah let me do the other day in the music room.

"If we weren't in public, I'd kiss you right now." His green eyes darkened with passion.

But there, at the edge of my vision, there he was again… Micah… walking in my direction. And looking straight at me! My heart beat furiously as his long, confident strides drew him closer and closer. Our gazes locked, his hot and piercing. It felt as if he could somehow see straight through to my soul. Right to the deepest, most treacherous parts of me. The parts even I was too afraid to acknowledge. Even so, I could not look away from him.

His dark, thick eyebrows haloed mesmerizing eyes I had not previously noticed. Deep hues of soft amber and olive green. Hazel. He reached us in what felt like mere seconds but passed by without breaking stride, snapping me out of my trance. With effort, I willed my head not to turn to track him, but I couldn't face Jason just yet. I felt naked and exposed and ashamed.

The hand pie suddenly became my focus, so I took a bite of the fried pastry, chewed slowly, and mumbled, "This tastes amazing." I mumbled through bites.

"Do you know Micah Fox?" Jason looked past me in the direction Micah walked.

Oh no! He saw me staring!

"No, not really. He was with a group of guys who came by my house one morning after Mama passed. Remember, I told you about that?" Whew, so glad there was a point of connection.

"Yeah. I remember," he murmured. "Anyway, he's the Champion's nephew, not that you could tell. The two are nothing alike."

"How do you mean?" What did Jason know about Micah, anyway? He wasn't the type of person Jason would willingly associate with. Even I didn't associate with him.

"He lives in the community but doesn't follow the Faith. It's insulting, since he went through Examination to become a Trainee. It's disrespectful to the purpose of the Community and undermines our Champion's family." His lips twisted as if the words tasted bad leaving his mouth. "I don't know why Malachi lets him stay." He bit off a chunk of his hand-pie then chewed aggressively.

"If he went through Examination, why isn't he a Trainee or Elder by now?"

"Because he dropped out in the last two months. And he's not married. Some people are just too weak to handle hard truths."

I had no idea what that was supposed to mean but quickly decided it was better not to ask. Didn't want to draw any additional attention to my curiosity about the man.

We sat in silence for a breath or two, watching the busyness surrounding us. It was enough time to allow the heat in my body to return to its normal temperature and for me to appreciate the tangy, sweet deliciousness of the peach pie.

A couple walked past staring at us and I overheard the woman tell the man "I hope those Bright Lord people eventually realize they're in a cult."

I shifted in my seat and glanced at Jason. He was looking off in the distance and clearly didn't hear the woman. It wasn't the first time I'd heard comments like that but the pity in her eyes and the recent events since Mama's passing made it sting this time.

Why did Micah stay in the community if he had no intention of following the Faith? Come to think of it, when a resident didn't follow Community Rules for two consecutive months without acceptable cause, they were promptly and discreetly evicted.

Maybe that's what had happened to the Winters family. When a rule breaker moved out, no one ever spoke of that person or family again. I learned that the hard way when I was a child. I mentioned my friend Analisa's family, and the adults rushed to answer with versions of, *"Oh, honey, not everyone is faithful enough to stay in this community, so we don't need to ask about them."* So, I stopped asking. But the removal of the unfaithful was happening too frequently, and it seemed to mostly occur with families who had daughters.

After devouring his pie, Jason wiped the cinnamon sugar off his lips. "We should tell my mom immediately. She'll want to meet with the Pillars and help with wedding planning."

"That's right." Mrs. Tucker was well known for her sense of style and eye for detail. Having her help plan the ceremony would be a bonus for me since I'll be spending my free time packing up the house and shipping strawberries.

"Okay. How about I come to your house for dinner tonight?" I suggested.

"Yeah, let's plan for that. I'll text you later." Jason stood then took my hand. "We should get back. I know you have work to do at the admin building, and I've got to help my dad with some briefs before noon." He whispered in my ear, "You look beautiful in that dress. I'm sorry I didn't tell you sooner."

What? It was extremely rare for him to compliment my appearance. Before Mama died, I'd spend hours trying on dress after dress before our dates, but he never acknowledged the effort, so I stopped trying these last few months. Today—for some reason—I made an effort, donning a navy-blue fit-and-flare dress. It complimented my figure perfectly, even with the addition of a cardigan to avoid drawing too much attention to my breasts. I'd hoped for such affection for months but finally accepted that wasn't his style. Now that he graced me with the compliment, I didn't know how to feel about it and definitely didn't know how to respond.

Before I let too much time pass, I settled on the safest response I could muster.

"That's sweet of you to say."

TWELVE

A SHORT STACK of rental applications and facility request forms sat on the desk I manned on volunteer days.

No doubt Gladys placed them there. The older woman didn't believe in wasting time and therefore spared me the few seconds it would take to ask questions like, "What would you like me to work on?" or "Where are the forms?" Even though the work I did at the Admin Building was voluntary, it was no less productive or more relaxed than if I were employed.

My role was to greet members and potential members with a smile. Even if I didn't feel like it, smiling was an essential part of the job. I had a very basic script to follow. If asked any questions, my instructions were to take down that person's information and set up a meeting with Gladys, Kendall Patterson, or Tamika Hill. If Gladys had no openings, I always choose Kendall. She asked fewer probing questions and didn't share personal information with the rest of the community like Tamika did.

Gladys limped toward me from the copy room. She wore a powder pink blazer over a floral dress. Her bright smile was always welcoming, and her presence was warm and cuddly. She was the grandma everyone wanted. "How did it go, sweetheart?"

"It went great. We settled on a date." I forced myself to sound more cheerful than I felt.

Through the years, I'd learned to react the way people in the community believed I should, whether the feelings were authentic or not. Once Lady Maribelle gifted me with a teakwood scented candle. When I merely replied, "Thank you," she gave me the stink eye. The next mandatory topic for Ladies Study Hour was on "Ways to Respectfully Express Gratitude."

I didn't believe Gladys would respond that harshly to my genuine feelings, but why chance it?

"I am glad to hear that, dear. I won't ask you anything further, as I'm sure others need the details before I do." She pulled a piece of paper from the metal file cabinet behind her desk. "I believe you'll be needing this."

I'd seen the form hundreds of times but scanned it as if it were the first. Now that there was a personal reason for filling out the wedding facility rental form, every question felt like an invasion of privacy, and the sudden desire to ball it up and throw it in the trash came to mind.

"I suppose I will. Thanks, Mrs. Gladys. You're the first person I've told."

੪০৫

THE ELDERS' RESIDENCES were located at the far east end of our community, closest to Malachi's mansion.

Their homes, much larger than those on my block, were perfectly situated around the three-mile perimeter of the man-made lake in which the name *Bright Lakes* was derived. The location afforded each home a boat dock to the lake along with front gate entrance onto the tree-lined walking trail encircling the lake. Men from newer families found the housing perk an attractive incentive to volunteer to become Trainees, in hopes of eventually achieving Elder status.

The Tuckers' home had floor-to-ceiling windows in the dining room, showcasing the beauty of the lake and providing an abundance of soft, natural light. Jason's warm hand took mine as we approached from the parlor. I immediately halted, stared wide-eyed at him, then looked to my left where his mom and dad were also stepping into the room, just a pace or two ahead of us. What if they caught us holding hands? It was fine in public spaces but not in private.

Jason gave a little smirk and guided me to the plush seat next to his at the oblong cherry wood dining table. Gentlemanly as always, he pulled out my chair just as Mr. Tucker did for his wife. Her position was at the head of the table to my immediate left. We exchanged warm smiles.

We all held hands and closed our eyes as Mr. Tucker said a short prayer of gratitude, thanking the Bright Lord for food, health, and family.

Mrs. Tucker removed the decorative lid from the porcelain butter dish and placed it gently on the ivory linen table runner, careful not to knock over the nearby candlestick. Their dining table was fully set in a traditional English style, a formality which always puts me on edge.

She buttered her yeast roll with a gold-handled knife. "July twenty-third is perfect. Robert doesn't leave for his business trip to Washington until the following Monday. And since it's two months away, there's plenty of time to send invitations and gather the items I'll need for your bridal retreat."

Soon to be mothers-in-law were responsible for hosting bridal retreats. In addition to helping new brides prepare for marriage, this tradition showed the community unity between the two prospective families. No one was to speak of what occurred during those retreats, as it was an honor only discussed amongst the married women of the community. I wondered if Mama, having been a widow who hadn't remarried, would have been allowed to join. The idea of spending a weekend with Mrs. Tucker wasn't so bad but spending it with other married women of her choosing made me sick to my stomach.

"Can I come too?" Kimberly beamed at Mrs. Tucker.

"No, you may not." Her mother shot her a knowing look. "The retreats are for brides only."

Ugh, so that probably meant Maureen wouldn't be able to join either.

"Pass the green beans, dear," she said to her husband.

He handed the ornate porcelain serving platter to his wife. "Jason tells us you have to vacate your mother's house." That non-question came from Mr. Tucker. I didn't want to talk about it with anyone, least of all Jason's dad.

"Yes." I turned to face him at the other end of the table. "It's all very sudden."

"Not so sudden. The Champion is allowing you to stay longer than regulations permit." He looked at me pointedly.

Just like that, I was no longer hungry. He was right, of course. The entire community was making an allowance for me, yet somehow being forced from my home felt like a betrayal, not a kindness.

"But they should have told you sooner." He turned his attention back to his plate and sliced into the salmon. "My son has been working diligently to expedite a house for you both, but if things don't proceed as planned, you may stay here until it's finished." He looked at me again. "Contingent upon you two being married, of course." He popped the delicate fish into his mouth.

"We have a spare room that used to be Jason and Kimberly's playroom, but obviously they don't play in there anymore," Mrs. Tucker said. "We could convert it to something more comfortable for you two, even if it is temporary."

"I'd love it if you could live with us, Nikki!" Kimberly smiled.

I loved her and Mrs. Tucker for always making me feel so welcomed. Unfortunately, it seemed her husband was determined to make me feel the opposite.

"That's very generous of you both. Thank you so much for being willing to let us stay here." I looked at Jason's father and mother in turn, trying to infuse as much honor and humility into my gaze as possible. If I had to be thrown out of the only home I'd known, it eased my nerves to know I'd have somewhere else to live within Bright Lakes—if I married Jason.

As if sensing my worry, Jason rubbed the top of my thigh. "We won't need it, Dad, but thanks. The Champion is helping make sure things go according to plan." He turned and winked at me, pride in his gaze.

I smiled back but wondered what the real cost would be for Malachi's help.

THIRTEEN

This darkness doesn't make me tremble.
It invites me to gestate in its womb,
welcomes my immature form and unevolved stature.
Pain rips from me and extends its length to it.
Sadness twists itself into a knot alongside.
Bitter, self-directed words link arms with loathing.
Midnight caresses have magnetic pull into warmth.

This darkness does not frighten me.
Penetrating eyes. Omnipotence of no escape.
No muscle, no sinew, no imagining.
No idea unturned.
Microscope of microscopes.
Surrendered to the depth.
Bury me in the grit.

Fire-hot branding upon my soul.
A scorching to claim and guide anew.

This darkness does not hurt me.
A tearing from within.
New extensions of my form.
Stretching, seeking, reaching for nourishment.
Fierce, unknown hunger,
no longer satisfied with the deep, greedy for light.
An aching thirst.
Transcendent shades of scarlet,
bursting with the promise of sweetness.
Formed without light, now seeded with hope.

This darkness gave birth to the new me.

ഇരു

I DIDN'T REALIZE I was holding my breath until I'd finished reading the last line of my latest poem to Reen.

A solitary tear slid from her eye.

We were sitting cross-legged on my living room floor after having packed everything except the larger furniture and enough silverware and dishes for four people to dine. I'd decided I wouldn't entertain others during the packing process, so there wasn't a need for bulky equipment like the stand mixer or food processor. Two medium-sized boxes labeled "donate" sat stacked in a corner. There wasn't much to take with me, bringing to light how little Mama and I actually owned in the way of stuff. With no photos on the walls and no items in the armoire, the house felt... empty.

"Nikki, your poems speak to me in a way I know other people—girls, women—could also appreciate." Her tone was more gentle than normal, and she had that look in her eyes that stunk of pity and disappointment. "I know you've said you don't want to share them, but do you really think these poems wouldn't be a gift to others as well? I still have the phone number to that magazine editor if you ever reconsider printing these."

She'd never tell me what she really thought—that I was a coward, too afraid of my own shadow to freely choose to stand in the light. These poems were mine. My deepest feelings, forged together through tears and laughter, bitterness and hope, isolation and grief. Only a masochistic fool would dare invite haughty eyes to look upon these words. But Reen couldn't understand this. She was a hummingbird. A magical creature of beauty and wonder, formed in such a way that left no room for insecurity. Made to be seen and admired. She couldn't understand that wasn't what I wanted, nor what anyone wanted from me.

"Thanks, Friend. I'm glad you like it. Maybe one day I'll have them all published, but for now, I'll keep them in this journal."

I hated disappointing her, but I'd hate even more sharing my private thoughts only to have someone tell me how stupid I was.

"But there is something I've wanted to tell you for the past few days." Now was as good a time as ever, since the thoughts weren't going away.

She looked at me with a raised brow. "Okay, the way you just said that…"

"I know, I know" Man, I was blushing hard even before I could let the words out.

"Hurry up and tell me then!" She shouted, adding a slap to my arm.

"Do you remember that guy who turned the water fountain on and got you ladies wet?"

"Of course. It's not every day the Pillars and the bougie ladies invite me out only to get soaked. Shawn knows him better than I do. What about him?"

"Well, I've run into him a few times recently, and it's been… weird."

"What kind of weird? Weird, good? Or weird, creepy?" She frowned.

"I honestly don't know, and maybe *weird* isn't the right word. He makes me feel something… different when he's around. Like I want to get close to him and admit every secret to him and run away from him all at the same time."

She sat up straight and stared at me for a moment. "Hold on a minute." She raised her palm in the air facing me. "Are we talking about Micah Fox? The Unfaithful dude who builds all kinds of stuff around here?"

I nodded.

"Why the hell are you just now telling me this?"

"There's been too much going on with the house and strawberries. Now I'm planning a wedding. Besides, I kind of didn't want to admit, even to myself, any feelings I could possibly have for another man."

"This makes no sense! How do you have feelings for a man you've barely bumped into? You're obviously skipping on some details from this story, so get to it." She shifted her weight on the floor and looked like she was ready to watch a movie.

I shared every embarrassing detail of both encounters. She gasped and laughed throughout the whole story.

"Lord, that feels good to get off my chest," I said once I finished telling her everything.

"Wow. I don't even know where to start. I can't believe you cried in front of him, let alone on the floor. Then got caught staring at him while with Jason." She laughed, loudly, shaking her head as if she couldn't believe all that I'd said. "He really said you didn't have to pretend with him? That's kinda sexy. And all this time, I thought I was the wild one. Meanwhile, you're breaking rules left and right." Her shoulders shook at how hard she's laughing.

I couldn't help but laugh too, partly because it felt good to share her amusement, but mostly because I couldn't dare admit I thought the same thing. Not aloud, anyway.

"I can't believe I cried like that either, and that's probably why I feel so naked around him now. My emotions are heightened, and nothing makes sense. I find myself actually wanting to see him, wanting to be around him. Why? It's stupid and shameful because I'm engaged! I love Jason. He's literally buying us a house, and I'm over here thinking about another man." I buried my face in my hands and shook my head at the confession.

"First of all, Micah is handsome. Second, he's got that whole I'm-an-asshole-and-mysterious-but-I-do-helpful-things-for-the-community-and-help-defenseless-women vibe going for him."

We both burst out laughing because it's true.

"I've kept my mouth shut from day one, and I've been even more careful since you accepted his proposal, but it's time to come clean. We both know Jason has a lot to be desired."

"Hold up. What are you talking about? I thought you liked Jason."

"As a friend! For you, anyway. But I didn't think you'd actually marry the guy!"

I looked at her like she had two heads. My mind jogged through every conversation we'd had about Jason over the past year, trying to find one where she said something negative about him. My quick mental search came up empty. "What do you honestly think about me marrying Jason, Reen?"

"I don't think we should talk about this right now. My opinion isn't always the most popular, and I don't want to make you mad."

"Why would I get mad over your opinion unless you think I shouldn't marry him?" The words felt heavy on my tongue as each one left my mouth slower than the previous.

A few seconds passed, and the heifer just looked at me without saying a single word.

I stood, knees wobbling, body trembling, heart pounding. My feet somehow carried me through the empty dining room, past the kitchen, and out the back door, then into the strawberry field. My hands swooped up my straw hat and bushel basket, hanging on a hook, and without thinking, I took to the task of seeking out and plucking ripe berries.

FOURTEEN

THE STRAWBERRIES GROWING in the garden towers grabbed my attention first.

I scanned each pot, performing a quick visual check of its moisture level. Unlike the garden beds, there wasn't a drip irrigation system along the length of the towers.

The planters on the top layers looked the driest. I plunged my fingers into the soil to test it. They needed water. I exchanged my bushel basket for a hose then mindlessly watched the showering stream of water fall onto the parched soil.

After thoroughly soaking the first tower from top to bottom, I did another soil test. It felt moist and supple between my fingers, like wet sand. Perfect.

As I moved on to the next tower, my thoughts drifted.

All this time. All this time, and she'd said nothing about me marrying Jason. It felt like a slap in the face. I expected polite dishonesty from others, but not Maureen. I'd depended on her candor to keep me on track. I'd trusted her.

I checked the soil. Perfectly moist. On to the next.

"I didn't know how to tell you, Nikki."

I jumped, as I hadn't heard her approach.

"How was I supposed to tell you I didn't think he was right for you *after* you already agreed to marry him?"

I whipped my head to face her. "You should've said something when I was still *dating* him!"

"I tried to! Many times. You didn't take me seriously."

She had the nerve to look hurt. Like I had done something to her, not the other way around.

"What times? You only mentioned that he's boring and can't take a joke. Of course I wouldn't take that seriously. You never said you didn't like him."

"He is boring, and no, he can't take a joke. He can't take anything lightly and takes himself way too seriously."

"What's wrong with that? He's a responsible man."

"What's wrong with that? What about last summer when I told you what he said about Danielle? That a fat girl like her needs to realize a man will only see her as a housemaid." She raised her eyebrow at me knowingly. "Or the time he asked me—me! —if you'd had sex with anyone before."

"He was just joking." He had to be. There was no way he'd seriously think that about me, nor be so dense to expect Reen to answer him.

"Was he? Didn't we just establish he doesn't joke around?"

I rolled my eyes.

"How about the time he made you go back inside the house and change your clothes to something 'less scandalous' because your shoulder was showing? He made y'all late to your own birthday party."

"He *asked* me! He didn't *make* me."

"What about the time you parked his truck on the other side of the street, and he said, '*I guess I need to talk to you like I talk to kids*' Don't you remember? He talked down to you. Made you feel so stupid. And he was *not* joking."

"No, he wasn't, but those are small things. None of that—"

"What about that day he made you *walk*?" I could see the pain in her eyes that said she felt sorry for me.

My feet felt soggy. The ground underneath me had turned soft and mushy. I'd been squeezing the nozzle, hose pointing downward, and now was standing in mud. My shoes were soaked.

I released the lever, walked to the water spigot, then twisted it off.

Reen trailed a few paces behind me. "I'm not trying to be mean, Nikki. You know I love you, and I know you think you love Jason—"

I put my hand up to silence her. I was tired of talking about him.

She pressed on. "You asked me what I really thought, so I'm going to tell you. I think he's turning you into a white-washed version of yourself. I think he's not kind nor godly nor spiritual. I think he's mean. And I think… I just think he's not a good man for you. You deserve better."

"I hope you feel better getting all of that off your chest because basically you're telling me you'd rather I be *homeless* than marry him. I know he isn't perfect, but no one is, Maureen. Not you, not me, not Shawn even though you act like he is, and no, not Jason. But he *is* taking care of me. He's *been* taking care of me, and just like all couples, if we have a few disagreements, we'll work through them—because we love each other, whether you believe it or not."

"See, this is why I never said anything." Reen opened the sliding glass door leading back into the kitchen. After wiping her shoes on the mat, she walked inside, leaving the door open.

My head hurt.

"Nikki!" she called a few seconds later.

"What?" I followed her inside. If she was going to leave, she didn't need to wait for me.

I found her at the front door, which she held open. Jason stood at the threshold, but she didn't allow him inside.

"Your *fiancé* is here." She rolled her eyes at me.

"Someone's in a cheerful mood today." Jason mumbled, one eyebrow raised at me but obviously talking to Maureen.

And she knew it.

"Either be passive or be aggressive, but stop being so fucking passive-aggressive, Jason." She shoved past him out the door.

My hands flew to my mouth, muting the gasp. She was highly pissed. The last time I heard her say anything that forceful was when the children's school principal denied her art teacher application for the second time.

Jason stared at her back as she strode down the street, then he closed the door while glaring at me as if I was the one who cursed at him.

"She didn't—" I stopped myself from apologizing for Maureen's words. My head hurt, and nothing about me felt composed, kind, or patient. I didn't feel like apologizing to him or her. And if he expected me to, well… that wasn't happening.

"What's her problem? Shawn finally broke up with her?"

Finally? Ugh, why is he proving her point right now? As furious as I was at Reen, I knew she didn't mean to hurt my feelings, but with Jason, I couldn't tell. I wasn't sure of his intentions when he said hurtful things—like right now—and I didn't want to figure it out.

"What are you doing here?" I asked.

He gave me a look that said he didn't need a reason to come over.

"I was around the corner at the Henderson's and figured I'd stop by. I did text you."

"I was in the garden."

"Obviously." He looked at my muddy shoes. I'd forgotten to step out of them before entering the house. Yup, I'd tracked a path of mud behind me.

"I'm about to take a shower. Can we talk later?"

"You want me to leave?" He grimaced.

"It's not that I want you to leave. I'm filthy, and I'm just not in a good mood." I pleaded.

"Okay, you want me to leave. I'll leave." He turned toward the door.

"It's not like that." I didn't want to fight. I just wanted to be left alone. I wanted to shout.

"Fine. Call me later." He walked out then closed the door behind him.

I didn't bother continuing to water the strawberries. I took off my tennis shoes, walked toward the bathroom, stripped off my clothes, then got straight into the steaming shower.

The hot water was so soothing, but despite how amazing it felt running down my body, it failed to ease my scattered thoughts. I couldn't stop thinking about the day Jason made me walk from the farmer's market in the rain.

We'd been dating a little more than four months at that time, and everything had been perfect. He was perfect, and I was happy. He'd buy me cute little gifts, diligently got Mama's permission for everything, took me places I'd never been, and treated me like a lady. I was falling in love with him.

That day, I felt giddy and girly and joyous. We browsed the furniture store and had fun pretending we were shopping for our home. He wandered ahead of me to look at the dining sets, and I hung back in the bedroom section. I'd seen a giant pillow in the shape of cherry red lips and thought they were funny, so I brought it to Jason and said, "This will be perfect for your office so you can imagine me kissing you while you work."

I admit it was a silly comment.

He looked at me with pure disgust then turned and walked away.

I stood there for a bit, unsure what his problem was. I was confused. I set the pillow on the dining room table then hurried after him. When I caught up, I grabbed his arm. "Jason?"

He yanked free of my grasp and continued walking toward the door. "Jason? What's wrong?"

He didn't say anything to me until we were outside the shop.

I followed him outside. The sky was darkening with thick clouds, and I could smell moisture gathering in the air.

"Are you mad at me?"

"Why would you say that to me in public? In front of all those people?" He finally asked. "Why would you even think to pick up that stupid pillow?"

I didn't know what to say. He was mad about the pillow?

"I need to know that you have more sense than that, Nikki." He started walking to the parking lot, so I walked alongside him.

"You're mad because of the pillow or because of what I said?"

"If you don't know the difference, that's your problem." We reached the truck, and he stood by the passenger door. Revulsion darkened his features…because of me.

Over a pillow?

"I need a few minutes alone. I'll see you back at the community."

"You're leaving me here?" No way would he do that.

"It's not that far, Nikki. Next time, don't wear hooker shoes." He hopped behind the wheel, turned on the engine, then drove off.

He actually left me there. In the parking lot of the farmer's market. While a storm was brewing.

I stood in that spot, watching until the glare from his taillights disappeared. After walking a few steps towards home, a light sprinkle fell from the sky. By the time I made it to the entry of the market—the quarter mile mark to the residential area—a steady stream of rain fell. I'd tried to look extra cute that day by wearing a pair of black high heels, but by the time I'd made it near Mr. Bagwell's place, my feet were killing me.

I lied to Mama about why I was soaking wet but couldn't help telling Maureen the next day.

She was speechless for a while then eventually asked, "Are you okay with being treated like that?"

"Nope," I confidently replied. "I'm breaking up with him."

But he called later that day and apologized. He confessed he'd been stressed out that week and was embarrassed that people might think we were having an impure courtship if they overheard what I said, especially when I brought him the bright, red-lipped pillow. It looked like we were more intimate than we were, and he didn't want people to question my virtue. He sounded so sincere in his apology, and I could kinda understand his perspective if not his reaction. People in the community gossiped—a lot. More than a few courtships had abruptly ended when rumors spread of a lady's behavior violating the Guidelines. With Jason being a Trainee, he had to be more cautious about things like that. His anger I could forgive but making me walk home was harder to get past. He promised he'd never do anything like that again and begged me to forgive him.

So, I did.

When I told Reen I hadn't broken up with him, she simply said, "If that's what you really want."

Jason never treated me that way again, and over time, I somehow forgot it even happened.

Until today.

Now, all I could think of was that I'd lied to my mama for his sake. For his sake. For his good-guy image and so she wouldn't think I chose wrong. Because deep down, I must have known that telling her the truth meant admitting my own shortcomings. I'd *allowed* him to mistreat me.

Those memories, coupled with the steaming water soaking onto my skin, made anger rise from deep within. A velvety sensation flowed through the blood vessels in my head, highlighting each moment, each suppressed feeling from that evening's conversation with Jason.

His disgusted face. His walking away from me. His dismissal of my questions. His calling my heels "hooker shoes."

His leaving me.

Even his pathetic excuse for an apology throbbed in my mind.

How could I not see things clearly before?

It was like a small, jagged crack started to spread throughout my soul. Light seeped through that small fissure until it became a brilliant, blinding glow. For the first time in my life, I wasn't afraid to recognize and acknowledge it.

Self-respect.

FIFTEEN

THE MID-AFTERNOON SUN felt like flames upon my skin.

Why did I think it was a good idea to walk instead of drive today? I'd forgotten to check the forecast before leaving the house. A mere two hours ago the temperature was warm but lovely.

Stupid weather.

At least I was on the garden trail. The vibrant flower bushes and trees let me imagine I was somewhere exotic. Honeysuckle was a dominant plant, and its sweet perfume led me down the path. Pleasant as it was, it couldn't erase my confusion from the brief meeting I'd just left.

Even though we had an appointment set for noon, Matron Kirk didn't see me until one. I'd call that very un-Pillar-like behavior. I'd scheduled the appointment over a week ago after seeing the disturbing entry in Mama's journal. I wanted to know what she said to my mom and what she found behind the flap in our Champion's office.

Matron Kirk gave vague answers. I showed her the journal and let her read the same entry Maureen and I read, hoping it would jog her memory. Ignoring the fact the flap was in Malachi's office, she insisted the photos were from one of our former community members—an "unstable man" who was caught taking photographs of people without their consent. "It's nothing to worry about, dear. All was handled a long time ago." When I reminded her that one of the photos was of me, she changed the subject to my wedding and asked for details about the ceremony.

I let myself in the black iron screen gate then walked up the two steps leading to the front door. More than enough days had passed for me to gather my thoughts, and now was the time to face reality. Relationships required honesty, and as much as I dreaded discussing emotionally complex topics, honesty was a virtue I wanted to uphold. Who knew what the outcome would be? I pressed the bell and hoped for the best.

Mr. Johnson came to the door, his graying hair and lined face making him look older than his fifty years. Between travel for work and his obligations as an Elder, he wasn't often home. He was the last person I expected to greet me.

When he saw me, his expression brightened. "Nicolette, it's so nice to see you. Please, come on in. Is Maureen expecting you?"

I stepped into the foyer. "No, she's not expecting me. I hope it's okay that I dropped by."

"She just got in and has some exciting news I'm sure you'll be happy to hear." He led me into the living room.

Maureen's family sat side-by-side on their pewter grey sectional. Her mom and twin brothers, already in a joyous mood, greeted me warmly. Maureen's smile, however, faded. We hadn't spoken since our argument about Jason. I didn't blame her for still being mad at me and deserved more than a dark expression. Hopefully she'd accept my apology and her festive mood would return.

"Nicolette, sweetheart." Her mother beamed at me. "Are you here to congratulate Maureen? I'm sure she already texted you the news."

"It's *okay* news. I wouldn't call it great." Thomas laughed.

"I'd call it *all right* news." Timothy, his twin, grinned. The two of them had a part-time job making fun of Maureen and they did it well.

Their constant ribbing made me glad to not have brothers.

I glanced at Reen then back to Mrs. Johnson. "What news? Whatever it is seems exciting."

"I mean, I wouldn't call it *exciting*," Tom said.

His mom pointed at him, her message clear—stop or suffer the consequences.

Had she finally been hired to teach art? The old art instructor died three years ago, and the role remained vacant. We thought Maureen would be a shoe-in because she's one of the few people in the community who holds teaching credentials and knows about the arts, but she'd applied twice each year and had never been offered the position.

It would be wonderful for her and the children. My heart warmed just thinking about it.

Then I saw it.

A shining gold band with a sparkling jewel in the center encircled her left ring finger.

A lump formed in my throat as tears welled. My jaw dropped. Covering my mouth, I gaped at my friend, eliciting laughter from most of the room. I hurried to Reen then bent to wrap my arms around her. I squeezed her tight, surprised she let me.

But there was nothing—not even her lingering anger—that would keep me from celebrating for and with her.

"Congratulations, Friend. I'm so… so happy for you. Shawn is lucky to have you." I stepped back and took her left hand in mine, looking at the stunning oval-cut diamond. It was beautiful. Perfect. Just like her. She deserved to be happy, and Shawn would work to make sure she was, yet I couldn't deny a twinge of pain. Another person I loved would be leaving me. She'd still be in the community, but her free time—usually spent with me—would drastically decrease. We wouldn't have the strawberry field anymore anyway, so what would keep us together?

Funny how I never considered the demands my impending marriage would place on me, how my availability would also diminish and impact Reen.

That realization brought Jason back to mind. He'd been taking up too many of my thoughts lately. After our last conversation a few days ago, doubts beat at me day and night. I repeatedly replayed concerning incidents with him. I tried to block them out with all of his wonderful, loving qualities, but it was getting harder to do.

I pushed aside those thoughts. Now wasn't the time for me to think about myself. I needed to be happy for my friend.

"It's a beautiful ring, isn't it?" Mrs. Johnson beamed.

I was still holding Maureen's hand. "It really is."

Reen stood. "Mama, Nikki and I are going to talk in my room for a bit. I won't be long."

&OG&

REEN'S BEDROOM LOOKED just like her—wild and free. Odds and ends hung and in the most random places, but everything was arranged in such a way that even the most unique items looked beautiful and intentionally designed for its exact placement.

The second she closed the door, I blurted, "I'm sorry. I didn't mean to interrupt your celebration. I only came over to apologize." Unburdening myself didn't help. I still felt like crap, so I rushed to continue. "I am so happy Shawn proposed. You deserve to be happy, and he really is a good guy. A very good guy."

She sat at the white wooden desk next to her heap of watercolor paint books. "Is he? You didn't think so the other day. Remember? You said he's not perfect, even if I act like he is."

Bright Lord, I loved her. The boldness she possessed, even with me, to say and ask exactly what she was thinking. To speak the truth to me because she loved me and she respected herself.

"I'm sorry for everything I said. Especially about Shawn. I didn't even mean it." I scooted over the bulk of laundry items strewn across the sage green sheets then sat at the foot of her bed. "You've been the *best* friend to me, Reen and I haven't been a great friend to you. You were right. About everything. I never put together all the things Jason has said and done until you mentioned them. Hearing it all listed out like that made me feel… stupid. I don't know how I overlooked all of it."

A brief, uncomfortable silence passed between us.

She sighed. "You ever heard that saying about the frog and the boiling water? They put the frog in a pot of cold water then turn on the fire. The water slowly heats, and the frog just sits there, not realizing it's getting hotter. By the time it's boiling, it's too late."

"Poor frog," I said.

"Yeah. Poor frog."

We say nothing because there's nothing else to say. Reen knew me better than I knew myself.

I finally broke the silence. "Will you please tell me about you and Shawn and this proposal?"

She smiled… big. Teeth and all. A rare thing of beauty.

"It was beautiful. We went to Sequoia National Park for a hike. When we reached the summit of Moro Rock, he got down on one knee and held up the ring. I was so surprised! There were a bunch of other hikers around, and they all cheered for us. One couple was on their honeymoon and shared the contact information for the wedding venue and florist they used just the week before. Shawn packed us a delicious lunch, so we began planning right there as we ate, though we haven't chosen a date yet. There are a few things we need to discuss before I can decide."

"I'm truly so happy for you."

Reen smiled. "Thanks. I'm glad you came by today. I was worried about you."

"Don't be. I'm doing okay. Besides, it's been too much about me lately. It's my turn to be there for you." And I was determined to be there, no matter what.

SIXTEEN

DESPITE THE SICKENING late-afternoon heat, walking home was more appealing than allowing Reen to drive me.

I needed space and time to think. I didn't tell her anything about my disappointing meeting with Matron Kirk or any of my growing concerns about Jason. He'd taken up more than enough attention lately.

As I endured the inhumane heat, thoughts of being homeless and excommunicated chased me. That was my unsettling future should I choose not to marry him. His father would make sure of that. If I knew nothing else about Jason and Mr. Tucker, it was that neither of them wanted to be embarrassed in front of the community.

Regardless of my feelings about being wed to Jason, I'd hate to cause them shame.

I simply needed to work up the courage to confront Jason and respectfully share my concerns. My *fears*. I owed him that since I agreed to his proposal and told the Pillars there was no other reason for the delay. And if I didn't try, I'd never again get to see Reen or anyone else within the Community. This place was Mama's refuge for many years. I couldn't give it up so easily. Not without careful consideration from all angles. Besides, Mrs. Tucker was a kind, happy woman, so things in their household couldn't be that bad. Their marriage gave me hope for my own happiness with Jason. Surely there was a way to build a life with him without sacrificing my newfound self-respect.

I continued walking, slowly shifting from abhorring the heat to enjoying my surroundings. Nature was therapeutic. The trees, the flower bushes, the clear sky above, the scurrying groundhogs... all of it resonated with me. There was a deep "knowing" within my soul, a spiritual vibration that solidified resolve in the marrow of my bones. Resolve to come clean and share every dark thought and doubt I had with Jason. Resolve to speak up, fully, completely, holding nothing back this time.

Resolve to make a contingency plan in case his response was unloving.

I rounded the tree-lined curve of the trail and was happy to find no other residents in sight. No doubt due to the heat during the time of day. Then, just behind a row of trees, I noticed one. A man, squatting. Head down, hands busy.

Micah.

I'd not seen him since the farmer's market, but to my embarrassment, I'd thought of him often. Almost daily. My pace slowed as I watched him work, debating if I should approach or pretend like I didn't see him.

The rational side of me demanded I keep walking and pretend I saw nothing. No need to add more drama into my life. I told myself he meant nothing to me. But the blossoming side of curiosity, the side that remembered how *seen* he'd made me feel, wouldn't be denied.

Before I could entertain another opposing thought, my feet pivoted toward him, into the grass.

His head turned toward me as I neared, his intense hazel eyes dared me to speak.

An unexpected fear washed through me. What was I doing? We weren't friends. He owed me nothing, and I had no reason to disturb him. Not even two minutes ago, I'd decided to try to make things work with Jason, so speaking to another man—especially this compelling, attractive man—was inappropriate. Irrational. Unnecessary.

So why did my heart betray me by racing? And I couldn't ignore the twinge of nervous anticipation that ran through my body.

"Hi, Micah." The tone of my voice was cheerier than I planned. In the brief that followed, I wondered how my hair looked and if what I wore was flattering.

He finally spoke. "I hear you're marrying Tucker in a few weeks."

He'd already surmised that the day we met in the music room. I'd been one of the engaged ladies who spoke with Pillars about the wedding date. I shrugged. "No surprise there."

"Guess not."

I didn't know what else to say. "What do they have you doing out here in this heat?"

"Fixing some leaks." Never taking his eyes off of me, he gestured to an irrigation drain, loaded his tool bag, then stood to his full, impressive height.

"Why are you always fixing things around here?"

"You're full of questions today."

"I was just trying to be polite. I'll go." I took a step toward the path.

"Are you headed home?" He stepped onto the trail then began walking with me.

If anyone saw us together, there would be gossip. I looked and quickly calculated the chances of us being seen. In this heat, the odds were low.

We strolled side by side for a bit, the silence filled by the sound of his boots hitting the pavement and birds chirping in the trees. I looked straight ahead but saw a lot through peripheral vision. The shift of his body. His measured stride. He exuded strength without even trying.

Gosh, what did the guy eat to be built like that?

"Last time I saw you, I didn't get to say anything," I rambled. "And the time before that, well… It was a stressful day." To say the least.

"I got a work Faith to clear out and repair any damage to your house by the end of next month."

I nodded. He knew I was moving out, and I didn't want to talk about it. Only then did I realize if I didn't want to answer him, he wouldn't press me or express disappointment. He accepted my silence, and I found that kindness refreshing.

"Why did you drop out of Examination?" I blurted.

He'd just given me privacy without being asked, and I repaid him by prying into his personal business. What was wrong with me?

His eyes cut toward me, and he halted as if I'd just uncovered a dark secret.

I knew I should apologize for asking such a blunt question, but I held it in. His answer mattered. Besides, if he didn't want to answer me, he wouldn't. And if he could mention my eviction and impending marriage, then I could ask this.

He began walking again. "There are things I'm not willing to compromise on. Not for anyone."

I didn't know what I expected his response to be, but that certainly wasn't it.

"What kind of things?" I probed.

Another short pause. "What kind of man I am. My purpose in this life."

"What is your purpose?"

"You really are full of questions." He stopped again and looked at me.

"That's because your answers make me want to know more." I smiled, then we continued our stroll.

He was right. I was full of questions, had many more to ask, and didn't know when or if I'd have the chance again. Why was he allowed to remain in the Community? What happened during Examination? What did he think of his uncle Malachi?

And the questions I had for myself—why did I enjoy talking to him? Why was I so excited and nervous being this close to him?

"My purpose is a topic for another day."

But would there be another day? Another day that we'd be alone like this?

"You're the first Community resident in three years who has *willingly* spoken to me outside of discussing work orders."

His invisible scarlet letter. That must have been when he dropped out of Examination. As shocking as his confession sounded, I wasn't entirely surprised. Micah looked different than the rest of us, and no one in the community would ever associate with someone who didn't fit in—especially someone who didn't attend Service or Lunch. Those repeated offenses would not be overlooked.

But there was something in his confession that made my heart sad. A familiar knowing, the painful experience of not being fully accepted, even—or especially—by those who professed love. I knew the pressure to hide the imperfect, unique, individual pieces of ourselves. I'd felt this way, and I'd empathized with Reen, who suffered it more. The respected ladies in our community treated her with disdain when she'd express a hint of her quirky, artistic personality.

It seemed Micah endured worse. He'd been all but shunned.

And like Reen, he was one of the few people with whom I could authentically be myself. I didn't feel like he was trying to get something from me or make me do something for him.

That realization unsettled me.

We neared a fork in the trail. One path would continue toward my house, the other led to the Admin Building. I stopped again and tipped my head to look directly at him. Something about him ignited an uncharacteristic boldness within me, and I took a chance on joking with him. "Well," I could feel the heat sprinting up to my cheeks, "I'm sure it's because you give off such warm and cuddly vibes. It's so welcoming."

"Warm and cuddly, huh?" His eyebrows lifted slightly, then he smiled.

My cheeks flamed. Bright Lord, the man was stunning.

His gaze moved past me toward the path leading to my house, and that gorgeous smile faded into neutrality. "It was good to see you again, Nikki. I gotta go."

I looked in the direction of my home and saw a woman in her early thirties approaching from a short distance away.

"Yeah, me too."

He headed down the path toward the Admin Building, and I took the other. Mrs. Hanson—whose first name I always forgot—waved at me as she passed.

I hoped she didn't see me walking with Micah.

SEVENTEEN

WEDNESDAY MORNING WAS my scheduled day to clean the bathrooms in the Service Hall.

I believed my janitorial contributions mattered just as much as those of the teachers giving lessons during the evening Study Sessions. Almost no one volunteered for restroom maintenance, so I knew what I was doing had value. Besides, cleaning was the next best thing to exercise for me. It felt as strenuous and satisfying as kickboxing or lifting weights—which I knew from last year's two-week stint to get healthier. Any built-up frustrations were released upon whatever I scrubbed or scoured. I'd tackle every stain until the surface gleamed. The way I saw it, few would sign-up for this detail, and I benefitted from it, so my efforts were beneficial to all parties.

Angelica Martinez and I were often partnered together, a smart move on the planning committees' part, as our work styles were complementary. The twenty-year-old was two years younger than me and currently not dating anyone. Married women had different volunteer responsibilities, and public restrooms weren't one of them. This honor was reserved for single ladies.

"I wish they gave us a medal for how awesome we cleaned," I joked as we walked down the corridor from the lady's restroom to the men's.

"Right?" Angelica placed the CLOSED sign on the men's restroom door. "Whenever they pair me with someone else, I double check her work and there's always something she missed."

"The base of the toilet?" I gave her a knowing look.

"Yup. It makes me wonder what the bathrooms in their houses smell like."

We exchanged nods and frowns.

"So, are you ready for the big day?" she asked with genuine excitement. "It's coming up soon."

During Service last Saturday, our wedding date was announced. Ever since then, everyone who saw me stopped to congratulate me and ask about our wedding. I'd waited the full two weeks before meeting with the Pillars, and at Mrs. Tucker's request brought her with me. Boy was I glad I did. During that meeting, I saw a side of her I'd never witnessed before. The woman was fierce. She knew what she wanted, when she wanted it, and would most definitely have it.

Before meeting with the Pillars, she and I had a lengthy discussion about my desires for the ceremony—which were few—and she insisted on all of them during our meeting. I sat by in awe as she gracefully navigated the conversation with subtle demands consisting of silence, well-placed eye contact, delicate laughter, and feigned disinterest. It was like a balanced but beautiful dance—a conversational ritual of dominance performed between women of power and influence. One I'd not been adequately taught but observed on occasion. This particular tango was cunning yet cordial—sharp-edged twirls, graceful sways, and flowy pirouettes.

I'd left that room feeling quite the opposite from my prior meeting. My gratitude and admiration for Mrs. Tucker couldn't be expressed in words. I just widened my eyes and gave her a wide grin. I couldn't think of a single person I'd rather have planning my bridal retreat. It also gave me a glimmer of hope and a sense of relief that her son might not be a lost cause. In fact, it strengthened my decision to speak with him about all my concerns and hope for the best. No one could have a mom like her and be as bad as I was making Jason out to be. She was a big reason for postponing that difficult, inevitable conversation. The other was that I'd simply been so busy.

"As ready as I'll ever be. Time is flying by!"

We were already in the second week of June. Wedding planning had become a full-time job, leaving little time for me and Jason to sit and talk about our future. We'd only spoken about the who, when, and where of ceremony preparations, as those matters were most pressing. The only other decision we made was to honeymoon on the beaches of San Diego.

Angelica dipped her cloth into our sudsy water bucket then began wiping the door of a stall. "I bet it is. There's so much to do, and everyone is talking about how lucky you are to have Mrs. Tucker helping."

So true. Just as she had in the meeting with the Pillars, Mrs. Tucker had taken the reins on coordinating the details of flowers, contractors, caterers, etc. As much as I appreciated her for doing it, I was even more grateful because she took into consideration what I wanted. She'd checked in with me almost every day over the past two weeks. We decided to hold the ceremony in front of the fountain then take the reception indoors of the Clubhouse. It would require extra labor to move chairs from one location to the other.

To my surprise, and discomfort, Micah managed the workers for the event. When we met to discuss the placement of the tent for the ceremony and the timing for moving chairs inside, he confirmed and re-confirmed the plan was what I wanted and not what someone else stipulated. Once the details were set, he handed me the contract. When his arm brushed mine, chills ran down my spine and heat flooded my entire body. I'd immediately put space between us and was careful not to make any prolonged eye contact for the rest of that conversation.

"I honestly don't know what I'd do without her. She seems to know exactly what to do before it even happens."

After we thoroughly cleaned the stalls, toilets, and sinks, we placed scented urinal cakes into each urinal. I was proud of us for making that place sparkle. Finished for the week, I grabbed my cleaning tote and supply holder. We exited the men's restroom, then I took the CLOSED sign off the door.

"Nicolette."

I turned.

There stood our Champion in a grey suit and a striped tie. His imposing presence overwhelmed the narrow corridor.

My body tensed, my breath hitched. I hated how I reacted to him, like I needed to hide because I'd just been caught being bad.

Angelica looked as off-balance as I felt. Her attention was on Jeremy, who stood directly behind Malachi, two small books in hand. There hadn't been many instances where he appeared approachable, but as his predatory gaze prowled over Angelica—head to toe and back—he looked almost menacing. It made me squirm.

Logically, I knew I hadn't done anything wrong, so I forced myself to at least appear calm and made myself smile. "Bright Blessings to you, Champion. Do you need anything from us?"

He looked down at me from his towering height. "I need to speak with you. Do you have a minute? I promise it won't take long." Though phrased as a question, there was no mistaking it for a demand.

"Of course." I replied, because saying no was certainly not an option.

Angelica stared at the floor as she tiptoed past the three of us then headed toward the main service hall. I wish she could've stayed and waited while we talked. My stomach felt queasy.

"We'll go right in here." Malachi pointed to a door to my left on which the word INFANTS had been engraved. This was the room new mothers brought their children into during services so congregants could enjoy the teaching without interruption.

What could he possibly want with me? I ran through the myriad of possibilities but nothing stood out that would warrant a personal conversation with the Champion.

Jeremy stood to the side as Malachi, and I stepped inside. The walls were painted in pastel blues, pinks, and yellows. Calming colors. Hopefully our conversation would match the tranquility of the room.

Malachi closed the door and told me to sit. I chose a cushioned rocking chair, the kind intended for mothers or volunteers who helped quiet restless babies.

He remained standing, making me feel small, insignificant. Malachi had to weigh no less than three hundred pounds and stood perhaps six feet tall. He was shorter than Micah but taller than Jason, and his girth made him appear more powerful than the two of them combined.

"Your mother was a smart woman. Regina." He said her name as if he were remembering how it sounded. "She kept the books for Bright Lakes Residential Community, including this hall, the administration, and the Faith. I respected her knowledge and knew she respected the Faith. Regina was good at what she did, and everyone knew it. We even gave her a seat in the third row." His stare bore into me. "She respected and understood the value—the gift—of this Community. We took her in, gave her a beautiful place to live even though she was widowed and had a daughter, and didn't require her to re-marry. I eventually realized it was better for the Community if she didn't. New wives have many responsibilities… to their husbands."

He walked toward the bookcase and picked up a thin book. *Goodnight Moon.*

"When you came of age to marry, it was perfect timing that Jason Tucker fell in love with you. He's a promising young man who respects the community just as much as your mother did. You, on the other hand, Nicolette… I'm beginning to wonder if you value this Community as much as your mother did. As much as your fiancé does." He pinned me with a demanding gaze from across the room, a look indicating a choice needed to be made right then.

My whole body tensed, and a lump formed in my throat.

Where was the resolve I had last week? The resolve of knowing I had a contingency plan should things not work out in my favor with Jason. In this moment, there was no Plan B. There was only our Champion, the pull to obey him, and the fear of disappointing him or worse, making him angry. Something deep inside of me desperately demanded I not make him angry or there would be hell to pay.

I sensed it was a hell I'd experienced a very long time ago, and something deep and dark, hidden in an alcove of my soul, sought safety from its clutches.

On some level, I knew the only way to feel safe again was to obey the Champion.

The words flew out of my mouth as if on cue, "I love this community. Bright Lakes is the only home I've known. I'm sorry if I've made you doubt my faithfulness."

He smiled wide, but I knew a fake smile when I saw one. "I'm glad to hear that. Matron Kirk thought you might be having some doubts about the safety of the community. That you may have seen something in a notebook?"

Mama's journal. Was that what this was about?

I stared at him like he was crazy. Like I didn't know what he was talking about. Because I wasn't completely sure if that's what he meant.

"Ah, right. I'm sure it was nothing." He stepped toward the door. "We best be going. I'm glad we were able to clear things up quickly."

He opened the door and gestured for me to walk through it.

My knees trembled, but I ignored that inconvenience. Freedom waited, so I grabbed my cleaning tote then exited the anything-but-calming room.

Malachi's tremendous shadow loomed over me until he stepped around me then strode down the hall without another word. The woodsy fragrance of his cologne lingered, choking me—a silent but potent reminder he was an unbeatable force of nature.

And I was not.

EIGHTEEN

I SAT ON a pillow on the floor of Reen's bedroom while she perched on her bed behind me, braiding extensions into my hair.

Time was flying by. My bridal retreat was in just a few days, and she'd agreed to braid my hair as a gift for the trip.

"Don't worry about the strawberries." Reen reached for the next thin bundle of loose hair on the braiding hook. "Tim and Tom are going to help me package and deliver them while you're gone."

"Aww, look at them helping out." I teased.

"Helping out? Yeah, right." She continued intertwining the extension hair with my own braid.

I hissed.

"Sorry, did that hurt?"

My tender-head never responded well to this hairstyle, but despite my extra sensitive scalp, she was my only friend who actually knew how to braid my hair without killing me in the process.

"No, I'm fine." I was not but telling her the truth wouldn't help. It would only frustrate her.

"In exchange for their services, I had to promise them I'd do their chores this week."

"Dang." I shook my head then quickly regretted the movement as I felt the pull of a few strands of hair. "So, what did you and Shawn decide about a honeymoon?"

"We haven't. We have some other pretty big decisions we need to make, so a lot of our conversations have been about that."

"What kind of big decisions? Are ya'll planning to have kids right away?" I beamed at the idea of becoming an aunt.

"Naw, girl! Don't be saying stuff like that." She pulled my hair.

I slapped her on the leg. We both laughed.

"No. Nothing like that. We're just trying to decide exactly where we'll live, what we can afford." She continued wrapping strands of hair into a braid. "Even some of the smaller houses closer to Mr. Bagwell's farm are pretty pricey, so it's hard to make a decision."

She was right. When the Pillars told me I had to move out of my house, I'd searched available listings. The most modest home was way beyond anything I could afford.

"It's not like we want to live that close to his farm. Or close to any of the Matrons or Pillars."

"That doesn't leave many options."

Since neither she nor Shawn were Faithful's, they couldn't live in my neighborhood or take over my house after I moved out.

"Anyway, I'll let you know once we decide on something. And hey, I wasn't sure if you wanted to know or not, but your Micah has been having Shawn work with him on a few projects around here lately."

My heart skipped at the mention of his name, and I whipped my head around. The braid Reen was working on dropped out of her hand, pulling my hair in the process, but I didn't care. "What? Shawn's working with Micah?"

Reen raised an eyebrow and stared at me. "I guess this is a topic that interests you?"

She knew good and well it wasn't, or so I told myself. I couldn't manage to control my words or actions when it came to him. The man just made me feel... things.

I repositioned myself on the pillow so she could continue working, my head tipping back as she tugged.

"Shawn seems to really like working with him, and apparently they have a few things in common."

"Oh." I tried, and failed, to sound aloof. "Like what?"

She chuckled. "For starters, they both like fixing things."

I'd forgotten Shawn had repaired her parents' fence when the neighbor's dog knocked out a few posts. He'd also helped us make the garden boxes.

She kept working.

When I couldn't take the silence any longer, I said, "Okay, and?"

"Oh, so you are interested in hearing about him?" She laughed, clearly making fun of me and playing with my emotions.

"You ain't no good." I crossed my arms and pretended to be mad while she tried to catch her breath from laughing so hard.

"I don't see anything funny about this."

"I do." She laughed again. "Other than building things, they both like outdoorsy stuff. That's really all I know. But Shawn says they're talking about starting a real business together."

"After only this short amount of time?" That didn't make any sense. I wasn't CEO of a Fortune 500 company, but I knew going into business with someone was not a decision to be taken lightly. Reen and I got along better than most people, and even we disagreed on things related to the strawberry business.

"Well, they've known each other for a long time. Whenever Shawn had questions about fixing something, he'd ask Micah, and Shawn's helped him with projects for years, though never as consistently as he has been lately."

So, Micah's known Shawn for a while? I knew they knew each other, but I didn't realize they were friends. I'd never seen Micah talk to anyone, but then again, I'd never paid him much attention. He wasn't a Faithful, so the direction my life was going would never include conversing or paying attention to someone like him. And if I were honest with myself, until Shawn asked Reen to officially court him, I didn't pay him much attention either. And he's kept scarce when I'm around.

"That's interesting," I eventually whispered.

"What's interesting is that *you're* interested, considering you're heading to your bridal retreat."

Leave it to Reen not to avoid potentially awkward conversations but to go for the jugular. I'd hoped she wouldn't mention it, but avoiding uncomfortable subjects had never been her style.

"What happened when you finally spoke to Jason, anyway?"

Case in point—another uncomfortable subject she wasn't avoiding.

I stared at the pink polish chipping on my toenails as I thought about the conversation we had just the night before.

I'd finally said everything I ever wanted to say. I poured my heart out and shared every fear and every hurtful thing he did that I never previously addressed. Surprisingly, he sat there quietly and listened.

"It wasn't what I expected. He apologized for hurting my feelings and asked if we could start fresh." His apology and his response caught me off guard. I expected him to deflect or dismiss my concerns, but he didn't. "He said he didn't know that's how I felt and I should have told him sooner. And he's right. I ignored anything that hurt my feelings and chose not to say anything in the moment and afterward. It's my fault things got so out of hand. I mindlessly followed his lead and numbed myself to the impact his words and actions caused me."

Reen grunted in response.

"He admitted he wants to be an Elder. Malachi has singled him out to be his apprentice." I sped past that last part because it filled me with worry.

"Humph."

"He thinks once I spend enough time with his mom and the other matrons I'll understand why he felt so strongly about the way I dressed or how other women behave. But I told him I'll never become a matron."

"I see."

"We decided to continue the conversation once both of our retreats are over." I twirled the shining diamond ring on my finger and remembered the "yes" I'd said to him. The "yes" Mama had also said.

"Sounds like you've made a decision," Reen said.

"I think so."

She sighed and continued braiding my hair.

NINETEEN

THE BLINDFOLD ITCHED my nose.

Without being able to see, I could only guess at the time and distance. I estimated we'd left two hours ago. Mrs. Tucker had arrived at my house at two in the afternoon, as promised. I'd thoughtfully packed my toiletries and underclothes into my favorite black-and-white striped tote bag, but she insisted she'd provide everything else—clothing, journals, books, pens, etc. All the items I'd need while we were away. As I didn't know where we were going or what we'd be doing, I had no idea what those items were. The entire event was a secret. I wasn't even supposed to know the location.

The van slowed to a stop, then a woman announced, "We're almost there, Nicolette!"

I wasn't sure who spoke. Throughout the entire ride, ladies chatted nonstop about everything—and nothing interested me. The lack of inclusion felt intentional, but instead of keeping me in excited suspense, I vacillated between annoyance at trying to figure out who was in the van and worrying about whether it would be an enjoyable trip. Odds of that were slim given neither Reen nor Mama would be there.

I knew Mrs. Tucker sat to my left because I recognized the smell of her sweet rose-scented perfume. Also, she patted my thigh a few times just to reassure me. I appreciated that minor consideration. I didn't recognize the voice of the woman to my right, but there was another very familiar voice, one that made me clench my teeth and secretly wish I was somewhere else.

Lady Maribelle.

I tried to come up with plans to avoid her over the next three days.

The van eventually came to a complete stop, and everyone fell silent. The women began exiting the vehicle, rocking it as they gathered their belongings.

Mrs. Tucker patted my thigh. "Nicolette, we're going to scoot out now. Hold my hand. I'll tell you when to step down."

I followed her instructions, exiting the van without issue. The muscles in my legs were grateful to be stretched out.

"Stay right here. I'll return to remove the blindfold in just a minute."

"Okay." I stood motionless, still unable to see and relying on my other senses. Cheery bird songs sounded close by, warming my heart. A cool breeze swept past me, a welcoming sensation not often enjoyed in the middle of the valley summer. The temperature here was perfect. I inhaled the sweet fragrance of pine and fresh earth and smoke. Feet crunched gravel as people approached me, circling around me.

Finally, Mrs. Tucker spoke, her voice full of childlike excitement. "Okay, dear. I'm going to remove your blindfold."

The pressure from the band eased. My eyes stung from the bright sun. I squinted a few times until the shapes around me came into focus. We were in the mountains, standing outside of a large log cabin.

I was surprised to see two vans, not one, which explained how there were a dozen smiling women in front of me, each holding a single white rose. In the center of them stood Lady Maribelle. Her dark hair was swept up in a high bun, and her makeup was perfect. She wore a simple, blush pink dress. In fact, they all wore various shades of pink.

Mrs. Tucker, beaming, clasped my shoulders then kissed me on my cheek. "Blessings over your bridal weekend, Nicolette."

Lady Maribelle approached me with the white rose extended, her smile as big and bright as I could ever recall. She handed me the flower, kissed me on my other cheek, repeated, "Blessings over your bridal weekend Nicolette," then stepped to the side.

Tamika Crawford from the Admin Building approached next, followed by Sheila Carmichael. I stood there in complete astonishment as each woman, twelve in total, repeated the process. By the time the last woman, Matron Patterson, stepped to the side, I clutched a dozen roses and was completely stunned.

Mrs. Tucker said, "Normally, as the mother-in-law to be, I would have the honor of opening your bridal weekend. But our gracious Lady is here with us today and has personally requested the honor."

The women smiled and expressed quick comments about what a blessing her attendance was.

"We are truly favored, and it is with joy that I pass the rest of this opening to our beloved Lady Maribelle."

They broke into applause.

She slightly bowed her head in a gesture of reverent humility then waited for the clapping to die down. "Bright blessings to you Matron Tucker for allowing me to give the opening."

Mrs. Tucker nodded.

Lady Maribelle continued, "It is true I wanted to be a part of Nicolette's bridal retreat just as the Champion desired to be part of

Jason's groom retreat. Nicolette, in your hands you hold twelve white roses, gifted to you from twelve brides wearing pink. The white symbolizes purity. As a new bride, it is your obligation to present yourself in your most purified form to your husband, for it is only in this virtuous state that he is able to recognize and accept you as his wife. The rose represents you, my dear. As you see, they are not fully blossomed. They have bloomed but not fully opened. The rose is the most sacred and coveted of all flowers. As are you."

All the women smiled with genuine expressions of pride on their faces.

"You will notice there are no thorns on the roses you hold. That is because we have trimmed them off for you. We brides who have been married at least five years, your elders, are here to encourage you when moments become unpleasant. We will help remove any thorns that grow in your marriage and help nurture your wounds when you feel confused or exhausted with the duties required of you within a marital union."

All the women nodded.

Mrs. Tucker stepped forward. "And I, as your husband's mother, will be there when you need to understand the more challenging aspects of his character. I, who have seen him grow from a boy into a man, who nursed him and first taught him, have wisdom and experience that I willingly share with you when needed. This next few days, Nicolette, your only job is to rest and receive. That is why I took your cell phone. We've prepared everything in advance. Seven ladies arrived ahead of us to set up"—she gestured to the cabin behind her—"and all was done with love and care. You may rest assured while here, there is nothing for you to worry about."

I didn't know what to say. Wouldn't have been able to speak if I did.

"And so, Nicolette…" She turned to look at the ladies surrounding her.

They all shouted in unison, "Welcome to being a bride!"

By the time they completed the opening ceremony, my face was hot and covered in tears. The thoughtfully crafted welcoming was more beautiful than I could have expected. I had judged these women too harshly. It was clear Mrs. Tucker carefully chose ladies who she thought I liked. Even if I didn't actually like them, I could still appreciate her thoughtfulness in the choice.

Mrs. Tucker chatted about how special this weekend would be as she guided me toward the cabin. We walked arm in arm while the other brides busied themselves with our luggage.

TWENTY

WAS IT A log cabin or mansion?

Whatever it was sat at the base of a lake. In every direction I turned, there were no other houses in sight. It was the perfect place to escape the busyness of the world. We climbed the five steps leading up to the wide porch, which wrapped around the entire structure. Mrs. Tucker unlaced her arm from mine, opened the thick glass door, and with a wink and a grand sweep of her hand, gestured for me to enter.

She seemed genuinely happy to be here... with me. It tugged at my heart and loosened the tension in my chest.

The huge foyer had a high ceiling upheld by thick beams of light-colored wood. Beyond that, the great room was casually furnished with two large, cozy-looking couches, an oversized chair, and a chunky ottoman that could double as additional seating. Behind the furniture stood a massive unlit fireplace. Throw pillows printed with bears and woodland scenes were propped against the arms of all the furniture, and fuzzy blankets stretched across the backs of the sofas. A generous coffee table held wildlife magazines, books, and a set of coasters. The walls were mostly floor-to-ceiling windows of thick glass, trimmed in the same light-colored wood as the door which led back out to the deck.

Everything about the place invited relaxation.

To the left of the great room was an open-concept kitchen. An island of grey-and-black marbled granite stood in the center with barstools positioned along it. A farmhouse sink sat under the only window. The rest of the walls were lined with wooden cabinets, their expanse broken only by a dishwasher, gas stove, microwave-and-oven combo, and refrigerator, all high-end stainless steel appliances. In the back was a door to a full-sized pantry. It was the perfect kitchen for entertaining large groups.

The dining room was directly to the right of the kitchen, which also had a sliding glass door leading out to the porch. On the right side of the great room was a game room, the centerpiece of which was a pool table with burgundy felt. Behind it, built-in cabinets housed board and card games, puzzles, and more books.

"We can place those in here, Dear." Mrs. Tucker retrieved a glass vase from one of the kitchen cabinets and motioned for the flowers still clutched in my hands.

A quick tour of the upstairs ended in our room. Apparently, she and I would share the space, a tradition of the bridal retreat. At least it was the master suite, which had an attached private bathroom. I was grateful we wouldn't have to share a bathroom with the other brides. I was also grateful there were two full-sized beds. All the other rooms were twin-sized.

My bed was adorned with another set of flowers—pink carnations—and appointed with white sheets, a white comforter, and white pillows.

"Give it a whiff," Mrs. Tucker said as she placed my overnight bag on the luggage stand.

I giggled and bent down to smell the pillow.

"I added a spritz of lavender essential oil. I thought you might like it." She beamed at me, waiting for confirmation that she'd done a good job.

It was the cutest thing. I couldn't remember a time I'd ever seen her so jovial.

"It smells great. Thanks for doing that." I smiled back, and I truly meant it. "I can't believe you did all of this." It felt like too much, and I hadn't earned this amount of affection from her. From any of these women. I'd never done anything for them, not voluntarily. Yes, I followed their instructions—whether it was fixing things, improving posture, or speaking correctly—but I never intentionally cultivated their friendship. Certainly not enough to inspire them to plan such a wonderful retreat for me.

"Well, my dear, we have much more planned for you, so I'm glad it's starting off well. Take a moment to gather yourself before we move on to the next portion of the day. Your bag is there." She pointed at the luggage stand. "Either I or one of the other ladies will come get you when we're ready for you."

"Okay."

I stood there after she left and took in the room, appreciating my thoughtfully made bed, the door leading out to the deck, and the breath-taking view beyond. Everything was beautiful, peaceful. I picked up the flowers and inhaled their sweet essence. I loved flowers, and Mama loved them even more. Spring was different this year since she wasn't here to tend to the front garden. Flowers felt like a foggy dream, the joy they imparted forever gone along with my mother. The shifting seasons were a reminder of her rather than time I could share with her, empty but for nostalgia and happy memories.

As wonderful as it was being here at this cabin with these women, my heart anguished. I hadn't felt a motherly presence in many months. The way Mrs. Tucker now doted on me left me feeling emotionally raw.

By the time Sheila Carmichael came to retrieve me, I had splashed water on my face and reapplied my lipstick, ready for whatever festivities awaited below.

"Don't you look cute?" Sheila muttered in a tone that said I didn't look cute at all but more like I was trying, and failed, to look acceptable enough for her. I'd twisted my long, tiny braids into a crown that wrapped around the perimeter of my head and donned a midi length, button-down, white linen dress with puffed sleeves and a flattering square neckline that showed off my collarbone and decolletage. I did look cute.

"Thank you." I fully smiled at her, ignoring the taunt.

She didn't return the smile. "I'm supposed to take you down. Do you have everything you need?"

"I think so. Do I need anything specific?"

Without answering, she turned and began walking down the carpeted staircase. I followed, admiring the huge beams and trusses on the ceiling. As we neared the ground floor, I caught a whiff of some type of grilled meat and heard boisterous chatter. The atmosphere felt so lively, I couldn't help the goofy smile spreading across my face.

"Hello, Bride!" Some of the women sang in unison as I reached the bottom step.

"Hi." I replied sheepishly, feeling ridiculously out-of-place being around these married women. Married women had special privileges within the community, and they also hosted exclusive events and trips I'd always wondered about. Hearing them calling me "bride" before I walked down the aisle, especially while I was still coming to terms with the conversation Jason and I had the other day, felt like opening a present before Christmas.

I approached Misty Gonzalez, my fellow volunteer at the Admin Building and a childhood friend. She was humming a familiar hymn while chopping cucumbers at the kitchen counter. Misty was on the cooking team and often helped organize Lunch after Service. Her food was always good, and knowing she chose to come to my bridal retreat melted my heart.

"Can I help you with anything?" I asked.

"Nope." She smiled and shooed me away. "This time away is *for* you. You get to relax. If you need anything, just let one of us know and we'll be happy to get it for you."

But did they really mean that?

"But if you'd like to chat, I'm curious to know how plans are coming along for your ceremony."

I didn't mind talking about my wedding, especially with other married women. They always had helpful advice. Just as I was sharing a few updates with her, someone squeezed my shoulders. I turned around.

Lady Maribelle smiled at me. "How are you feeling Nicolette?"

"Grateful for all of this." I gestured to the entirety of the house. "I never expected you all to do this for bridal retreats."

"Every woman's bridal weekend is a little different, but yours is extra special because I'm here." She playfully tilted her head.

Behind her, Misty rolled her eyes. She continued humming and preparing meat items on a beautifully carved charcuterie board shaped like a rose.

They really liked to keep to a theme.

After an extravagant and delicious dinner of grilled fish, veggie kabobs, rice pilaf, a garden salad, and all the yummy fixings from the charcuterie, I was stuffed. Mrs. Tucker escorted me to the great room, where we all gathered. These women who I treated with distant respect at home seemed relaxed here. Approachable. Real. It was in complete contrast to what I encountered throughout the community. Weirdest of all was *they* were serving *me*. If I got up to get anything, one of them would quickly ask what I needed then retrieve it for me, even a glass of water; accompanied with a straw.

The evening passed with laughter as each woman shared meaningful high points and hilarious low points of their first year of marriage. It was fun. I was having fun with Matrons and Pillars and Lady Maribelle and even Sheila... kinda. I felt so incredibly accepted, and I couldn't remember laughing so much since Mama died. This was the Community my heart yearned for. It was why I lived in Bright Lakes, why I loved the people there, and why I would marry Jason.

TWENTY-ONE

"**N**O! PLEASE!"

My mouth moves, but sound doesn't come.

I shove hard, commanding my elbows to strike at least one of them. Neither man budges at my attempt, but I won't stop fighting. I thrash and buck while glaring at the two other men, shadowed and faceless, who pick up the little girl I tried to rescue. The taller of them hauls her limp form over his shoulder, then they melt into the deeper darkness of the night.

Demanding fingers dig into my shoulders, lifting me off the muddy ground. Fire hot tremors of pain shoot through me, splintering up from my tailbone through my hips, back, and arms. I'm bruised and sore where they tackled and pinned me to the ground, and my throat is raw from screaming.

About thirty yards away is another shadowed figure—a man running toward me. As he nears, shadows fall away, and his form and features come into focus. He's someone I know… someone I trust.

ಸಂಐ

A LOUD BOOM jolted me awake.

My heart beat wildly, and I sprung to an upright position on my bed. The blinding fluorescent lights stung my eyes as I tried to peel them open. This wasn't my bed. This wasn't my room! I whirled to my left.

Another bed was there.

A *crash* reverberated through the room.

"Time to get up, sleeping beauty," a woman sweetly sang.

My head whipped around.

Three fully dressed women stood in front of me—two smiling, one smirking.

Right. My bridal retreat. I was at my bridal retreat, and that was a dream... a nightmare. The faceless men caught me again. Caught the last little girl I tried to save. Though I knew it was only a dream, my heart was breaking for her even now. I shook my head as the frightening images flipped through my mind like a sadistic slideshow.

I had to remember I was safe, unhurt, and in a beautiful mountain cabin filled with loving women. There was no girl to save and no wicked men trying to capture me.

But why were these women in my room? I couldn't be that late in the day.

Someone started clapping. "Wakey, wakey! You have ten minutes to use the restroom, get dressed, and meet us downstairs in the great room."

My vision adjusted, and my gaze landed on Lady Maribelle. She wore a deep pink dress, make-up perfectly applied, and a peculiar smile. She was accompanied by Matron Jordan, the gong-pounder, and Tamika Crawford. I could hear bustling throughout the house as if everyone was already awake, but there was no sunlight streaming through the window, so it could not possibly be morning.

"What time is it?" I managed to ask.

Lady Maribelle chuckled. "Don't mind the time this weekend. We're here to take care of all those pesky little details. Now, hurry and get dressed. We'll see you in the great room in ten minutes."

"How am I supposed to know when ten minutes is?" They'd taken my cell phone and didn't allow me to have a watch, so there was no way for me to tell time.

"Use your heart, dear. Your heart will tell you. And don't be late." Lady Maribelle shooed everyone out then closed the door behind her.

I freshened up, threw on the white dress Mrs. Tucker packed for me, then made it downstairs in what I imagined had been less than ten minutes to find all twelve brides again clad in various shades of pink. They stood in what appeared to be Faith of rank within the community, with Lady Maribelle front and center, and Mrs. Tucker directly next to her. I felt frantic as I waited for someone to speak and let me know what the emergency was.

Mrs. Tucker gave me a sincere smile. "Good morning, Nicolette, we hope you slept well."

I might have if I hadn't been so rudely awakened before dawn.

She continued, "You will now join Luz Padilla, Matron Smith, and Matron Calhoun for a time of Sacred Text reflection." She gestured to each of the ladies standing next to her. "As you were awakened with the sound of the gong this morning as a symbol of the power of spirit, this sound—"

Matron Jordan tapped the gong with a soft-looking mallet, smiling. No doubt pleased with herself for having been selected to be the gong-tapper and disruptor of my sleep.

"—will also alert you when it is time for a shift. As we mentioned before, the bridal retreat is a time for you to simply receive. Receive love, receive food, receive care. There is no need for you to keep track of anything. We will gladly do it for you. If you need something, just ask, and we will see to it."

More sleep would be great.

Just receive? That sounded well and good, but why were they waking me so early and giving me such a short amount of time to prepare myself? I wasn't stupid enough to argue with women above my station, and Mrs. Tucker looked so happy. I would never embarrass her by being rude. But I hated not knowing what was happening.

Morning dew was sprinkled about the cushion as the three ladies, and I sat on the east end of the front porch. I took my time inhaling the sweet, piney, woodsy air—a reminder that nature is soul medicine. A cure-all for any ailment, including pushy women. The crisp morning air was so refreshing, it wiped away all residue of agitation and carried me through the beautiful, thoughtfully crafted reflective.

Each lady was tasked with choosing a portion of the Text to reflect upon and share their thoughts with me from their personal life experience. It was a discussion method I'd never experienced before. I listened with rapt attention as these women explained how they had been trying to be the best follower of the Bright Lord by applying certain portions of the text to their lives.

When the disruptive gong sounded, the three ladies immediately stood.

Matron Smith said, "Now we'll escort you to breakfast."

I followed them inside. Though I wasn't quite hungry, the undeniable smell of bacon made my mouth water. Classical music poured through in-wall speakers. The large dining table was covered with a bright yellow cloth, and two tall crystal vases sat on each side, bursting with a variety of yellow, white, and purple flowers. I was greeted by a sea of pink dresses and warm smiles.

Porcelain serving trays neatly lined with sliced melon, strawberries, and grapes sat on the kitchen island along with trays of breakfast sausage and crispy bacon, two pitchers of orange juice, and a carafe of coffee. I knew not to ask if they needed help. I was to wait until the ladies served me and ask if I needed something. It was a strange concept to me, the complete opposite of what I've experienced my entire life. But since it was my bridal trip, I did as they said, sat at the head of the table, and admired the beautiful decor.

"Would you like some coffee, Bride?" Misty held a ceramic mug in one hand and a porcelain container in the other.

It felt good to give her a genuine smile in return. Why hadn't I spent more time with her since we graduated from high school? She was just a year ahead of me and Reen, but we used to hang out during lunch break.

"I would. Thank you, Misty." She placed the steaming mug full of black coffee in front of me. "Cream and sugar?"

"Just cream, please."

She poured the cream but making that request to her felt so weird. I felt like I was at a fine dining establishment, and she was my pretty waitress.

"Mind if I sit with you this morning?" she asked.

"Please do!" With Misty, I felt more comfortable than with any of the others, even Tamika. "I'm sure I said it already, but I can't believe you ladies do all of this for bridal weekends. It's a little overwhelming."

"Yeah, it can be overwhelming. But not everyone's bridal weekend is as lovely as this. You've got Mrs. Tucker to thank for that."

My heart filled with gratitude and humility at the thought of all Mrs. Tucker had done for me. How long had she been planning all of this?

"Before she approached me about this, I hadn't spent much time with her, but I can tell she really likes you, Nikki. I've been to a few of these since Chris and I got married, and let me tell you"—she leaned in closer—"there is a huge difference when the mother-in-law likes the bride versus when she merely tolerates the bride."

I'd heard horror stories of bridal weekends. Some were so bad, engagements ended shortly thereafter. But I'd not heard any details, just the aftermath of the breakup. I ignored the compliment and gave free rein to my nosey side. "Like what?"

Before she could answer, Mrs. Tucker announced it was time to eat, then she placed a plate of food on the lace-rimmed placemat in front of me. All the other ladies filled in the empty chairs around the table, each with their own dishes. Lady Maribelle sat across from me. When everyone had settled, she said a simple prayer of gratitude before we began eating.

The breakfast was heavenly. The food was delicious, and conversation flowed easily amongst myself and the other ladies—until the irritating bang of the gong sounded.

Lady Maribelle stood.

The other ladies immediately followed suit. Not wanting to look like the odd-one-out, I abandoned my apricot tartlet and rose.

"Thank you, brides, for preparing such a tasty breakfast for our dear Nicolette."

I squirmed at her announcement. I really wished they'd all stop saying they were doing all of this for me.

The afternoon passed much the same as the morning, with three ladies leading a reflective conversation immediately after breakfast, followed by another. I was in the middle of the third when I stood and turned toward the house. We were sitting on the west side of the front porch this time, which granted us an unhindered view of the beautiful river. The whole time we sat, I had the pleasure of hearing the rushing water, and it had an undesired effect.

"Nicolette, what do you need, dear? You just need to ask and one of us will get it for you," Elizabeth Patterson said. She was one of Mrs. Tucker's best friends and the mother of Lilliana, the student I tutored.

"I'm just going to the bathroom. I'll be right back."

"Oh. Can it wait until we're finished with the reflective?"

Can it wait? What a strange question. Who would get up in the middle of a reading to go to the restroom unless they needed to go? I glanced around the group.

The expressions on the other two brides' faces mirrored Mrs. Patterson's—incredulous surprise.

"I… I suppose it can wait a little while longer."

"Excellent." Mrs. Patterson smiled again. "Please get comfortable again."

"How much longer will this take?" I asked while still standing.

"You don't have to worry about the time, Nicolette. The gong will announce when it's over." Her tone was lighter and higher pitched than normal.

"Yeah, but I do still need to go to the restroom, so I'd like to know how much longer I'll have to hold it."

The incredulous looks returned to each woman's face.

"You'll be just fine, dear," Matron Martin said. "It won't be too much longer. Remember, we're here for you, and we have things in excellent control." She smiled brightly and patted the seat I'd vacated.

Biting my tongue and fighting the urge to run, I took my chair.

TWENTY-TWO

B Y THE TIME the gong sounded, cramp-like pain was throbbing through my lady parts.

We all stood as Mrs. Patterson announced, "Thank you, ladies, for helping facilitate this powerful time of reflection and thank you Nicolette, for being such a thoughtful contributor to the conversation. We'll escort you into the house for lunch."

When we stepped inside the house, I made a beeline toward the stairs. I needed some time away from them, just a few moments alone before lunch began.

Someone called my name, but I tuned them out as I began my climb. Then a hand was upon my shoulder. I turned to see Lady Maribelle standing behind me.

"Nicolette dear, did your escorts forget to tell you it's time for lunch?" She wore a look of confusion, which nipped at that growing crack of anger hidden within me. I didn't know how I knew her question wasn't genuine, but I did. I'd walked into the great room with my escorts and had obviously seen the ladies in the kitchen putting final touches on lunch.

"Yes, I just need to use the restroom. I'll be right back down."

"It'll be faster if you use the one right here behind the great room."
A few other ladies now looked at us.

"I also need to get something from my bag," I lied.

As soon as the lie came out of my mouth, fiery heat rose up within me, quick and demanding. That spark of self-respecting anger I hadn't felt since the day Reen and I argued. When I stood in the shower and allowed myself to feel everything Jason ever said and did to make me feel small, stupid, insignificant. That's what I was feeling right now. Why couldn't I just go use the bathroom?

"Whatever you need out of your bag, one of us can—"

"It's fine, Lady Maribelle. I'll use the restroom right here. Thanks for mentioning it."

I walked past her as quickly as I could, feeling the muscles in my face tensing too much to smile. Besides, my bladder couldn't keep up with this pointless conversation any longer.

"Okay, if you could hurry that would be great. We'll all be waiting for you at the table."

If only I could slap the smile off her face.

I nodded and looked up at the number of steps, realizing I probably couldn't have made it up all of them without putting myself in an even more precarious situation.

After I took care of business, I spent two extra minutes gathering my composure. When I returned to the dining room, all the brides were standing around the table, waiting for me, just as Lady Maribelle said.

I walked toward my seat, ashamed for making them wait. But more than that, I was pissed off. "I'm sorry for making you all wait."

"It's okay, Nikki," Mrs. Tucker said. "We just finished preparations. Now, who would like to say the prayer of gratitude for our lunch?"

The rest of the day passed by in a fashion similar to the morning and afternoon, back-to-back reflectives and overlapping groups of brides of three. I'd met with the same group twice, then a mixture of other women. I asked for things I needed, they happily obliged, and I waited to use the bathroom until they told me I could go. During one of the sessions, muscles in my legs began to stiffen from all the sitting so I stood to stretch a bit. That was a mistake. The brides in my group politely asked me to sit. It clearly didn't matter to them that I wasn't used to being sedentary all day. Apparently, it wasn't only the bathroom that required permission.

At one point, I dared ask why women were singled out in the Guidelines but not men?

Lilliana's mom, Matron Patterson, cleared her throat. "First of all, it's not a woman's place to be concerned about what men are or are not wearing."

"But they're concerned about what we're wearing. Why is that acceptable?" I challenged.

Her eyes narrowed.

I was happy to see I'd hit a nerve.

"A lady must be concerned about purity, virtue, and the vulnerable fragility of her being. She must understand these values make a woman both a danger and a subject of prey to men. If her focus is on others, she does not properly guard her virtue and willingly exposes herself to harm through either ignorance or loose morals. The Guidelines are in place to help protect all women. So, you should clearly see it's in your best interest to not focus on men but on yourself. Men can protect themselves. Now, let's continue with the reflective." She turned her attention to Tamika. "Mrs. Crawford, where were you in the Text?"

By the time dinner began, Misty was the only person I could tolerate without my face broadcasting my true thoughts.

"How are you enjoying the retreat so far?" she asked.

"It's been… surprising."

"Yeah, a lot of us felt the same way during our trips too, since we didn't have any clue before we arrived. But you'll understand everything by the time we leave tomorrow."

"That's what everyone keeps saying."

Mrs. Tucker was waiting for us at the foot of the stairs. The creases in her forehead and tightness of her smile was clue enough that I might really be in trouble.

She was the last person I'd ever want to disappoint. I reconsidered my "no more apologies" stance and prepared to offer one.

"My Jason tells me one of Nicolette's favorite treats is fried hand pies. So…" She gestured toward the countertop in the kitchen. The few brides who stood earlier were now coming back out with trays in their hands. Trays of freshly fried fruit pies! I thought I smelled cinnamon and sugar earlier.

"She shall have her favorite treat at her bridal retreat! I want to thank our dear Mrs. Gonzalez for making them exactly as Nicolette likes them, sprinkled with cinnamon and sugar. Enjoy, ladies, and don't worry about the calories. Remember, they don't count during retreats."

"Ahh, thank you Misty." I said to her directly.

"I was happy to do it, Nikki. These retreats can get a little… intense, so it's good to have something that brings you comfort."

She wasn't lying.

I'd just finished eating my delicious pie when again, the gong clanged, announcing another transition to the evening. I squeezed my eyes tight to prevent them from accidentally rolling in front of everyone. The only transition I wanted into bed, with hours of peace and quiet ahead of me.

Mrs. Tucker stood. "Okay brides and bride-to-be, let's all move to the great room for our final reflective of the evening. I'm sure our Nicolette is getting tired after so much excitement."

Not exactly the word I would've used.

The evening ended as it began, with one of the Matrons telling me exactly what to do and when.

"Lights out in fifteen minutes," Mrs. Tucker announced when our evening's *excitement* came to an end. At the sixteenth minute, three of them stood in the doorway until I lay in my bed. One woman turned off the lights.

As I lay there, I imagined my life with Jason. Imagined following the guidelines and being the best version of myself. Imagined leaning upon these brides for advice and comfort.

The more I imagined the word *comfort*, the more vivid the image of Micah came into focus.

TWENTY-THREE

THROUGHOUT THE NIGHT, I'd woken hot and flung off the sheet only to wake again—cold—and have to search for it.

I'd repeated this routine multiple times.

As my body cycled between temperatures, my restless mind also whirled. I replayed every word and action of the brides, shocked at how many things were contrary to what I believed.

When Mrs. Tucker tiptoed out, overnight bag in hand, I realized I didn't have much longer to rest. About thirty minutes later, she reappeared with all the other brides. They wore white cotton gowns with white sashes tied at the waist, and each held flickering candles. She stood front and center, holding something circular in her hand.

They began singing.

I was grateful to have already been awake. Once again, the sun had not yet risen. The sight of the women in white, holding candles in the dark, might have startled me into having what would've been deemed an inappropriate reaction.

The hymn they crooned was one I'd loved. A soft, swaying melody reminding people to view their lives in light of how well they served others. I sat up and watched as they filled the room. Mrs. Tucker was the only one who walked toward me, arms outstretched. She placed a twisted crown of flowers atop my head. It was such a sweet gesture.

Probably would have made a prettier image if I didn't sleep with a silk scarf around my hair.

She took her place at the center of the group, and they continued singing. It truly was a beautiful moment, being serenaded by these women, though Lady Maribelle wasn't with them.

When the hymn came to an end, Mrs. Tucker said, "Dear Nicolette, please take fifteen minutes to dress and freshen up. Then meet us in the great room."

I understood fifteen minutes, without the use of a watch, simply meant I needed to hurry.

After they left, I removed the flower crown. Something stabbed my finger. On closer inspection, I discovered thorns. There were thorns in my crown. How did they even manage to twist it together? I placed it on the bed and just stared at it. Wildflowers interwoven with white roses. The vase on the desk held the white roses they handed me on the first day. Still intact, fully blossomed. No thorns on those.

I dragged myself to the restroom, lack of sleep pulling me down. At least I got to go home today. I'd get my watch. My phone too. The first thing I planned to do was text Reen.

I readied myself quicker than the previous day. Yay me. The flower crown of thorns taunted me from my bed as I deliberated how to place it on my head without hurting myself. A few minutes later, I strategically placed it back on my head with a combination of bobby pins and tweezers and even managed to have the ribbon dangling in the back. Then I made my way downstairs to the great room.

There was no music playing, and I smelled no breakfast cooking. In fact, the ladies I normally saw scuttling about preparing food and setting the decor were all gathered in the great room as well. All wearing white, like me. It was still unsettling to walk amongst so many married women and be the center of their attention. After a deep breath, I walked toward them.

Mrs. Tucker gestured her hand to my chair, the oversized one near the fireplace. The chair wrapped me in its squishy warmth, and I was ready to hear the morning reflective.

Mrs. Tucker remained standing.

"As brides, you all know it is customary for the mother of the bride-to-be to lead us in the reflective this morning. But with the passing of our dear Regina, it is incumbent upon me, as mother-in-law, to lead it in her absence."

All the other ladies turned sympathetic eyes in my direction. At that moment, the loss of Mama felt like a blow, and I couldn't look at anyone. I turned my focus to my engagement ring and tried to compose myself. I desperately wished my mom could've been there with me. To help me understand all the unasked and unanswered questions disturbing my peace, preventing me from fully receiving the gift of this time spent with other married women. But she was gone, and I didn't know why. Her death was so sudden, so unexpected. So pointless. I wasn't sure I'd ever move past it. Moments like these made her absence even harder to bear.

I braced for whatever Mrs. Tucker was about to reflect upon.

Bright Lord, please give me strength and help me not to make a fool of myself anymore.

"The reflective today will be brief and is titled 'Be free and give love.' The Sacred Text teaches us many ways to receive love when it is given to us. As brides, we must be willing to help our grooms in many ways. We must be willing to help our children in many ways.

And we must be willing to help our community in many ways. An honorable bride is constantly helping others, just as she is commanded.

"Upon your head, Nicolette, is a crown of flowers. They are beautiful to look upon, and their fragrance can fill a room. This represents you, my dear. I can attest that my son, Jason, did well by choosing you as his intended bride."

Murmurs of agreement fill the room.

"You may also have noticed that unlike the white roses we handed to you upon your arrival, the crown upon your head has thorns. Allow me to explain. A bride's beauty is precious and even more valuable because it needs protection. Should she waywardly expose her beauty, both she and her husband may be hurt in doing so. It is the woman's responsibility—the wife's—to ensure her virtue is protected at any cost. Yesterday, you asked a question that many brides-to-be have asked before. I hope you can now understand.

"You have seen how I treat my husband, how I hold myself, and how these other brides represent their husbands and their families. They are respected by everyone in the Community, and that is why they are here now. You have been the center of our attention this entire trip. The decorations were selected with your favorite colors and designs in mind. The meals have been prepared in a way that you like, based upon the feedback from your friends, colleagues, and fiancé. You have sat at the head of the table, and we have all waited upon you. All of this was done to help you understand how valuable you are to us all. How valuable you will be to your family.

"Now, my dear, take all that you have received from this trip and give it to your husband, my son. In the same way we honored you, your role as a wife will be to honor and uphold him. As we styled this home with you in mind, you will prepare your home for him. You will cook meals that he enjoys, play music he likes. If he wants anything, you will retrieve it."

My mouth gaped so wide, my chin nearly hit the floor.

"When he is in the home, he should feel welcomed and comfortable because you have taken the time to get up early, sometimes before the sun rises, to ensure it is so. Brides are not only beautiful, they are helpful."

In unison all the brides said, "When we give love, we are also receiving it."

"This is the expectation of a wife in the Bright Lord's Faith. It is what we have all committed to. It is what I have committed to, and if your mother had remarried, it would have been what she committed to. We said it upon arrival, but we repeat it now in the hope that you will truly understand. We are here for you. Any advice you may need, any help we can offer. We take care of one another the way only women can. Men have their own struggles, and that is what the groom's trip is for. The same way you are receiving what you need to be the best wife you can be to Jason, he will receive what he needs to be the best husband he can be to you."

They were right—I would understand what the fuss was about by the last day.

PART 2

TWENTY-FOUR

ESTINATION SIGNS DURING the ride home confirmed the bridal
retreat was within Yosemite National Park.

I was glad to be free of my blindfold and relieved Misty
chose to sit next to me. She was more grounded than when we were
in high school, and I could tell she was genuinely happy. Hearing
updates about her life, her toddler, and the joy she gets from
cooking for others was the distraction I needed to keep my jumbled
thoughts at bay. I felt raw, irritable. Like at any moment I could
burst out crying or screaming depending on the next thing someone
said to me.

They dropped me off first, and I was grateful for it. I was desperate
for a thorough shower, a cheeseburger, and time to be by myself, moving
at my own pace. I dropped my overnight bag on the living room floor
then rushed to the backyard. My strawberries were calling me. I'd missed
them. The blazing sun presented an illusion of mid-day, but now that I
had my phone privileges back, I knew it was past six. Reen said she would

take care of the berries, but the pots in vertical towers were dry as if they hadn't been watered at all.

No problem. I enjoyed watering them, feeling the soil come back to life between my fingers.

After watering them all and enjoying that time with my babies, I felt a little energized. I grabbed an apple, chopped it into six slices, popped one in my mouth, then made my way to the shower. The steam filled the room, and I went to the effort of placing four drops of lavender oil inside of my diffuser, allowing the soothing aroma to fill the enclosed space. It smelled wonderful, like a spa. What the fragrance didn't do to help me relax, the water did. I melted under the spray, glorying in the therapeutic haven it offered.

I was glad to be home. Glad not to have a gong directing me to get up, move, sit, and eat. Glad not to have people around me all day. Glad to have space to think and digest all that occurred. Glad to be able to feel my own heartbeat, hear my own thoughts. Glad to satisfy my own hunger with whatever I wanted.

Time for a cheeseburger! I slipped on an oversized soft sage and tan maxi dress in a geometric print that I loved. Cozy and quick. I grabbed my brown leather purse from the coat hook on my closet door then headed back to the kitchen for another apple slice.

The sun was barely setting by the time I stepped outside. Deep gold mixed with cotton candy pink on the horizon. We had the best sunsets in this city. I looked forward to feeling the warm breeze during my quick drive to Johnny's Burger Palace. It was a favorite of mine for both proximity and taste. I didn't eat there when I was on a health-food kick, but today I wanted comfort in the form of salty, meaty calories. I would add a strawberry milkshake to my order too. But not fries!

I fumbled around in my purse, searching for my overcrowded keyring.

Okay, maybe a small order of fries.

As soon as I found it, it slipped from my fingers and clanked to the ground. I really needed to sweep the stray leaves from my front porch before the Administration sent a warning. As I picked them up, I noticed a crisp white envelope tucked under my mat.

It had no name, no address. No identification at all. I ripped it open. Inside was a folded piece of lined paper. I didn't recognize the handwriting.

They took your friend. Try to act normal.

-M

I flipped the paper over, but it was blank. I looked left, then right. No one was there.

Took whom? And who was M?

I looked around the porch, maybe I missed something. I read the note again and wondered if Sheila left this here as a joke—a final test from my bridal retreat. I took two steps toward her house then remembered the berries. Reen hadn't watered them like she promised. I took my cellphone from my purse. Not one text message from her over the past three days. I pressed the button to call her. It immediately went to voicemail.

Fine. I'd just go to her house.

I rushed to my carport and tried to ignore the thumping of my heartbeat. This was just someone playing a mean joke. I slid into my car. Before I knew it, I was knocking on the Johnsons' front door and stabbing the bell. No light shone on the porch to illuminate the front steps, and even with my ear pressed to the iron gate, I couldn't hear signs of movement. It wasn't late, but the sun had fully set. There should have been lights on inside, but all the windows were dark.

I was aware of how inappropriate I was being by banging on the door and didn't want to draw attention from the neighbors. Mr.

Johnson was an Elder, granted housing in a special neighborhood among his peers. Here more than anywhere else, no misconduct or breach of community rules would be tolerated.

But if something really had happened, I couldn't be faulted for my concern.

I rang the bell again. With each press of the button, the familiar sinking feeling beckoned me deeper into its embrace and control of my breath was slipping. I pressed it two times, then a third. Knocked at the door, a little harder than before.

This couldn't be happening to me. Not again.

Memories assaulted me—waiting in Mama's hospital room, holding her hand, praying the Bright Lord would restore her consciousness. Believing my worst nightmare would not come true. Believing each visitor's kind words of encouragement. Believing everyone's prayers would be granted. Hoping I could take a break from sleeping at the hospital. Hoping this mysterious illness would blow over and bring us both closer to the Bright Lord. Why wouldn't it? Mama was still young, just in her late forties, and she had no pre-existing conditions or diseases.

The memories were bad enough. How could I face this new reality?

My breath stuck in my throat. Moving oxygen through my lungs was a strain. It burned. I could only manage short spurts of air at a time.

Please, not again. Not another person taken from me. Another thing I loved. The only person left who loved me.

I knew this wasn't nothing and no prayer didn't help when I lost Mama, and it wouldn't help now. I needed action, not words.

My head swam. I clutched my chest, certain my heart was going to burst.

TWENTY-FIVE

WHEN HANDS GRIPPED my shoulders, I yelped. I looked up to find Micah, eyes wide, staring at me. When did he appear? I didn't hear him approach.

He was shaking me gently. "Nikki, can you hear me?"

I shoved his hands off me and took a wobbly step back. I pulled in a stream of air. A second, longer than the last. I had to steady my breath and my head. "Wh-what are you doing here?"

"Are you okay? You looked like you were about to pass out." His voice was calm and full of concern.

I placed my palm on my head, a pathetic attempt to ease the throbbing. "I think my friend, Maureen Johnson…" Why was the air so thin? "I think something bad happened to her. She's not here. No one's here. That's not normal."

Micah gripped me by the arm then led me to the passenger side of my car. I let him guide me to the seat.

He scanned the block. "You can't be seen here after dark, especially behaving this way. Give me your keys."

He was right. I handed him my crowded keychain.

He scooped up my calves, spun me so I faced the windshield, tucked my legs inside, then shut the door.

My gaze remained on Reen's front door. I was desperate to see some sign of life. Movement, a light. Something indicating she and her family were okay.

The weight of Micah's frame made the car go down when he climbed behind the wheel. Only after he drove away did I close my eyes, hoping that by doing so, the pounding in my head would stop.

When I opened them again, we were rounding the space between Mr. Bagwell's farm and the city. I recognized the field of wild dandelions. This was where Jason proposed last year. Back when my life made sense. When everything felt whole and safe and beautiful.

Not anymore. The field was a stark reminder of all I'd lost... of all I still had to lose.

Micah parked my car along Fruit Road, an isolated stretch with just enough space for one car to pass at a time. It was more accurate to call it a dirt path formed by the frequent passage of farm suppliers and kids from the community who dared walk this far to glimpse what the world outside looked like from the safety of Bright Lakes.

He cut the engine, then we sat in my car under the cover of orange trees.

"What were you doing at Maureen's house?" I asked.

"I figured you'd go there after you got my note."

"Right. Okay, you're M. Tell me what happened to Maureen. Where is she? And where is her family?"

"I knew they wouldn't tell you, so I left that note and hoped you'd start asking questions."

"What do you mean *they* wouldn't tell me? Tell me what? And who's they?" Heat rushed through my body as anger roiled through me, hot and uncapped. There was no reason to hold back. No reason to keep my composure or pretend like I was anything but pissed off.

"This isn't anything new. You've seen families at Service one day then gone the next."

Of course I had. Clarissa's family disappeared a few months ago, and it was as if their family never existed. Like a damned fool, I played right along. A barrage of other families ran through my mind like a slideshow. How could I have been so apathetic? How many times had I turned a blind eye to the unkind, unloving things that happened within our Faithful community? In the ten years Mama and I lived here, a startling pattern had emerged, and I'd ignored it until now. Other than the elderly—those grandfathered into the community because they were here before it was established—most of the residents were related to the Elders, on the path to Leadership positions, or new members. People who didn't fall into one of those categories often moved into one.

Or they disappeared.

Panic reared up again. It took a while before I calmed, and Micah gave me the time, space, and silence to settle.

Once my breathing was stable and my thoughts were clear, I became aware of my surroundings. Fruit Road had no streetlights, and since the sun had set, it was completely dark. I was in a car, on a deserted back road, with a man who wasn't my fiancé. It was scandalous! I was asking for trouble, but that paled compared to the fact I still didn't know what happened to Reen and her family.

I reached down to the floor of the passenger seat, grabbing my phone from my purse. My texts remained unanswered, and I didn't have any missed calls. Again, I sent her a message.

Where are you? I'm getting really worried.

"I better get you home." Micah's deep voice broke through my ricocheting thoughts.

"No. Wait. Why would they just leave? Why wouldn't they say anything to me? Maureen is my best friend."

He stared into the night. His thick eyebrows pinched together between his forehead, and he looked like he was struggling to decide what to tell me. "People who leave like this don't have a chance to say anything to anyone."

"Why wouldn't they have a chance? Were they forced to move away?"

"Look, it's not for me to say. I'm only telling you this, so you don't cause a scene and make the situation worse."

I didn't ask him to help me, and I don't cause scenes. Well, I almost did.

He continued to look out into the distance.

"Micah, what are you not telling me? What is going on?"

"It's not for me to say." He said in a near growl, finally making eye contact with me.

I leaned away from him and pressed my body against the passenger door.

He looked pained. His expression didn't match what he was saying.

Even though I was afraid of what he might say or do, I couldn't drop the subject. My best friend and her entire family were the only people alive who truly loved me—I couldn't even say that about my fiancé. I wouldn't let fear keep me from seeking answers. Not anymore.

"Why do people leave suddenly, Micah? Why would Maureen's family be forced to move out?" My voice was as calm as I could make it.

"This isn't a sudden decision. Elders and Matrons meet in advance to plan these things."

"But Mr. Johnson is an Elder!"

He turned to search the road, looking in both directions. "Sometimes a higher-ranking Elder can make a move against someone like Mr. Johnson. The Matrons offer their advice, then the Elders vote. As you might imagine, it's almost guaranteed the higher-ranking Elder will get his way."

"But it's possible, right?"

"I can only recall one time where the higher-ranked Elder was outvoted—the time my uncle became Champion."

I was going to be sick. "Who all knows about this? And why would all the other Elders want to vote the Johnson family out?"

"My best guess? Maureen got engaged to another Unfaithful, leaving no spouses to bring them back to the flock."

"But Shawn's a good man. You know that. You know *him*." Reen recently told me they were going into business together. "Why would an engagement to an Unfaithful warrant a full-family eviction?" None of it made sense. Each answer peeled back another layer of anger. I was on fire.

"Look Nikki, I don't want to hurt your feelings and like I said, I've already told you too much." He was practically begging me to stop asking questions. I wouldn't.

"Stop trying to protect my feelings!" I screamed. "Stop trying to keep me ignorant of my own Community! I want to know the truth. I'm tired of feeling like everyone is in on a secret that's affecting my life. Mine, Micah! I'm not a little girl. Yes, my mom's death made me go quiet for a while, and even that left me with lingering questions, especially after I saw her journal entries, but this… what's happening with Maureen…"

Tears flowed, and I was too angry to wipe them away.

"If she's not hurt… if she's not… dead… then I want to know the truth. She's the only person left who loves me. I can't be left alone like this again. Not so soon."

Heat filled the space between us, then suddenly Micah's mouth was upon mine. The shock of the action didn't linger long before I closed my eyes and relaxed into his kiss. The scent of soap and wood chips filled my nostrils. His lips, warm and full, pressed into mine. Soft and gentle yet passionate.

I didn't just like it. I wanted it. Wanted *him*. And I had, for longer than I'd ever admit.

In the next heartbeat, the space between us was there again. He was fully in the driver's seat, clutching the wheel.

I was stunned. I looked down at my engagement ring, then out the window.

"You're not alone Nikki." His baritone voice was deep and low, and I liked that too. He turned the key, and the soft hum of the engine filled the silence. "It's getting late. I'll take you home."

I nodded and continued to look out the window. My heart raced for different reasons now. Out of the corner of my eye, a little further down the road past a row of orange trees, I spied two figures standing in the shadows, looking in our direction. I couldn't make out who they were, then the car began moving north, toward the residential area of the community.

"Micah, I just saw two people."

"If they're out here at this time of night, I doubt they'll say anything. Besides, they likely don't know who we are."

I kept my eyes on the road, not him. I couldn't look at him.

"Micah, who else knows about this? You said you didn't think they would tell me. Who did you mean?"

We passed through Mr. Bagwell's farm then turned onto Butler Street. We were three blocks from my house.

"Your fiancé, his family, and your neighbors... the Carmichaels."

TWENTY-SIX

I F I HAD venom, it would have been spewing from my mouth.

Instead, my heart dropped, and my stomach roiled. "Pull over!"

On the corner of Butler and Torrence, before the car had fully stopped, I threw open the door then hurled into the grass along the sidewalk in front of the Hernandez's' house. The seatbelt pressed into my belly and chest apple and acid reversed direction through my heaving body.

"Do you have napkins in here?" Micah asked, fumbling through the arm storage.

Still twisted over the side of the car, I pointed to my glove compartment and heaved again.

Micah's warm hand rubbed and patted my back. I retched until the rock in my stomach transformed into muscle pain, then I sat limp within my seat, one hand on my stomach, the other wiping my mouth with the napkin Micah gave me. The silence between us mirrored the silence in my mind as he drove the final blocks to my house.

He pulled into the carport then ran to my side of the car to open the door. My body was weak, and I felt more stupid than I ever had in my entire life. My fiancé—the man who committed his life to mine, who was the reason I'd just spent the past three days in utter discomfort and ridicule for—knew the person I loved most was taken away and didn't mention a word to me. He hadn't come to tell me in person. I had no missed calls or text messages from him. He knew, yet he kept this from me.

It was agonizing. And humiliating.

I reached for Micah's extended hand then stepped out of the car. The Carmichaels' lights were on in their home. Instead of the fear I'd typically feel in this compromised position, I seethed with unleashed anger. Let her say something. I wished she would.

"I wasn't going to say anything," Micah said, interrupting my thoughts. "I know you just got back from your bridal retreat, and I know you love him, but after seeing you, like this"—he pointed to my face— "I think you should know the truth about him."

What did that even mean? The truth. The term was laughably ridiculous.

"Thank you. And you're right. No one else would tell me."

"I better go before your neighbors see me." He turned and walked down the block.

I watched as he rounded Torrence then took a left toward the Elders' residences on Wolter Avenue. The sight of him leaving left me feeling more alone than when the day began. I turned to open the unlocked door to my house and saw a curtain swaying in Sheila Carmichael's house. Was that heifer spying on me again? Of course she was. I closed the door behind me and took a few deep breaths in an attempt to dull the pain in my head.

The time for second guessing myself was over. I'd wasted years tormenting myself for having reckless, unchecked thoughts—thoughts that caused me to doubt my instincts and hate myself because I couldn't agree with everything I heard and saw. All this time, I was pretending, and I hadn't even realized it. Pretending I believed what the Faith said I should. Pretending the societal roles were acceptable—no, desirable and deserved. Pretending the truths whispered to me weren't actually lies. But in my heart, I knew. And Reen knew too.

The luxury of ignorance and blind submission was no longer an option for me. Not after learning everything Micah told me. I didn't even want to think about Jason's betrayal. It was too much.

I reached for my phone again, checking for any replies from Reen. None. I texted her again, not expecting an answer.

Please call me.

Donation boxes lined the north and east sides of my empty living room. After freshening up and brewing a cup of tea, I took a mental inventory of the space and contemplated my next steps. Everyone I believed in had lied to me. I desperately wanted to hold out hope that Matron Kirk wasn't lying about Mama's journal entries, but her dismissive remarks and Malachi's discussion with me in the Infants' Room told me otherwise. If Leadership was brazen enough to evict Faithful members of Bright Lakes—and an Elder's family, no less—what *wouldn't* they do?

But why? I still didn't understand why any of this needed to happen.

Tomorrow I'd have to join Jason's family for Service. Since the bridal retreat was a success, I'd be expected to sit with them from now on. There was no getting out of it. I didn't know how I'd stand it knowing the whole time Mrs. Tucker planned my beautiful bridal retreat she simultaneously plotted against me. She knew Reen was my best friend, and she knew what was happening to the Johnsons while we were gone. The warmth and motherly affection I craved and received from her during the trip made the betrayal a gut punch.

And what was Jason's role in it? That's exactly what I'd find out tomorrow. How could I rectify this situation or make him see that doing things like this would only drive me to leave him?

છ૭ભ

I WORE THE dress he hated most while waiting for his family at the Service Hall steps.

A wide boat-necked, capped-sleeved, fit-and-flare dress in the color emerald green. The scandalous dress barely met our Ladies Styling Guidelines because the length skimmed my knees as opposed to reaching past them. The last time I wore it, he asked if I were looking for another boyfriend. The grumbled comment hurt my feelings, but because of my conditioned passivity, I said nothing and never wore the dress again. If it weren't for Mama convincing me to keep it, I'd have thrown it away. The dress was very flattering, but since my breasts were a bit too voluminous, he found it *inappropriate*.

Mr. and Mrs. Tucker approached arm in arm, looking like a poster couple for the Bright Lord's Faith and a perfect selling point for the Bright Lakes Residential Community.

"Nicolette, sweetheart, blessed morning!" She greeted me with a huge smile and extended arms.

I forced myself to return her embrace, then forced myself not to crush her. My mind reeled with thoughts of how she took the time to learn all my favorite things then smiled in my face, peppered me with compliments, and plied me with delicious foods—not out of love, but as a ruse. While she put on a show, she knew my dearest friend was being taken away.

"Good morning, Mrs. Tucker." I smiled, big and bright as I was taught. Just another day working at the Administration Building, silencing my disgust and replacing it with my goal. This time, it wasn't polite customer service. It was to find out why Jason did this to me, find out why he hated Reen so much that he sent her away, find out why he destroyed our future and ruined any hope that I'd ever trust him.

Mr. Tucker simply looked at me and nodded—a more enthusiastic greeting than he'd ever given. Directly behind him was Jason, also smiling, but his eyes didn't look like he was exactly happy to see me. I returned the look.

"Is Kimberly not joining us today?" I asked, noticing she wasn't trailing behind Jason.

"She isn't feeling well, so we let her stay home," Mrs. Tucker replied.

That was extremely rare. Faithful families, especially Elders weren't allowed to miss Service except in cases of emergencies, and we'd all know about such situations in advance. I didn't pry further. That wasn't my goal for the day, and I couldn't handle more conversation with them than necessary.

The four of us made our way into the Service Hall. As I entered, I looked around—half out of habit, half out of desperation—hoping to see Reen. Or at least the rest of the Johnsons. But none of them were present. It really was true. The row they sat in, with the other Elder families, was filled in by others. No space was left for them even if they showed up. If an Elder and his family was not present, simply absent, no one would ever take his family's seat. That meant everyone was in on this secret. Jason stepped up next to me, but he also made no mention of it.

I caught sight of the wives from my retreat. For the first time since I joined the community, they stood out to me. None of them looked disturbed by the Johnsons' absence either.

Service went on as usual, but my mind was occupied, leaving no room to hear the teaching. I think the Champion was prattling about focusing on the best in people and not dwelling on their imperfections.

I walked alongside Jason as we made our way out of the Service Hall towards the courtyard for Lunch. When he reached for my hand, I dodged it by fanning myself and complaining about the heat. He frowned at me but said nothing as we approached the tables. Today included a birthday celebration for Annabeth Hinsley. She was a Faithful member who married last year and was on her way to becoming a Matron. Everyone adored her, and I never had a negative encounter with her or her husband Brian.

I couldn't have been more grateful when Misty found me and dragged me away from Jason. "How've you been since the retreat? Were you able to sleep well last night?"

I stumbled over my words, trying not to lie. "It was difficult to rest last night, but I'm glad to be back home. No one prepared an amazing breakfast for me this morning, so I'm a little mad about that."

We both laughed.

"Yeah, it's hard to go from having food cooked for you all day to nothing." She giggled.

"Hi there, brides." Sheila Carmichael approached us. Her sly smile said she knew something scandalous about someone and was itching to share.

"Hey, Sheila," Misty replied.

I wouldn't give her the satisfaction of a greeting but instead returned her smile with a grimace.

"Is everything okay, Nikki? I saw you came home pretty late last night, even after we dropped you off."

That bitch. She *was* watching me when I returned home with Micah. Did she also notice him?

"Is she on house arrest?" Misty retorted.

My head slowly turned to Misty. She did not just say that to Sheila Carmichael.

"I didn't say anything about house arrest, Misty." Sheila now sized up Misty as an opponent.

"Good. We wouldn't want to think you'd keep our bride-to-be locked away in her empty house after spending the past three days with twelve women." Misty turned to look at me, her back facing Sheila. "Nikki, do you like cake? I made this one for Annabeth today." Misty wrapped her arm in mine, moving me away from Sheila toward Annabeth, who stood talking to two other ladies.

"In case you didn't know," Misty said under her breath, "Sheila is determined to become a Matron and will do anything to spy on and tell on anyone at any time. If I were you, I'd keep my distance from her."

I couldn't believe what I was hearing. Was Misty on my side? If there was a side to be had. Did she also know what happened with Reen? Better not to ask and ruin everything. I needed to be alone with Jason, and I needed to find out what he knew before the day was over. It was my last chance. He'd be leaving tomorrow for his groom's retreat.

"I did know. And thank you. She's told the Pillars a few things about me that aren't true, and it's caused some problems," I admitted.

"I'm sorry she did that to you, but it's not uncommon, you know."

"Yeah, I've just never had to live next door to a Trainee before, so it's been a little intense the past year with her."

"Ugh, I can imagine." She rolled her eyes.

The gesture made me miss Reen.

Elder Kirk, Matron Kirk's husband, stood in the center of the picnic tables, a sign he was prepared to say a blessing before Lunch began.

My curiosity got the better of me. "Misty, why didn't you become a Matron?"

She didn't hesitate to answer. "Many reasons, but most importantly, I like my life just the way it is. I didn't want to have to change into a version of myself that I wouldn't be able to respect. I need to sleep at night, in peace, without worrying I may have ruined someone else's life."

Wow. If she told me that three months ago, I wouldn't have believed it, but with all I've seen since Mama's passing, I couldn't agree more.

TWENTY-SEVEN

T THE SOUND of the bells, Elder Kirk raised his voice and began praying.

Everyone stood with bowed heads as he gave thanks for our food and the people who prepared it. But my gaze rested on Matron Kirk as he prayed. All my life, I trusted her above anyone else in the community. Mama trusted her. She stood there, perfect clothes, perfect hair, beautiful face, head down—the pinnacle of grace.

I gritted my teeth. Why would these people do all of this? That's what I wanted to get to the bottom of. Why were they keeping so many secrets and demanding all this obedience and creating all these rules?

"Thank you for always being honest with me," I said to Misty once the blessing ended. "I better find Jason before everybody takes seats."

"Anytime, Nikki. And hey, feel free to reach out sometime. You'll be married soon, and it won't be frowned upon for us to hang out more."

"I'd love that." It was only half true. I wouldn't be married soon.

We hugged, which felt like a goodbye to me. Then I turned to find my dear, sweet fiancé.

I took a few deep breaths to brace myself as I walked upon the grass toward Jason. I felt sick at the idea of confronting him, the idea of saying my thoughts out loud.

He was in conversation with Elder Brown, the most prestigious Elder in our Faith and husband of Matron Brown, the rude old woman who spoke about Reen with disgust. He was a dark-skinned Black man with a bald head and perfect posture. Average height and a little overweight, but not by much—it was obvious he took good care of himself despite his age, which I'd guess was late sixties to early seventies. As I neared, his scent carried to me on the breeze. He smelled like every old man I'd ever met—a combination of liberally applied cologne, mouthwash, and arthritis cream.

If memory served, Elder Brown was an astute rule follower and no one, not even his kids, could stop him from following the Guidelines to a T. If anyone had a question about the Bright Lakes Community Rules or the Sacred Text, he would know the answer.

"Ah, Nikki, there you are." Jason reached out to me.

I placed my hand in his, offered them both a tight-lipped smile, then gave a slight nod—as etiquette dictated girls did as a show of respect to older men—before greeting him with his proper title. "Elder Brown."

He eyed me from my face down to my shoes without saying a word.

I shifted my weight, disgusted by his examination.

The older man finally shifted his gaze to Jason. "We can continue this conversation later, Trainee Tucker."

"Thank you for your advice, Grand Elder."

The two men shook hands before Elder Brown walked toward his mean wife.

"I heard Misty joined you on your bridal retreat," Jason said.

"What were you and the Grand Elder talking about?" I didn't have energy for his questions. Rather, his statements. My stomach felt queasy, but I couldn't let that stop me from asking what I needed before Lunch ended. And I couldn't let on how angry and betrayed I felt. No matter what, I still needed a place to live. If he had enough power to evict an entire family, what could he do to me? I didn't have a contingency plan in place, and unlike Reen, I didn't have a family. I had no one to lean on. My future depended on Jason—at least until I knew the whole truth.

"Just stuff for the groom's retreat. He's happy I'm finally getting married."

A Trainee could never become an Elder unless he was established and married. The rule popped into my mind.

"Why would that concern him?" I asked sweetly, trying not to sound bitter or suspicious.

"He's helping my father prepare for the retreat. My dad couldn't do it all on his own."

It occurred to me that in normal situations, under normal circumstances, it would have been my father leading Jason's groom's retreat. The thought made me feel inferior. And sad for Jason. He'd done so much just to marry me. My background and family situation added additional hurdles to his process, and there was nothing I could do about it.

"Let's get something to eat." I didn't want to dwell on that thought and refused to feel sorry for him. I wasn't hungry, but food made for a good distraction.

Mr. Winters, his wife, and their young son Patrick were ahead of us in the buffet line.

"Are you two excited for the wedding?" Mr. Winters smiled at us. "It's in just a couple weeks, isn't it?"

Jason nodded. "We couldn't be more excited. Nikki just returned from her bridal retreat last night."

Mrs. Winters leaned in a little closer. "Ooh. Did you learn a lot at your bridal retreat?"

"I'm sure every woman does." I pasted on a wide smile. "It was definitely memorable, and Mrs. Tucker made everything so beautiful." To think all the married women in our community participated in that horrible ritual made me want to throw up.

We made it through the line fairly quickly. My plate was piled with food I knew I wouldn't eat. I needed to find the perfect opportunity to ask Jason the question, and I was running out of time. The muscles in my neck tensed, and my senses were heightened. I studied the people around us—every smiling face, every laugh, every head bent in private conversation. I found myself wondering what everyone was talking about, laughing about, grinning about. Was Reen and her family on everyone's mind, or was I the only one who cared? Who else knew about the shady deals the Elders made? How many people have suffered at their whims over the years?

Jason and I sat next to a couple I didn't know well, but we smiled and said our hellos. His parents sat at a table to our right with other Matron and Elder families. Were they talking about the Johnsons? I didn't want to make eye contact with any of them for fear my expression would reveal more than I was willing to share. I poked at the potato salad on my plate and pretended to listen to the conversation happening between Jason and the man next to him. I contributed an occasional, "Oh, that's nice" until their conversation ended.

Jason turned to face me. "My uncle Scott is coming to live in the community. He's currently an Elder from the community in Los Angeles and just got approval to move here. He'll arrive next week."

"Oh, that's nice," I responded mindlessly.

"I haven't seen him in three years. He's the one who helped my dad become an Elder."

It was now or never.

"I didn't see Reen's family at Service today, and she hasn't answered any of my texts." I pulled out my phone and clicked on her name within my text messages. "I'm starting to get worried."

He didn't respond.

Ask. Just ask.

"Have you heard anything about why her family isn't here today? It doesn't make sense for her to not be here nor answer my texts."

No answer. He gnawed off a chunk of his barbecued drumstick then made a show of chewing, all the while avoiding eye contact with me.

"Jason, did you hear me?"

"No. What did you say?" He tore off another chuck of the saucy meat.

He was lying. I could tell. Of all the nerve!

"I asked if you've heard anything about Maureen's family not being here today." My tone was laced with anger. That was an accident. I didn't want him to know I was mad.

Finally, he looked directly at me.

I couldn't will my expression into something softer, less accusing.

"She misses one day and you're worried? Will you miss me when I leave tomorrow for the next three days?"

Oh, Bright Lord. Micah was right. Jason was involved.

"Jason, I asked you a question. Please answer it. Do you know anything about why neither Reen nor her family are here today?" I could no longer mask my anger. The energy required to keep my voice low was all I could manage.

"Yes." He replied, glaring at me. "They moved out, and my uncle is moving into their house."

"Your uncle?" I repeat because I'm obviously missing something here.

"I just told you he's moving into the community. He'll be taking their place. And since he's already an Elder and has a great relationship with the Champion, it will be an easy transition."

"You knew about this and didn't say anything to me?" My voice shook. My legs trembled under the table.

"In case you haven't noticed, I've been busy working and planning for our house and our life together Nikki. I haven't had time to think about your friend when I've only been thinking of you."

He not only knew about this, but he also planned for it. And he's blaming me?

"You've been *thinking* of me? How could you have been thinking of me? If you had, you would have told me that my best friend in the entire world was leaving."

His fingers dug into my thigh.

"Stop causing a scene," he snarled through gritted teeth. Then he smiled pleasantly at me.

I turned away from him. Directly across from us sat the Prescott's, and they were staring at me. My heart beat wildly. I couldn't put into words how the sharp pain twisted in my chest, in my head. My eyes burned. Still, I managed a smile at the Prescott's and apologized, then I sipped the overly tart lemonade.

Jason continued talking. "She was ruining you, Nikki. As your husband, it's my job to protect you, even from yourself and your unwise decisions. Trust me, you'll be happier without her dragging you down all the time. I would have never said this before, but she was just following you. Using you. You need people in your life who want to help you, people who have positive things to contribute. Like my mother and the other matrons. And you'll love my aunt. She also likes to garden."

He grabbed my hand. It took everything in me to let his skin touch mine. I would not cause a scene. I would be smart.

"Trust me on this, Nikki. I promise you won't regret it."

I nodded. I was numb. I felt nothing but bitter betrayal and flaming hatred for this man. He didn't know me at all let alone love me. If it hadn't been clear before, it was crystal clear now. I was a means to an end. He needed a wife so he could ascend through the ranks of the Faith. He wanted to become an Elder—the youngest ever appointed—and I was a step on the rung. Reen was an obstacle to his ambition, and my association with her would tarnish his reputation. But if he was in favor with the Grand Elder…

Why did he receive favor with the Grand Elder?

I sat through the rest of lunch like a mannequin. There, presentable, but completely vacant within. Other brides from my retreat stopped by to say hello and chit chat, and I recited scripts I'd learned over the years. Scripts that kept me agreeable and in favor with everyone in the community. Scripts that didn't represent anything true or meaningful but were perfectly acceptable and expected from a nice girl like me.

TWENTY-EIGHT

MY STOMACH GROWLED once I reached the safety of my home—a reminder I hadn't eaten a meal since breakfast yesterday before leaving my retreat.

The apple I snacked on was expunged last night on the side of the curb, and I'd only pushed food around my plate at Lunch.

My empty refrigerator mocked me. I had nothing but some stray veggies in the bottom tray, a carton of eggs, butter, and a quart of milk.

"Eggs it is."

I made a soft scramble and toasted the heel of the bread. Coffee wasn't my thing, but my usual lavender tea wasn't going to cut it today. Thankfully, I kept some in the freezer for the rare occasion of Jason visiting in the morning. As I ground the dark beans, my whole kitchen filled with the intoxicating aroma of coffee. I loved the smell more than the taste, but today I'd indulge in both. While the coffee brewed, I sat at the table to journal.

I stared out the kitchen window, looking at my neglected strawberry plants. Every year, I looked forward to growing them, but this year, they were the one thing that brought me both joy and a sense of purpose. Now, they too were a reminder of my myriad losses. Another thing—the last thing—to be taken away from me. Not just the *thing* but the *person*. Maureen wasn't here to help. No one would laugh with me as we got dirty and complained about what the buyers were saying. It was just me and an abandoned garden of berries.

I poured my heart out into the journal, recording everything that had transpired in the past four days—from the loss of my home through the loss of my best friend. I wrote about what was revealed at my retreat and what was revealed afterward.

And Micah. I wrote about every encounter with him, from the music room to the kiss.

All my senses heightened at the mention of his name. I thrilled as images of him whirled through my head. Smiled at the deep, rich timber of his voice. My skin tingled as I recalled his touch—calloused fingers and warm palms holding my hand, gripping my shoulders. I could smell his earthy scent, taste his mouth on mine. I ran a finger over my lips at the memory. That *was* real. He was so… real. So honest and thoughtful. He awakened something inside me. Made me things I'd never dreamed of.

Four pages of thoughts later, I found myself in my mama's bed. Except for the larger pieces of furniture, it now sat empty. Not even sheets covered the mattress.

When I woke, it was dark.

I had no desire to turn on the lights. Didn't want to see. Even after journaling, my mind still swirled. For the first time, the tool which helped provide clarity and illicit courage failed me. My situation felt too big, and I was drowning in a sea of overwhelm.

I trudged through the hallway to the bathroom then stared at my reflection in the mirror. Even in the darkness, I could tell my eyes were puffy and shadowed, my hair was wild from sleeping without a scarf, and my cheeks were marred from the wrinkles on Mama's pillows. I looked as miserable as I felt.

I splashed my face with water then combed through the tangles. The air conditioning was set to sixty-eight degrees—typically quite comfortable. Now it made me feel clammy and cold.

I needed to get out.

After locking my front door, I hesitated. Starting the engine would bring unwanted attention, and Sheila didn't need more fuel for the Pillars. I decided to walk and secured my purse across my body. It was a far better choice, as the exercise would be good for me after sitting all weekend, and solutions came easier when I walked. Besides, no matter the temperature, I always felt better in the end, and since I had no destination in mind and no schedule to keep, I could take my time and go anywhere I wanted.

My aimless stroll guided me to the lesser populated area of the community, toward the field of wild dandelions. Sweet and bitter memories vied for prominence in my thoughts. It was where I got engaged to a selfish, opportunistic liar. It was also where Micah kissed me.

That's what I chose to dwell on. The memory played again and again as I walked through Mr. Bagwell's farm. At first, it warmed me, but at some point, I realized I'd been so surprised by the kiss, I'd forgotten to ask how Micah knew about the Johnsons.

When I reached the threshold of the field of wild dandelions, I realized I'd never walked that far alone at night before. When Reen and I were kids, we raced here one day after Service. By the time we made it to this spot—the divider between Bright Lakes Residential Community and the rest of Fresno—we were completely winded. We'd never run, nor walked, so far again.

The last two times I came here was when Jason proposed, then with Micah. Tonight, it was just me and my thoughts. I felt so raw, so brittle, that the slightest breeze gave me goosebumps.

Fruit from the budding orange trees smelled sweeter than usual. The dandelions looked more like flowers than weeds, and I felt they were inviting me to join in their wildness. I took the narrow trail through them, one I'd never taken before, down a path I knew would lead me to a destination I'd not ventured to with Mama, Reen, or anyone.

The distant croak of crickets sounded like music, the opening number to the dramatic play of my life. Normally I'd flee, afraid one would jump on me if I got too close, but tonight, I wanted their attention and their song. Delicate dandelion tufts lay on the ground like flakes of snow, guiding me toward my destination—the city. I plucked a flower then twirled the stem between my fingers.

It represented my feelings perfectly.

Dandelions are considered a nuisance, a weed we battle with pesticides to eradicate them from our carefully tended gardens. But in truth, they aren't weeds. They're wildflowers. We tend not to appreciate them because they're so prolific. How strange that we despise them just because they're everywhere. No matter how hard we try to diminish them, they endure.

They're like women. They're like me.

Some in the Community would have everyone follow the Lady Styling Guidelines. They would contort a woman's very nature until she became what they wanted to cultivate. Something more acceptable, like a rose. But the dandelion is fierce and strong. She grows under tough conditions, even after being trampled upon. And when her seeds are scattered, whether by a gentle breeze or a gale-force wind, her sisters grow all around her.

Just like the field I stood upon. When untouched and left to natural conditions, the flower flourished.

At that moment, I felt beautiful too. Graceful in my flowy dress. Elegant despite the sadness and deceit surrounding me. Grateful to appreciate the contrary moment I was living. The awareness filled me with energy and transformed my wandering gait into a meaningful stride.

I was going to the city.

TWENTY-NINE

B Y THE TIME I reached downtown, it was almost ten o'clock, late by Community standards.

But in the city, activity abounded. Everything was bustling and bright.

I stood at the corner of Van Ness and Olive. The dark of night couldn't hide the age of my surroundings. Cracks splintered portions of the sidewalks. Crumbled papers and broken bottles littered the curbs. Yet there was beauty too. The walkways were covered in art. Colored tiles arranged in a stunning mosaic guided me through the crosswalk to the other side of the street.

Buildings were nestled close together and stood no more than fifteen feet high. They were identical in size and shape, differing only in the wares displayed in storefront windows and the signage on the doors. A shop for smog checks and repairs was on the southeast corner, across from the market. Opposite that stood a tattoo parlor. And on the northeast corner, a smoke shop. A literal shop for smoking. Did people go there because they wanted to smoke together?

Murals decorated the sides of buildings—walls of sketchy-looking characters and vulgar words and phrases. The streetlights illuminated the "artwork," spotlighting the pale white face of a man wearing a black mask and smoking a cigar.

Even the air around me was different than what I was used to, redolent with dirt, spices, and liberation. People, young and not-so-young, walked in every direction. Some stood in groups, chatting or posing for pictures. T-shirts, flip flops, ripped jeans, shorts... they wore whatever they wanted.

A massive red sign flashed the word TOWER as people left a theatre. Its windows advertised upcoming events like graduations, plays, and neighborhood activities. Twinkle lights adorned the entries of restaurants, and food trucks lined the sidewalks.

A group of girls around my age walked past. Two had brightly dyed hair and multiple piercings. The other two looked... like me. Despite their differences, they all seemed at ease with each other.

My pulse quickened, and a jolt of adrenaline surged through my body. I don't know why, but I was compelled to follow them.

The main street, Olive, was narrow. Stop signs were posted at the end of each block so cars slowly cruised by. Every sight and every sound caught my attention, and soon I'd lost track of the girls. Not that I minded. I was distracted by the sound of music. A lively, jazzy melody pouring from a building beside a nearby restaurant.

The taqueria's extended patio took up a portion of the sidewalk. Patrons sat at round tables, engaging in conversation and laughter between bites of tacos, beans, and rice and sips of colorful drinks. Nothing about this place, these people, was muted or tidy. It was real. Authentic. Genuine. The air was thick with it, thick with...

freedom. Freedom to be happy and hungry and angry and wary. And it was glorious.

A man, maybe late twenties, stared at me as I watched people living out loud.

I stopped my shameless gawking, focused on the music, then followed the sound to its source. A line of people waited to enter a building. A beefy guy sat on a stool by the door. He kept shining his flashlight on things held up or handed to him. I joined the queue behind the last couple. I'd never entered a bar, never been outside of the Community alone at night. Though this experience should have given me pause, none of it bothered me. I was too overcome with excitement and wonder. I wanted to see what was inside. Wanted to know what it smelled like, sounded like, felt like. Wanted to know what people did inside and whether it was fun. And I wanted to be closer to that music—one of many forbidden forms of expression behind the gates of Bright Lakes.

"ID?" gruffed the burly ginger blocking the entrance.

"Oh, right." I fumbled in my purse. The simple question was a stark reminder that I was quite out of place. Anyone who'd been to a bar before would know to have their ID ready. I quickly handed mine to Mr. Gruff, who shone his flashlight on it, then my face before gesturing to the black door.

"Thank you." I scuttled inside.

This darkness was different. Outside, bright lights shone from buildings and street lamps, giving nighttime a glow. This darkness felt heady, intimate. Dimmed beams of red light slashed across the entryway. Further in the back, an indigo beam glowed. Black leather booths lined the wall, anemic running lights illuminating the walkway past them. The floor was dotted with high-top tables big enough for two and lower ones that could seat four. Across the room stretched a wall-length bar. Behind it, shelves displayed dozens of bottles with various colors of liquid at different levels of fullness. A neon sign above them proclaimed the name of the establishment—*Leti's Lounge*.

Some patrons sat, others danced. Groups clustered together, these in deep conversation, those joking and laughing. All trusting their companions. This was completely foreign to me. I felt like I was in another world. Another dimension. I'd seen bars on television, of course, but experiencing it was different. I could see why people would enjoy time spent in places like this. There was an aura of mystery here. A knowing and a telling of secrets. A sharing and a withholding. A tilted head and alluring eyes.

I spied an empty barstool and darted for it before someone else claimed it. A woman wearing a deep red dress sat next to it. She was engaged in an intimate conversation with a man on her other side.

I tapped her on the shoulder. "Is anyone sitting here?"

She turned toward me, shook her curly blonde head, then returned to her companion.

I smiled and hopped on the stool, proud of myself. I'd done it. I actually freaking walked into this place… by myself! On purpose! My actions both surprised and pleased me. This was so unlike me, yet something inside said it was very much like me. Even acknowledging that part of my personality was gratifying, and now that I'd let it out to play, I didn't think I'd ever be able to force it back into its cage. Yes, I felt naughty. Perhaps someday the novelty would wear off and take with it my joy. But tonight? This felt right. I didn't know a soul here, yet I was part of this group in a way I'd never been part of Bright Lakes.

I had no idea what I looked like to those around me, nor did I care enough to give the thought more than a micro-second of consideration. I was too enthralled with my surroundings—with the hum of conversation, the tinkle of laughter, the melody of the intoxicating music.

The music. That was the reason I was drawn here. A band was setting up in the corner—singer, guitarist, bassist. I didn't see a drummer, and no one sat behind the piano. Still, a live band was probably even better than what was being piped through the speakers. I swiveled my chair around so I could watch their performance.

A man's voice pierced through the chatter and instruments. His words were directed at me, though I couldn't make them out.

I swiveled toward him—a bartender with questioning eyes. Did I do something wrong? Was this someone else's seat? I held my hand to my ear and said, "Excuse me?"

"What would you like to drink?" he yelled.

Right! I'm sitting at the bar. People drink drinks at the bar! I guess the puzzled expression on my face answered the bartender's question because he handed me a laminated menu then walked away toward a beckoning patron—someone who obviously knew what they wanted. Unlike me.

Holding the menu in my hand made the experience a little more real. A little… dirty. A little wrong. I shifted in my seat, grateful that the stool had an iron back, so I didn't fall to the floor. That wouldn't be a good look. There were so many options on the menu, so many types of drinks, and I didn't know the difference between beer, wine, cocktails, and specials. Heck, they were all special to me. If Reen were with me, she'd ask for one of each. The thought made me smile, then frown, then my lip trembled. Despite my sadness, I wouldn't cry *here*.

I stared at the menu without seeing the words. My best friend really was gone, and I was sitting in a bar in the city, alone, because I didn't want to be in the place that caused her disappearance.

"Nicolette?" a male voice asked.

I snapped back into my body. My blood chilled, drained from my face. Pooled in a sickening mass in the pit of my stomach. Slowly, I spun. Then my jaw dropped.

"Micah?"

What the heck was he doing here?

"What are you doing here?" He looked as shocked as I felt.

"I could ask you the same thing." Was he mad at finding me in a place like this? Or was *he* on a date and worried that I'd tell on him?

The bartender returned. "What can I get you?"

"I'll have that." I pointed at a purple-colored drink sitting in front of a lady three seats down from me. It was pretty, with a flower on top and a slice of lime on the rim. If it tasted half as good as it looked, it would be delicious. He nodded then looked at Micah.

Micah jutted his chin then returned his attention to me.

Worse than guilty, I felt *caught*. I couldn't bear his gaze, so I focused on the overwhelming menu in my lap.

And if he was on a date…

Nope. None of my business!

I chanced a glance at him. He'd dressed in all black—shirt, jeans, and shoes. His eyes, amber and sage, held a heat, an intensity that couldn't be denied. He looked good. Real good. Then he smiled, and just like that, my whole body softened.

He stood with his arms folded across his chest and feet spread apart, like he was preparing to stand there for a while. Considering all other seats were taken, that was his only option.

"What's the difference between beer, wine, and cocktails?" I asked.

"So, you don't even know what you just ordered?"

"I have no idea, but I'm sure I'll enjoy it." I smiled. Of all the people to catch me here, I couldn't be happier.

"How did you end up here?"

"I walked." I replied, proud of myself.

"All the way?" His brows arched, and his lips quirked.

"Yup. And I'm glad I did. What is this place?"

"You've asked me that question before."

"No, I haven't." I squinted at him.

"Not about this place, but your words are the same as when I found you in the music room." He smiled again. "This is Leti's Lounge. We're in the part of town called the Tower District."

"The Tower District." I repeated aloud. "I've heard people in the community mention it before, always with a warning to stay away." Was he here with another girl or not? That's what I needed to know.

"And now I guess you know why."

He was right. Nothing here was permitted. Drinking alcohol, women wearing pants, men alone with women, fraternizing in the dark, laughing loudly, colored hair, tattoos, body piercings… just one of these things would be grounds for immediate eviction.

The thought made me wonder about Reen again. Did she come here and a Matron found out? And even so, her whole family wouldn't have been punished for that. Not when she was nearly married to Shawn.

The bartender slid a wide-rimmed, short-stemmed glass in front of me. It was filled to the rim with purple liquid and topped with a lavender sprig and a slice of lemon. If someone saw me with this… What was I thinking? Someone was watching me. Then again, Micah wasn't one of the Faithful. Besides, he was here too!

Putting all thoughts of the community and retribution out of mind, I reached for the glass. I held it to my nose and inhaled. Mmm, citrus and sugar—such an invitation to drink. So I did.

"Oh, man. That's delicious." It was fruity and tangy and didn't taste horrible at all. I took another sip so it wouldn't spill then held the drink out to Micah. "Here, taste it."

"I'll take your word for it. That stuff's too sweet for me."

Good, more for me. He looked at a black leather watch clasped around his wrist. "I'll be back."

"I'll be here!"

Micah shook his head, turned, then walked toward the band in the far corner of the room and sat down at the piano.

THIRTY

THERE WERE SEVERAL musicians, but my attention belonged to Micah. He conversed with the singer and other musicians until everyone took their positions.

The bassist—tall, thin, White—ran his fingers over his instrument. A succession of chords, deep and grounded, reverberated through the bar. My head instinctually nodded to the beat. The guitarist's fingers flew over his strings, strumming a fast and infectious melody. Then the keyboard came to life, Micah pounding out a fun and upbeat, ding ding ding tune. The lady singer shook a hand-held instrument—a tambourine, if memory served. The metal discs around the edge jingled. It was the most cheerful sound I'd ever heard. Loud and clangy and perfect.

Then it was just the keys. Micah played the notes faster than I thought possible. His head bobbed, his body swayed. He was having fun, and I was having a blast watching. I rocked side-to-side and tapped my toes, stopping only for the occasional sip of the best drink ever. I danced in my seat, relished my cocktail, and simply enjoyed life. Who knew being in an environment like this could be so much fun?! And I couldn't imagine returning to one that wasn't.

In the center aisle of the bar, a group of ladies danced. They moved and twirled and laughed. Held hands and spun around. No one stopped them. No one side-eyed and mumbled about their inappropriate behavior. No one cared what they wore or what they looked like. They were happy and carefree. It was beautiful to behold.

I turned my attention back to Micah. To my surprise, he was looking at me. And I didn't look away. My heart fluttered at the intensity of our connection. At the importance of that moment, in that place. He wasn't just *looking* at me. He was *seeing* me. Only recently had I realized how invisible I'd been and how I yearned to be noticed. To matter. And not because I wasn't being scrutinized and shamed for a ridiculous indiscretion, but because someone was interested. Someone cared.

Not only was I unafraid of his gaze, I desired it. Welcomed it. Reveled in it.

I watched as his fingers danced across the keyboard, and it wasn't until he broke eye contact that I looked away. My pulse was wild, my breaths fast and shallow. I reached for my tasty drink and took another sip.

Mmm, so good! No wonder people came to these places.

When the song ended, I waved at the bartender. "Excuse me. What is this called?"

"A blueberry cosmopolitan. You want another?"

"Yes, please."

He nodded and returned moments later.

The next song featured more vocals. They played three more songs, five altogether, a pleasant mix of instrumental music and numbers with lyrics. When they took a break, Micah walked past me to the back of the lounge. It stung a bit to be ignored, but I was feeling a little too mellow to dwell on the pain. When he returned a short while later, he tapped me on my shoulder then motioned for me to come with him.

He'd found an empty booth for us near the back of the room where the indigo light cast an otherworldly hue upon the lounge. I sat on the cushioned side of the booth.

Micah dropped into the chair across from me. He nodded toward the band. "What did you think?"

"That was absolutely amazing! And so much fun! I've never heard anything like it."

The way his mouth moved when he spoke was equally amazing.

"I gotta admit, I'm surprised you ended up here of all places in Fresno."

"Yeah, me too. It wasn't in my plans for the day." I laughed. And laughed again. "I can't believe I'm here. I can't believe you play music here. How long have you been doing this? And how have you not been caught?"

"I'm not worried about anyone from Bright Lakes coming here."

"Except me!" I said through laughter. I couldn't stop laughing. I took another sip of my magical beverage.

"Yes. Except you." His gaze raked over me. "You look beautiful in that dress."

His voice was beautiful.

"Thank you." I couldn't stop staring at his mouth. Heat rose from my belly into my face. "Jason hates this dress, so I decided to wear it today. You know, you were right about him. You were right about everything. He knew about Reen. I made him tell me today at Lunch. His uncle is moving into their house."

"Yeah. I heard about that."

"How do you hear about all of these things?"

He didn't answer right away, which I was starting to realize was his norm. It was like he calculated the cost of each word before sharing and had to decide how much he could afford to tell me.

"Because I listen for things and I make it my business to know what's going on."

"What does that even mean, make it your business? What are you? A detective or something?" I laughed again. Goodness, why was everything so funny? "Hey, what was that music you started with? That first song."

"You're funny tonight. I think that drink is getting to you." He pointed at my empty glass.

When did I drink the last sip? I should definitely order another one.

"The first song was 'What I Say' by Ray Charles. He was a blind pianist and singer back in the sixties."

"A blind pianist? How is that even possible? What a talent! Like you! Oh, my gosh. You're so good. And your fingers were moving so fast. It was amazing to watch." I leaned in, propping my elbows on the table. "Did you see the people dancing? Dancing! In the middle of the walkway?" I shook my head in disbelief.

Micah's hazel eyes brightened as he laughed, and dimples popped out. Dimples! The man had dimples. The indigo lightening gave his normally golden face a bronzed effect, and fleeting wondered how to get a statue made of him. The thought made me laugh again, and cocooned in the booth, I couldn't have felt safer. Sitting with him, I couldn't have felt happier.

"Yes, people dance sometimes."

"So, all of this is just *normal* to you? Hey, you didn't answer my question. How long have you been doing this?" I waved my hand to encompass the whole scene.

"You're asking a lot of questions all at once, some are bound to get lost. But to answer that one... four years. Right before I signed on to become a Trainee." His expression grew serious.

I could tell that was still a sensitive topic for him. But why? Curious as I was, I couldn't bring myself to pry. Instead, I wiggled my empty glass at him. "Can you get me another one of these?"

He chuckled then walked toward the bar. I watched his back, watched him. Watched people watch him. Watched other women watch him.

He returned with a glass of clear liquid. With no flower.

I frowned. Sniffed it. Scowled. "Water?"

He smiled. "It's your first time. That stuff sneaks up on you."

I'd heard that somewhere before, so although I was tempted, I didn't argue and sipped my bland, boring water. "Thank you. Will you answer me truthfully if I ask you a personal question?"

"Depends on the question."

"Why do you live in Bright Lakes? Seeing you here, seeing you have interests that are explicitly prohibited... I don't understand why."

He didn't answer.

I couldn't take the silence. "I live there because it was my mom's dream come true. She lost hope when my dad died, but the people of Bright Lakes and the Faith kept her from falling apart. I guess it did that for me too. Until now, I never doubted that the Bright Lakes Community was good and honest and true, and the Faithful members were the pinnacle of what it meant to live out the Faith. I don't trust anything now." I looked at him, lost in his mesmerizing eyes. "You seem to have some sort of immunity to all of this. How do you do it? How can I?"

"It's not that I'm immune. I just have a purpose."

"What purpose?" I probed.

Again he calculated. Then he said, "My mom is sick. Has been for about two years. About ten months ago, we all thought she was going to die, but she pulled through. That's why I stayed. I'm the one who takes care of her."

"I had no idea. I'm sorry your mom is sick." My hand instinctively reached out to his. Upon realizing I was rubbing him, I pulled away. "Sorry."

"It's fine. You can touch me."

He really shouldn't tell me that.

I took a deep breath and tried to wrangle my thoughts. "Why do you want to leave? Did one of the Elders do the same thing to you as they're doing with the Johnsons? Did someone hurt your mom?"

"No. It's more complicated than that."

"What could be more complicated than what they did to Maureen's family?"

"Do you remember I told you they probably got evicted because Maureen and Shawn are both Unfaithful? Well, I meant that. You already know how they treated her. She was only getting away with breaking Guidelines because her dad was an Elder. If she married Shawn, whose father isn't an Elder, and Shawn is also not a Faithful, that posed a problem for the Faith. Do you really think the Bright Lakes Community would allow a family of Unfaithful's to live there?"

"No." I hadn't thought about it like that. The Bright Lakes Residential Community was only for Faithful members who had proven themselves over the years, just like Mama had to do for two years before they allowed us to move in.

"Exactly."

"But that doesn't explain why she hasn't returned any of my phone calls. Or why her whole family had to leave."

"Her whole family didn't have to leave. They must've chosen it once they realized she couldn't stay. I don't know the details, but since Mr. Johnson is an elder, he would've had the choice to sever ties with his daughter or go with her. As for her not answering your calls… anytime someone is evicted, their cell phones are immediately taken. They usually don't even have time to make arrangements. They're sent away immediately with whatever they can pack in suitcases. Everything else is sent through a moving company within a day or two."

So quickly. She couldn't return my calls if she didn't have a phone. And she couldn't have written a goodbye note if they only had time to pack a suitcase. As sad and unbelievable as it was, it made me feel a little better knowing she wasn't intentionally being unresponsive.

But she must have a new phone, a new number. How could I get in touch with her?

"Do you know where they are? Where they moved to?" I could at least go visit them if I knew.

"I don't know. No one knows that. I'm not even sure what they tell the moving company."

"What made you want to get out? You said you started coming here when you were a Trainee."

He looked over at the band. The musicians were gone, and recorded music was being piped through speakers. I took in his profile—his jawline, his mouth, the thick vein that ran down his neck.

I remembered our kiss, remembered his words. *You're not alone, Nikki.* Did he mean that?

Micah turned back to me. "When you become a Trainee, you spend a lot of time with select Elders and eventually the Champion. When your dad is already an Elder, your core training will come from him. I'm sure it's the same with Tucker."

The sound of Jason's name made my stomach ache. I sipped my water again.

"If you pass the first year of Training, with approval from Malachi, you get to move on to the second year. During the second year, you learn about the ins and outs, the foundation of the society, the reason why the community was built and the purpose of the guidelines and systems. You saw the ladies dancing here tonight, and said you liked it. Well, there's a reason music and dancing aren't allowed in Bright Lakes, and there's a reason restrictions are placed upon you ladies." He looked at me with an intense gaze, heated with anger. "It's about power and submission."

My throat felt tight, and I let out an exhale. I didn't realize I was holding my breath.

"If women don't behave in the community, the community would cease to exist." He added.

"What do women have to do with anything? Only the Pillars and the Matrons have any say."

"And why is that?" he asked.

"To keep us younger girls dignified and pure and ready for marriage. They teach us to treat our husbands with the utmost respect. At my bridal retreat, I found out a lot of what—"

"None of that matters, Nikki. Think about *why*. Why would they want you ladies to be dignified and pure and whatever else they say to you?"

I thought for a while. "Because if we aren't, we might end up like these women here. Free and laughing and choosing differently… about everything." About whom we married. About whom we befriended. About how we let others talk to us, discipline us.

"How do you take control over someone? You make them believe they need to be controlled. You make them not trust themselves. You make them fearful. And you start when they're young."

When they're young.

The words sounded louder in my head. When we first moved to Bright Lakes, I was very afraid and stayed very quiet. The only person I would talk to was Mama. Until I met Maureen. Even then, Reen was different. She wasn't afraid, she was angry—at everyone. Especially the Pillars and the men of the Community. Except Shawn. Shawn always took care of her, even when we were little. Even when she would lash out and push him down. He would get back up, ask why she was mad, then get her to play with him. As we got older, he became more of her protector, even when they weren't officially courting.

My head spun. "What are you saying?"

"You heard me. What do you think I'm saying?" He challenged.

"It sounds like you're saying when we girls are young, something happens to make us afraid and keeps us in that fear as we get older. And the older women"—Lord, my heart ached to say the words out loud—"the respected women in the community, the Pillars and the Matrons, are in on it."

We sat there in silence. Letting the weight of what I said aloud settle in. It was ridiculous, impossible.

"What exactly happened in your second year as a Trainee that caused you to drop out?"

"I found out the answer to your question and was expected to do what they wanted in order to keep the things operating as-is. Without question."

This was bullshit. I stood. "Where is the restroom?"

He pointed past our table, down the hall. "The second door on your left."

My knees wobbled. I braced myself on the table before attempting to take a step. My head felt light, woozy.

Micah sprung to his feet. He grabbed me by my waist. "Told you liquor catches up to you. Lean on me, I'll walk you to the restroom."

I didn't want to be touched. "Thanks, but I can manage."

Micah stood close by, watching me as I took a few breaths and steadied myself. Each step was a struggle. I walked down the dark corridor, the smell of urine indicating I was on the correct path.

THIRTY-ONE

I RETURNED TO the table. "Can you take me home?"

Worry clouded Micah's eyes. He should look worried. He just dropped an anvil on top of me while I was already standing in quicksand. How was it possible to breathe or believe in humanity after learning what he just told me?

How awful for him, torn between caring for his mother and his morals. No wonder he kept to the outskirts of our community.

The question was what would I now do?

Had my mom known any of this? Did any of the Faithful—other than the Pillars, Matrons, and Trainees—know? No way! Misty didn't seem like the type to fall in line with any of this. Nor did her husband.

"Yeah. I'll meet you outside after I cash out."

He walked to the bar then handed the bartender a bill. I'd forgotten to pay. Didn't even think about it earlier. I'd pay him back later. Now, certain I'd never return, I took one last look around before walking outside.

A warm and welcoming breeze fluttered my skirt. It was maybe around eighty degrees, and the air was perfect. Twinkling stars lit the night sky. Light shining amidst darkness. The beauty of it felt like an insult after what I just learned. I had no hope things would improve. If only there was a way I could reach out to Reen, or even Shawn. Yes, Shawn! His parents probably still lived in the community. They might have more information.

Micah's strong arm wrapped around me. He guided me down the sidewalk, gesturing toward a narrow walkway that likely led to a parking lot behind the store fronts. "I'm parked right behind here."

I wouldn't have believed it was possible, but the streets were more lively than when I arrived. The music was louder, also more vulgar. Aggressive. Curse words spewed from the speakers of the taqueria, where people pressed their bodies together, touching and swaying in inappropriate ways. This atmosphere was different—not like the lively, joyous environment in Leti's Lounge. This wasn't the type of excitement or escape I wanted.

My world was being turned inside out. Truths were lies, lies were truths, and their blurred lines twisted around my mind and heart like weeds tangling with flowers. There were only so many nutrients in the soil. Eventually one would choke out the other. I thought of the flowers in Mama's landscaping. The dandelions in the field. The thorns in my crown.

The dehumanization, the horrendous treatment, the abuse. It was too much, and it frightened me.

Micah's hand lingered on me causing goosebumps to sprout on my arms. He led us between the buildings to a back alleyway. My gaze darted left and right, then I turned to look behind me. The reality of what harm could have come to me, to any woman, soured my stomach. I had a reason to be afraid of dark passageways. A reason to be afraid of men. I inched away from Micah.

He looked at me as if he knew what I was thinking but didn't say anything. He simply lowered his arm and gave me space.

He led me to a big, black Ford truck with massive tires, opened the passenger side door for me, then offered his hand to help me.

A fear of men made sense, but I didn't fear him. He was the reason I knew what I knew. He wouldn't have told me if he wanted to hurt me. Wouldn't have distanced himself from the Faith if he believed what they did. Micah was safe. I placed my hand in his and used his strength to keep me stable as I climbed into the seat. He closed my door, circled to the driver's side, then hopped in with ease.

His truck smelled like him. Felt like him. Dark and mysterious. Calm and peaceful. The engine purred, then he began driving us home.

Home? I didn't know if I could call it that anymore. "Home" was where I was to marry a man who would violate women, deceive his fiancé, and Bright Lord knew what else. He kept so many secrets. What else had he done? The thought of being in the same room as him sickened me, let alone marrying him. It was inconceivable. Our relationship was truly over, and in the worst possible way. I never could have imagined this. Now I didn't know where home would be or where I could go. Who could I reach out to?

"What are you thinking about over there?" Micah's baritone voice broke my thoughts.

The least—or maybe most—important question popped out of my mouth. "Why did you kiss me last night?"

Without missing a beat, he replied, "You were afraid."

"Oh."

"And because I wanted to. I wanted you to know you weren't alone."

"But I am alone. Knowing what I now know, I feel trapped. I can't stay in Bright Lakes, but I have nowhere to go. And no matter what happens, I need to make sure no one else gets hurt."

"You're not alone. Tell me what you want, and I'll do my best to make sure you get it."

Such powerful words, such emphatic promises. I wanted to cry at the incomprehensible mix of his tenderness and strength. More than that, I wanted to lean on him and let him handle my problems. But I couldn't accept what he offered. It was time I handled things on my own. I'd be forced to soon enough.

I turned to face him. "How can you stand living there? And why does Malachi let you? Jason was pissed about me even talking to you. He believes you've insulted Malachi by living in the Community without embracing it, and I'm sure other Trainees and Elders must feel the same way."

"It's not like I'm happy there."

"Why haven't you done anything? How can you just let things continue to go on as they are like there isn't some sick, twisted shit happening every single day?" I was yelling, and though I thought I didn't have more tears to shed, they fell freely. "You've known this for years! I've known for five minutes and I'm sick to my stomach. I can't even think straight. I have no idea what I want other than to be free of this, but I don't have anywhere to go. No family, no friends who live outside. Only Reen, but I can't even reach her."

I was huffing and puffing after my rant. Glad to get it all out. Glad he let me.

After I caught my breath, he said, "If I leave, my mom will die. My dad won't take care of her. He's already secretly courting another woman."

"Oh, Micah, I had no idea." I needed to stop yelling at this man and blaming him for everything.

"I'm sorry this was the way you learned their secrets, but you told me you wanted answers. Most people think they want the truth only to end up just like you—angry, afraid. And that's normal. This isn't the life you thought you signed up for. I knew you were different. I used to see you around the community, always helping, and not because you're trying to get something from someone. It's genuine. You really are a kind person. There's a difference, and when your mom died… I knew what would happen to you. With the house, I mean. I wanted to help. Even though my uncle's timing was terrible, I knew it was my chance. So I organized extra men to come to your house that day. I wanted to see you for myself, make sure you were okay. And I wanted you to know people will help take care of you."

I didn't know what to say, so I just sat there.

Micah shook his head. "I've seen a lot of horrible things go on in Bright Lakes. Much as I'd like to stop all of it, I have my own problems to worry about. I have to put my mother first because no one else will. But when I heard you postponed your marriage, I wondered if you'd figured something out. So, I kept an eye on you, looking for an opportunity to talk. The day I saw you in the music room…" He sighed. "You looked so sad, so defeated. I didn't know if I could trust you, but I also couldn't leave you alone like that, especially if someone else found you there."

We were nearing Bright Lakes, and my heart raced like I'd sprinted there. I twirled my engagement ring around my finger—a reminder that I was claimed. Bright Lord knew how many rules I was breaking by sitting in another man's truck, alone, after dark, on the way home from the city, talking about Community secrets, and what we thought about each other. It was all scandalous, yet I couldn't imagine being with anyone else.

My pulse somehow pounded faster.

"I thought you'd left after I was rude to you that day. But when I turned around, you were on the floor, weeping. You said you liked my music, and you didn't try to turn me in for breaking the rules that day or any other day. That told me all I needed to know about you."

Anyone breaking the Rules was to be immediately reported, lest we be divided. Failure to turn someone in was as bad as being a rule breaker—because not doing so meant breaking the Rules.

Ugh. I don't know how I put up with this nonsense for so long.

We'd both broken the Rules that day. And he hadn't reported me either.

"I knew they'd told you to move out of your house. I'd received the work Faith to prepare it for new residents by the end of July. Then I saw you at the farmers market with that asshole. I don't know what you were talking about, but you didn't look happy."

We'd just settled on a wedding date, and Jason was making plans for our house.

"But you looked at me that day." His voice was like velvet.

The way those words rolled off his tongue made my skin feel tight and hot. I had to focus on controlling my breath. He'd looked at me that day too, and I'd never forget it. Like he *saw* me. Really saw me.

"When you approached me that day on the trail, you seemed… different, lighter. And I liked it."

"That day, you said you had a purpose. What is it?"

"It's to help as many people as I can before I leave Bright Lakes."

"So, you are leaving?"

"That's always been my plan. Once my mom…" He cleared his throat. "So, do you want me to drop you off at your front door or somewhere else? In case you didn't know, your neighbor reports everything you do."

"You're eventually leaving?"

"You can leave too Nikki."

"I want to, but I don't have anywhere to go." Why didn't he understand that?

"If that's what you're worried about, you'll never leave."

He turned the headlights off as we neared my block. The clock on his dash glared 1:33 a.m. I was certain the Carmichaels weren't peeking out the window looking for my transgressions at that hour. And I didn't like Micah's reply. I felt ashamed and ignorant. Late to learn about the world I was living in. The pit in my stomach grew heavier. It sank so low as my worst fear unfolded right before my eyes. This time, I couldn't run away from my problems or hide in my room for months pretending time would heal me. No, this time, unlike when Mama died, I had to act. I had to do something.

And I actually *could* do something.

I was more afraid of that than disappointing Micah, or pissing off Jason, or withstanding Shelia's sneer and snark. This time, I had a say in what happened to me. A choice I could make. It would reveal the truth in my heart, force me to accept responsibility for the path my life would follow.

Micah turned off the engine when we made it to my house.

"I would lose everything," I confessed one fear.

"What would you gain by staying?"

"I don't know anymore." Out of the blue, my mom's journal entry came to mind. The one Matron Kirk brushed off and told me was nothing.

"My mom wrote some disturbing entries in her journal before she died. She referred to pictures of little girls. One was of me."

Micah's face contorted with rage, but I knew his anger wasn't directed at me.

"When I asked Matron Kirk about it, she told me a man who used to live here was caught taking photos without permission, so they evicted him, and I had nothing to worry about. After everything you've told me, I don't believe her anymore."

"Did your mom say where those photos were?"

"Yes. In a flap behind Malachi's desk, in his office."

"I knew it! I knew that bastard kept records somewhere but didn't have any proof." He pounded his fist on the leather dashboard.

"My mom died so quickly. She was healthy, Micah. No matter what anyone says, my mom was healthy." The tears came. I hadn't given voice to the fears before. Doing so now broke that last bit of denial I held onto, shattered the last bit of hope I had of staying in Bright Lakes.

I sobbed into the softness of his cotton shirt.

"I have an idea," he said once my sobbing turned into silent tears and my breathing evened out. He rubbed my head in gentle strokes as I laid against the hardness of his chest. "Can you meet me tomorrow night, after dark? There's an abandoned treehouse behind the orange orchards. No one should be out there. Do you know where I'm talking about?"

Of course I did. It haunted my dreams.

I nodded into his chest. I wanted to melt into the warmth of him. Wrapped in his arms, I felt undeniably safe—something I hadn't experienced since I was a little girl sitting between Mama's legs as she combed the knots from my hair. Safe was a time long ago—when my dad was alive. When he'd read to me and tuck me into bed at night.

My jaw dropped. He was reading the Sacred Text—a passage we would rehearse whenever I was afraid of the dark.

I will always be with you. In the darkness of the night, at the dawning of the day, through the unforeseeable trials, I am the Way.

The weight of Micah's head rested atop mine for a long while, then his hands cupped my puffy face, and he stared into my eyes. Our gazes locked, and we sat there—unmoving, unspeaking, unhurried. And in that moment, we both knew a line had just been crossed. An agreement had just been made, and the surety of our focus on each other was its signature. The untethered spirit behind his confidence revealed sorrow and loneliness that mirrored mine. I was truly seeing him, the intangible Micah. And I allowed him to truly see me in my unguarded, transparent essence.

In that instance, for the first time since I was a child, my confidence rose. It was like a glowing surge of strength, a wildness within me that I'd buried so, so long ago. First, at the passing of my father, then again at the death of my mom. And inside I wanted to devour this man that was causing this stirring within me to erupt. Yearned to reach out, to consume him. To protect him and never let him go.

I knew the moment he felt my thoughts because his hazel eyes deepened and his once-gentle palms around my face stiffened. He drew me toward him, and I wanted everything he offered. I could smell his woodsy scent, see his jaw line sharpen like he was grinding his teeth, taming himself. Amid all that passion, he placed a tenderly sweet kiss atop my forehead then leaned away from me, back into the cushion of the driver's seat.

If I knew where he got that restraint, I'd buy it by the barrel.

He removed his cell phone from the compartment near the gear shift. "What's your phone number?"

I pulled myself back to my seat, shook off the intensity of that previous moment, then recited the familiar ten digits.

"Let's plan to meet at 9:30pm by the treehouse. I'll text you if anything changes, and you do the same."

"It's a plan." Smart or not, it was the first plan in a long while that I actually looked forward to.

THIRTY-TWO

THE NEXT DAY, I slept till noon.

Upon waking, I checked my phone hoping by some miracle I'd see a message from Reen. There was nothing from her, nor Jason or Micah. But there was one from Misty asking if there was anything she could help with for the wedding.

The day dragged on, granting too much time to replay the idea that my mom's death might not have been an accident. That possibility elevated my fear and sadness. I was terrified to step outside.

I took to my journal, detailing everything I'd need to accomplish within the next week. By the time the sun set, and the blistering heat became a tolerable warmth, I was seething. I wanted to punch something, throw something, stomp something. I wanted to hurt whoever hurt my mom and everyone who had anything to do with her death. I was more than ready to strategize with Micah and get on with... something.

I threw on the lightweight, long black skirt and black oversized t-shirt I wore when gardening, then I left my house. The walk was long, but anger fueled me, and I made it in record time.

Micah was standing under the treehouse when I arrived, and I couldn't remember the last time someone wanted me enough to wait for my arrival. It sent a thrill through me. A second jolt of excitement chased it as I took in his appearance—dark blue jeans and a charcoal grey t-shirt. He'd never looked better.

He towered over me—big, strong. But when he pulled me into him for a full embrace, he was gentle. I lay my head on his hard chest, basked in the feeling of protection, and breathed him in. He smelled fresh, like he'd just showered.

"I thought about you all night." He said into my hair. "I was worried you might not show up."

I could've cried at his compassionate admission. But I'd cried enough.

"I wasn't sure if I would make it either," I admitted.

The grief and fear that clung to me was heavy, but I'd weighed the benefits of meeting him against the costs of getting caught and realized he was more than worth the risk. His hug was a welcomed surprise and all the confirmation I needed that I'd made the right decision.

He grasped my shoulders, held me at arms' length, and met my gaze. There was no kindness in his eyes, only intense determination, but I wasn't afraid. Not with him by my side. I felt strong and brave and met his determination with my own.

"I have a plan." He said and slid one hand down my arm until my hand was cradled within his. The action felt so natural, like he'd been doing it for years. Everything with him was comfortable, easy. He led me behind the dilapidated treehouse, the same one that haunted my dreams, and continued. "You mentioned an entry in your mom's journal about pictures of kids. Of you."

I nodded.

"At the next Service, during Updates, bring the journal with you and share the information with the whole community."

I pulled my hand out of his. "Why would I do that? I don't have any proof."

"You work in the Admin Building. I have access to Malachi's office on Wednesdays and Saturdays during Services. This Wednesday, I'll look for the flap you mentioned. In the meantime, you volunteer tomorrow through Wednesday and look for whatever you can to find out about little girls between the ages five through eight. That's when…" Micah paused, and he looked like someone stole the life from him. "Eight is when they stop hurting them."

Oh, Lord. This is really happening.

He took a deep breath. "Around that time, some girls start having nightmares or not wanting to go to Service. Sometimes families move away. There has to be a record of those names in a file somewhere."

Nightmares?

"I don't have access to those, Micah. I don't even have keys. Those privileges are reserved for Gladys, Tamika, and Kendall."

"It's our only chance, Nikki."

"There has to be another way. I mean, what are we even trying to do here? Are we getting out? What about your mom? You said you can't leave her. What do we accomplish by sharing that journal?"

"Other people will know. Other people will leave—including my mom."

"So, let's just share it with her."

"They won't let me take her without a reason, a good reason like what you have. But with this, with proof, everyone will know what they're doing. They'll lose control, and we'll be free."

I paced in the dirt, shaking my head. "That's *if* we get proof. I don't even know where I'd look in the office. And say I did find records of people moving out. It doesn't prove abuse of their daughters. It doesn't prove what happened to me. And it doesn't prove they killed my mom."

"All the lay members need is a reason to doubt Malachi."

"Like my mom did?! Look what happened to her!" I whisper-yell.

"Nikki, others know something is wrong. They just don't know what. Sooner or later, those people get evicted or choose to leave or… disappear. Someone's keeping a record of it. I'll look for the photos. That should be enough leverage to protect anyone from Malachi or the Leadership."

I didn't want anyone else to go through what I went through. Didn't want harm to come to anyone. If little girls were being hurt and I could do something—even a little something—to prevent it, I had to at least try. I thought of my students Clarissa and Lilliana. They'd come to me for academic tutoring but really needed a good counselor. They weren't misbehaving or adjusting to the system—they'd been abused. They were crying for help, and no one was listening.

"There's an extra key kept in the lockbox behind Gladys' desk," I said. "If I can somehow get it, I should be able to look through the files. But I don't even know what files I'd be looking for." This was all too much. Where would I even begin?

And then I remembered.

"There's a black folder inside the lockbox. The last time Malachi stopped in while I was there, he was looking for it. I only noticed because it's rare that he comes to our office, so I watched him. That's when I saw Gladys open the lockbox and retrieve that folder. I thought it was odd."

"Good. Very good. You work on that. I'll break into his office on Wednesday during service to see if that flap is still there. They might have covered it after your mom found it."

"Do you really think he keeps pictures of young girls in there?" I realized we hadn't been talking in hushed tones the whole time. Worse, we were standing in the open and anyone could see us if they walked through the orchards. I tugged him into the shadows.

"Nikki." He tipped up my chin, forcing me to look at him. "You have your mother's journal. You have her words, her testimony. Do you believe she would write what she did if it wasn't true?"

Of course she wouldn't, but that didn't ease the aching in my heart or the sadness I felt for the girls.

How would I manage it? I always follow the rules. Doing this meant I had to break them. I had to disrupt the system that taught me, shaped me, and formed me into this muted, compliant version of myself. If I did this, I wouldn't be able to hide anymore, and all the people I loved would realize I'd hidden behind Reen, letting her take the hits all these years.

She may have been shunned and excommunicated, but in the end, she did exactly what she wanted. She'd been free even while trapped here, and she was free now.

It was me who was trapped. In Bright Lakes and within myself.

I nodded. "Okay. Let's do it."

He pulled me back into his arms.

This was it. We had a real plan, and I was choosing to help someone other than myself. I wasn't brave, but I would fight. Micah's courage and convictions would give me the strength to see things through.

"Nikki, there's something I've been wanting to ask you, but there hasn't been a good time. Even now isn't ideal."

I tilted my head to look up at him. The moonlight bathed him in a soft glow, and his eyes almost looked golden.

"What is it?" I breathed.

"Can I kiss you?"

I was not expecting that, but I would have been lying to myself if I said I hadn't thought about kissing him, touching him... every day since I saw him at the farmers market while I was making wedding plans with a man I didn't truly love.

"You've kissed me before."

"But not the way I want to."

My heart raced. Heat flushed my entire body. I felt nervous, shy, like a little girl. I nodded, still looking into those golden eyes. My breath quickened as he slid his hands up my arms to cup my face. His touch felt like lightning sparking through me until finally his lips were upon mine.

It was slow, sweet. Deep and passionate. A moan escaped me, and he took the opportunity to deepen the kiss. Our tongues tangled as he snaked his arms around the small of my back and pulled me closer.

I reached around his neck, toyed with the ends of his hair. When he groaned, the sound dissolved whatever sliver of decorum I had left. I was ravenous. I wanted to consume him. His reaction told me he wanted the same.

Why did I never feel such passion for Jason? I didn't even know I was capable of feeling... so much. So uninhibited by the shame of desire. Jason wanted more from me, but I didn't want that from him. Out of obligation I was willing, after we married, but I didn't feel secure enough, safe enough, to share that side of me with him. Doing so would admit I had emotions and desires of my own. That I was capable of more than smiles and obedience. It wasn't proper for a woman to express passion or anger or anything other than gratitude and humility—especially a woman engaged to a future Elder.

A twig snapped. I leaped away from Micah. My heart leapt into my throat as we turned to see who approached.

THIRTY-THREE

A SQUIRREL.

Relief sluiced through me, and I burst into laughter. I didn't even know squirrels weighed enough to snap a twig, but there the little fella was, dashing up the tree truck and into the abandoned treehouse.

The disruption was warranted though. We were being stupidly reckless, not that I regretted a single moment of it. What I did regret was the engagement ring wrapped around my finger. Sparkling with beauty as I tarnished its sacred meaning.

Micah walked me home. He stayed out of Sheila Carmichael's sight but made sure I got inside safely.

Come the morning, we'd enacted our plan.

I didn't sleep. All night I'd tossed and turned, imagining all the ways things could go wrong. Instead, things couldn't have been easier. When Gladys and Tamika went to lunch, I took the keys from Gladys's drawer. My nerves started to fray as each failed, but the very last one fit the lock.

A turn, a click, then I opened the box. The folder was propped against the wall beside the petty cash.

I hurried to retrieve it then put everything else back where I'd found it. Now I stood in the office, trying to settle my racing heart.

I hurried to tuck the black folder in my bag. Then the day wore on.

It nipped at the back of my mind as I smiled at Lilliana's mom, Matron Patterson, who was waiting for me to tell her my favorite shades of purple. She and Matron Butler had taken the lead in preparing my bridal quilt. I couldn't care less about it, but this wasn't the time or place for me to reveal that fact. I smiled and acted as sweet and compliant as ever. Even more so, as there was now a purpose behind my fake smile. Strategy and freedom waited on the other side of it, spurring me on. I felt a wicked sense of satisfaction as I spouted out colors and scrolled through the online inspiration board she showed me.

"What do you think of this sandy yellow and periwinkle purple?" She pointed at her tablet.

"Oh, Matron Patterson, that's just perfect. Let's go with that, please." I beamed.

"You're right, that is perfect, isn't it? Okay, we'll thread shades of these colors along with your other suggestions, and that'll be all the input we'll need from you." She closed the tablet then wedged it into her snakeskin tote. "How are you doing since the bridal retreat? I was a little concerned with some of your questions, but it seems you're managing just fine after we clarified things."

"Thank you for being so patient with me. I am blessed to have all of you wise brides to seek guidance from." I felt sick to my stomach at the lies coming so easily out of my mouth. Then I realized this wasn't new to me. That's exactly what I had been doing all these years—lying. We all were. Lying to ourselves, lying to others. We participated in a structured system of deception upheld by fear-motivated compliance. There were certain acceptable responses. Acceptable questions, acceptable thoughts, acceptable behavior, acceptable attire, and so on. Anything outside of "acceptable" marked a person as a threat to the system.

If women don't behave in the community, the community would cease to exist.

Micah had nailed it.

But why did it have to be like that? I wanted to scream inside.

"How is Lilliana?" I asked. "Are her math scores improving?"

"That reminds me, I've been meaning to ask if you can come by tomorrow or Wednesday afternoon to help her with a practice test?"

"Of course."

I loved Lilliana, and now that I suspected her attitude had to do with what she suffered at the hands of the Elders, I desperately wanted to see her. To help her. She was only nine!

My thoughts drifted back to the folder in my bag.

"I can come tomorrow at eleven. Would that work?"

"She'll be ready for you." Matron Patterson left the building.

I was good at my job and even better at lying.

Only one of those things was a good character trait. Soon, Bright Lord willing, it wouldn't matter.

‽⃺

I RANG THE King family's bell. Their house was two blocks from mine, but despite the proximity, I felt out of place.

A pool party was in progress three doors down, and cars lined the entire block. Moms carrying large beach bags shepherded children dressed in swimsuits from the street to the Drapers' house. Young Christopher was sure to have lots to talk about over the next few days.

The door swung open. Mrs. King did not look happy to see me. Or maybe she was just unhappy, period. Shawn's mom was always polite, quiet but kind. She didn't go out of her way to speak to others, but when approached was considerate. I liked her.

The dark circles under her eyes and scowl on her face told me what I already suspected—she'd been as shocked as I was about her son being evicted with Reen and her family.

"I'm sorry to bother you, Mrs. King." I stood as poised as possible, willing myself to do this. Micah had a plan for how we were going to expose the Elders and Malachi, but I had a plan of my own.

Mr. King's voice boomed from behind her. "Who's at the door, Alexis?"

A split second later, he opened the door wider and peered over her shoulder. Anger darkened and sharpened his features. He didn't resemble the kind father I'd known him to be, and I'd known him since I was little.

"If you're here to ask about Shawn and Maureen, don't." He began to close the door.

I placed my hand on the door, willing it to stay open. "Mr. King, please, I just want to know where I can find them."

"You need to leave," he growled.

"This is all your fault," Mrs. King snapped. "If you had just married Jason sooner, they wouldn't have had a reason to go after my son."

My mouth fell open. She slammed the door in my face, but I couldn't move. Couldn't think.

The sounds of splashing and children's laughter shoved me back into reality. When I turned around, Sheila Carmichael was looking at me. Her son, James, stood next to her wearing swim trunks and Spider-Man floaties on both of his tiny arms.

"Go ahead, sweetie, I'm going to talk to Miss Nikki for a quick minute."

James obediently turned toward the Drapers' house. He ran to catch up to the other kids.

I walked from the Kings' doorstep to my car, ignoring Sheila. I didn't have the time or the patience for her right now. "I'm just leaving, Sheila. Call me later if you need something."

"I don't need anything, but I am curious what you're doing at the King's house?"

"Like I said, if you need something, you can call me later. I have to go." I buckled my seat belt then drove off, leaving her slack-jawed in the street.

ℰℭ

Just two blocks to my house, and I didn't know if I'd make it.

My vision blurred. Nausea rolled through my belly as I passed one stop sign then the second one. Finally, I rounded the last corner. In the safety of my carport, I moved the gearshift into park then turned off the engine. It was difficult to breathe. My chest heaved. Was I hyperventilating? The late-afternoon heat felt like a boa constrictor wrapping itself around my body and cutting off my oxygen.

I need to get out of this car.

I snatched my bag from the passenger seat then stumbled inside, grateful for the privacy of my house.

Thank the Bright Lord for air conditioning.

I tossed my bag, containing the evidence, on the couch then stumbled to the bathroom. After steadying my breath, I splashed cool water on my face. The girl staring back at me in the mirror was unrecognizable. She looked worn, miserable. Beaten. Perhaps that is why she never fought before. She hadn't been fighting long, and it had irrevocably changed her.

Fighting wasn't pretty, wasn't tidy. It hurt like hell. It ripped out your soul and shoved it down your throat, forcing you to swallow it whole.

You knew with every cell of your body that you couldn't do it, not alone. If you tried it alone, you would certainly fail.

In this life you will have trouble, but be at peace, for I have overcome the world.

Low and deep, the passage of the Sacred Text reverberated in my heart. I didn't recall having read that one before, but I knew it was true. More than I'd ever known something to be true. I closed my eyes and placed my hand over my heart.

"If you're real, please be with me. Please help me. Please guide me. I don't know what I'm doing." Tears streamed down my face. "I don't know where I'm going. I don't know who to trust anymore. I need you."

Somehow, I made it to Mama's room. I fell asleep on her bed. When I awoke, it was dark, and I had a pounding headache.

Then I remembered the black folder. I was dying to see what was inside and darted into the living room.

On the couch, next to my bag, slept Micah.

THIRTY-FOUR

H E SPRANG FROM the couch when he heard me rush in.

"Are you okay?" He looked down the hall in the direction I just came from.

"What are you doing here?" I threw myself into his arms. Without hesitation, he held me. "How did you get in? Did anybody see you?"

"Nobody saw me, and I have a key to everyone's house who's being evicted."

Right, I almost forgot I was on that list.

"Why are you out of breath?" he asked.

"Come with me." I stepped from his embrace, grabbed my bag, then pulled him toward the kitchen. Talking in the kitchen is something I did with Reen. It was more comfortable there, and I desperately needed tea.

"You can sit there if you like." I pointed to the breakfast nook bench, but he didn't sit.

"What's in the bag?"

"I found Malachi's folder. The one I told you about." After putting water on to boil, I retrieved the heavy folder then gave it to Micah.

He finally sat.

"Would you like some tea or water? Sorry, I don't have anything else."

"Water's good Thanks." He opened the folder. "Have you looked through this yet?"

"No. I didn't want to risk it at work, then I had a run-in with Sheila Carmichael. When I got home, I was upset and took a nap. What made you risk coming over?"

"I texted and called you this afternoon. When you didn't respond, I thought something… bad happened."

"Oh." I hadn't checked my phone since I was with Matron Patterson earlier. It hadn't occurred to me that he might check on me. I liked that he did. And what we were doing was dangerous. The reality of that was still sinking in.

"When I saw you sleeping, I was relieved. I'd have left right then but thought it best to wait until the Carmichaels' lights were off. Sorry for scaring you. I didn't think I'd fall asleep."

"No, I'm glad to see you!" An image of our midnight interlude flashed in my mind, and I immediately became aware of my appearance. Last time I checked, I looked like crap!

The whistle of the kettle made me jump. I whirled around, filled a mug with hot water, then dropped a prepackaged chamomile lavender tea bag into it. The scent began to calm me. "Um, I'll be right back. Bottles of water are in the fridge. Help yourself!"

He looked at me like the weirdo I was and stood.

When I returned from tidying my appearance, Micah had three short stacks of paper laid on the table and his water bottle was empty. Had I been gone that long?

"What do you make of it?" I picked up my mug then sat on the opposite side of the bench.

He looked me up and down, smiled, then turned his attention to the pages, tapping each pile as he described their contents. "This is exactly what I hoped we would find. This stack is a log of girls either entering or born into the community. This stack is a record of those same girls whose families moved out. And this stack is a list of girls who at one point blamed Malachi or an Elder for *indecency*, reacted violently to being in their presence, or exhibited 'extreme emotion' when going to Service."

"They really did track everything." I said in disbelief. Was I in there too? My memory of the first years we lived here were all a blur. As I contemplated the depravity of the documents in front of me—rather, the depravity of what the documents represented—I jogged my mind for even a hint of a memory of being violated. I quickly stopped. The mere notion of it made me sick.

Micah nodded. "I haven't looked through the names, but I think we should start with this stack." He divided the last bundle of papers then passed half to me.

"What are we looking for?" I asked.

"I don't know. Let's begin with what these girls said. Maybe we'll find an overlap between their accounts and those of the girls whose families moved out."

Two cups of tea, another bottle of water, a bag of pretzels, and a bowl of strawberries later, we had a list and a plan. Micah used his cellphone to take photos of the documents we gathered, and I placed the originals back inside the folder. Not only was there a correlation, but the most vivid complaints came from the Elders' daughters. It seemed the leadership ensured their secrets were kept by offering promotions and awarding prime real estate along the lake.

I wondered if Gladys knew the contents of the folder or merely was the keeper of it.

Tomorrow, I would return the folder before anyone knew it was missing, then I'd tutor Lilliana as planned. While at the Pattersons' home, I'd try to gauge if she remembered being violated. Her name was on the list of girls who complained, but her singular comment was brief.

The Champion scares me. I don't like to see him.

My heart ached at her words. She must be suffering dreadfully. Did her mom or dad believe her? Were they punishing her for saying unkind things about the Champion?

Mr. Patterson would be at work, and Mrs. Patterson intended to run errands while I was there, so the timing couldn't be more perfect.

On Wednesday, Micah would search for the flap and hidden photos. If all went according to plan, and we prayed it did, by Saturday, we'd be ready to expose it all in front of every member.

THIRTY-FIVE

"How are you doing today, sweetie? You look a little under the weather." Gladys patted my shoulder and appeared genuinely concerned about my well-being.

I'm sure I did look under the weather. The nightmare I had last night woke me at four, and that was after kissing Micah goodbye at midnight.

I struggled to keep my composure under her careful study. It hurt to believe she played a role in all of this. That she could potentially be the one recording all the Elders' sins.

"I'm fine, thanks."

She looked skeptical but returned to her work.

The morning passed slowly. Finally, Kendall and Gladys left for lunch. Because I knew which key to use, returning the folder to the lockbox took even less time than removing it. Part of me was relieved while another was frustrated. I imagined getting caught so I could confront her, yell at her, demand answers. I craved revenge—now. It would be a sweet release, but doing so would ruin our plan and destroy all hope of helping others.

As the hours and the days rolled by, I realized holding secrets like this was more difficult than I imagined.

I'd decided they could have my physical presence but not a damn thing more. I would not smile. Gladys would think it was because I'm sick, but I had the satisfaction of knowing better. Today would be my last day in this office. I'd accomplished all I needed to move forward, and there was no reason to return. They wouldn't get one more fragment of my soul.

When they returned from lunch, Gladys studied me. "Are you sure you're okay, dear?"

"Just a little tired, I suppose." That wasn't a lie.

"Of course you are. Probably haven't slept well since Jason left. I'm sure you miss your fiancé, but he'll be back tonight, right? From his retreat?"

Right! He'd return tonight. I'd lost track, having been so busy gathering evidence and plotting my escape with another man.

I patted her hand and turned back around to my computer screen and continued recording entries of new member applications.

After finishing my hours and leaving the Administration Building for the last time, I drove to the Pattersons' house. I took Bright Lane, the street Maureen's family lived on. It was the first I'd been there since their eviction. Other than going to Jason's house, I had no reason to be in the Elders' neighborhood and so hadn't dared to drive through. Now I had a reason but found I didn't care. I should have come sooner.

I slowed as I neared her house. At Leti's Lounge, Micah told me the moving trucks had come the day after they left, so I was surprised to see a "Fernando's Transports" moving truck in front of their driveway. Men in beige and white uniforms hauled furniture from the truck into the house.

Someone was moving in already!

I glared at the men as they carried a large armoire up the steps, but I continued driving, forcing myself to focus on my goal and make it to Lillian's house on time. She was my priority for today, and Reen was safe. I hoped.

Lilliana looked annoyed. Her mom must've dressed her in the turquoise dress and matching shoes. Strong-willed for a nine-year-old, Lilliana had her own opinions and gave them voice. One she frequently shared with me was her dislike for frilly dresses. Her preference aside, I thought she looked rather cute in it.

I waved goodbye to Mrs. Patterson then proceeded to the library. Lilliana waited for me at the long mahogany table in the center of the room.

The space looked like something out of a gothic movie. Tall toffee-colored shelves lined two of the walls. The wood was intricately carved and topped with an arch. High-backed chairs sat on either side of the desk, an alcove along a window boasted a view of the lake. Shaded lamps were placed strategically near each chair to give readers light while not disturbing others in the room.

When Lilliana saw me, she jumped up, turned on the overhead light, and drew the curtains so the room was brightly lit this afternoon.

"How are you feeling today, Lilly?"

"She made me wear this stupid dress. Isn't it ugly?" She picked at the fabric and frowned.

"Did you tell your mom you didn't like it?"

"She doesn't listen. Hey, Nikki, when are you getting married?" She beamed.

"In two weeks." It hurt to lie to her, but it wasn't completely false. The ceremony was scheduled for two weeks from today. She'd been through enough and I wanted to be the one person she could trust.

"Wow! You're going to be the most beautiful bride. My mom's helping make the quilt. Matron Butler asked her. Do you know Matron Butler? She's the mean one."

She sure was.

I listened as she prattled on, flipping through the pages of her math book. "Mommy was telling her that she likes the color you chose. She doesn't really like to do the quilts, but she'll do it this time because Matron Tucker is her best friend."

"I'm glad your mom is doing my quilt. And that she likes the colors."

"Yeah, purple and yellow are her favorite colors too. Nikki, do we have to do math today?"

"What else did you want to do? Your mom wants you to get ready for an upcoming test." Every time I came over, Lilliana wanted to talk about anything except homework. Now I understood why. It wasn't that she was stupid or lazy or distracted. The poor girl just wanted to be seen and heard and loved, especially after what she'd just experienced.

Instead, her parents sent me.

She frowned.

"First, show me the assignments you did this week and anything your teacher gave you about the test. Then we can do other things, if you'd like."

"Can you tell me anything else about your wedding first?" She was so cute, so innocent. To think she still had enough joy to ask me about my wedding after something so terrible happened to her. I wouldn't deny her what little pleasure I could provide. I'd tell her whatever she wanted to hear.

I showed her pictures of my dress, shoes, flowers, and bridesmaids' gowns. It was the least I could do, knowing there wouldn't be a wedding. I didn't feel any hesitation about showing her everything. When we were done, I put away my phone and prepared to ask her questions about what had happened.

She went to the kitchen to grab a juice box for herself and a bottle of water for me.

"Lilly, why don't you like going to Service anymore?"

A brief silence passed before Lilly handed me the water, avoiding eye contact.

"Does it make you uncomfortable to talk about it, honey?"

"No." She fumbled with her juice box. "I don't know why. I just don't like it."

I understood. "That's okay. And sweetheart… if you don't like something or someone, please do your best to tell your parents? Can you do that for me? And if someone does something bad or wrong to you, tell them."

She shrugged.

I took a bright yellow journal with lilies printed on the cover from my bag. "I brought this for you."

"What is it? A pretty math book?"

"No, honey." I giggled past the lump in my throat "This is a diary. If no one will listen to you, write your thoughts in here. Write the good things and the bad things and everything in between. You don't have to keep secrets when you have a diary. It's for keeping your secrets safe."

THIRTY-SIX

MY BACK YARD reflected how I felt.

It was overrun with weeds. Over-ripe fruit decayed on the ground. If it weren't for the automatic watering system along the garden beds, all the branches and leaves would be dried and crispy. I came out here because it was my routine for the past five years and I loved it. But tonight, I came out not to work but to look. To *see* it. To remember who I was and what I was capable of. I created this amazing garden from nothing, and now, even though it needed some TLC, it was still alive.

After I returned from my retreat, I'd given up on salvaging anything. I didn't have the will to work without Reen. Community members whose Faiths I never fulfilled were extremely forgiving, believing I didn't deliver their strawberries because wedding preparations took my time. And all but two families insisted that I keep their payment and use it toward our wedding or honeymoon. Moments like that are what held people here. In times of need or celebration, the Bright Lakes Community came through for one another without hesitation. We were a big, messy family, and I loved them. Most of them. I understood why Mama moved us here. And as wonderful as most of the people were, I'd never get over the inhumane treatment and violation of our children.

Earlier in the day, I updated Micah on my successful replacement of the folder. He sounded more relieved than I felt. Although we wouldn't see each other tonight, we agreed to meet at the treehouse two hours after Service tomorrow evening.

The thought of what he had to do sent chills through my body. It was dangerous. But it was more damaging to remain silent. We were doing the right thing.

That thought was all that kept me going.

ഇന്ദ

WHEN JASON ARRIVED at my front door the next afternoon, he was not alone.

An older man slightly taller than him with a sharp jaw and sky blue eyes accompanied him. Slightly behind them stood a woman, also taller than Jason, but not by much. She had long, straight, beautiful black hair. It looked silky and shone in the light.

"Nikki, this is my uncle, Dr. Scott, and my aunt, Hailey."

Dr. Scott extended his hand to me. "I've heard so much about you. You prefer Nikki over Nicolette I hear?"

As we shook, I stumbled over my words "Yes… Yes, it's nice to meet you, Scott." Without thinking, I moved to the side so they could enter. "You're welcome to come in, but the house is pretty bare right now."

"Jason told us you'll be moving out soon." The three of them filed into the living room.

The woman looked at me with soft, kind eyes. Her smile revealed perfectly white teeth. She also shook my hand. "I'm Hailey. It's so good to meet you. Jason tells us you're quite the gardener."

I pictured the sad state of my "garden." Definitely didn't want to show her that. "It's good to meet you too, Hailey. I grow strawberries, but they're not in the best condition right now."

We stood in my pitifully empty living room with boxes piled in one corner, mail strewn about the couch, and my raggedy pair of house shoes in front of the chair. Why didn't he say he was bringing company? Bad enough I had to pretend everything was normal with him, but to do it around complete strangers? I wasn't prepared for the charade. Not today.

"I wanted you to meet my uncle and aunt before Service tonight. They'll be sitting with us. My uncle is a doctor and has been good friends with our Champion for as long as I can remember."

"That's right. We were Trainees together long, long ago," Dr. Scott added.

Friends with Malachi. I needed to get this man out of my house. I inched toward the door. "I'm glad you dropped by. I've been packing and clearing the house, so don't have anything to offer you, but it'll be nice to get to know you better when we can properly visit."

"We won't stay long," his uncle said. "We just wanted to introduce ourselves. Jason says you knew the family who lived in our new home."

A knife to the heart wouldn't have hurt less. My mouth wouldn't move.

Jason glowered at me when I didn't speak.

"Yes, Uncle. Nikki was great friends with Elder... Mr. Johnson's daughter. I was just telling her that you also garden, Aunt Hailey. Nikki, why don't you show her your strawberries?" He began walking through the hallway toward the back of the house.

I grabbed his hand, halting his movement.

That earned me another glare.

"Um, I'll be happy to show Mrs. Tucker another day. I really need to get a few things in order before Service tonight, but thanks so much for coming by. I'm glad I got to meet you."

His uncle's eyes turned from the soft expression into something more stern, and he looked at my hand upon his nephew's as if he disapproved. It was that look that snapped me out of my desperate, robotic actions and reminded me I didn't give a damn about what any of them thought. I marched toward the front door, opened it wide, then smiled big and bright. Keeping eye contact with Hailey, I said, "I'll see you tonight!"

Jason walked to the door first, looking at me with hurt in his eyes. I knew that look. He was sad. He was embarrassed. That small act of disobedience shamed him in front of his uncle. He pecked my cheek then mumbled, "See you tonight."

There was no way I was going to Service tonight. I had plans for my evening, and it didn't include spending time with them.

The wildflower-printed luggage set Mama bought me last year lay opened on my bedroom floor. It was 7:05 p.m., and my phone signaled a text. Jason, asking where I was. I ignored him. I'd never missed Service before. I'd never been late. Tonight, that changed. I needed to pack. Time was ticking, and our plan was entering its last phase. Who knew what would happen after we made the announcement Saturday morning? No matter what, I was leaving. *We* were leaving. The rest would figure itself out.

After all but three outfits were packed, I moved to Mama's room. Reen and I previously packed everything but the top shelf of her closet, where her big, elegant hats and shoe boxes remained. I'd go through those and donate everything tomorrow. And that would be that.

THIRTY-SEVEN

I<small>F IT WEREN'T</small> for Micah's earlier text message saying he "got it," I would've been worried.

He was ten minutes late. Okay. I was still a little worried.

I stood in the dark, hiding behind the abandoned treehouse. Evening didn't bring much relief from the scorching heat of the day. The quarter mile it took to get here had my forehead and back of my neck perspiring. There was no cool breeze tonight. It was one thing being out in the orchards with someone, quite another being alone. Every cricket, owl, and frog had me jumping out of my skin. I cowered at the sound of footsteps approaching.

"It's me, Nikki."

"Oh, Bright Lord, I'm so glad it's you." My breath came out in a whoosh. "What took you so long?"

He dropped a small, blue bag. "All the Elders were meeting at my house, including Jeremy, Malachi's guard dog."

It had never occurred to me that Jeremy was Malachi's bodyguard. I thought he was just the guy who held his things and stared at people. He was definitely creepy enough to be a bodyguard.

"They immediately noticed the items were missing. The flap and all the evidence was exactly where your mom said it was. It would've looked suspicious if I walked past them carrying this bag."

"Are you sure they didn't see you leave?"

"I'm sure. I would've let you know if I couldn't make it tonight." He squatted down and unzipped the bag. "I don't want to make you see anything you don't want to, so before we continue, I have to ask if you're sure you want to look. These photos are pretty disturbing."

Did I? What if I saw pictures of Lilliana or Maureen or myself? I don't know if I could handle it after everything that had happened. But I needed to. I'd hid my head in the sand long enough, pretended long enough.

"I need to see it… need to know. It'll ground me in reality. I've been blind and ignorant for too long and now isn't the time to close my eyes."

He squeezed my hand before I knelt. The beam of his flashlight illuminated the bag's contents. Inside were two large manilla envelopes, a plastic bag filled with half sheets of white paper, and a metal box. He picked up one of the manilla envelopes. "I separated out the photographs from some of the things I found. This one contains pictures."

He handed it to me. My heart raced. Before I could open the folder, my eyes filled with tears.

Saying nothing, he gently wiped them from my face.

I removed the top photo then dropped onto my butt, unable to support my weight. The first image was of a young girl I didn't know, but that didn't make it easier. She was asleep in the center of a mattress, stripped of her clothes.

A man I *did* recognize sat next to her. He was touching her inappropriately. I dropped the photograph. My hands flew to my mouth to muffle the scream.

Micah reached for me, but I swatted his hand away. I didn't want to be touched. Didn't want to see another photo. Didn't want this to be real.

He scooted next to me but didn't touch me again.

I counted backward from twenty. My breath slowly returned to normal.

Micah put the picture back inside the envelope. He didn't hand me another. Instead, he handed me several pieces of paper from the other envelope. "I found something else in that hole."

I studied them. I didn't know the words, but I recognized the format. "Prescriptions?"

"I looked it up on the internet. Rohypnol is a drug that makes people drowsy and hallucinate. It also makes recall difficult. I think this is why most of the young girls, including you, don't remember what happened to them. And look here,"

He pointed to the signature.

"They're all signed by the same doctor. S. Tucker. That's the new Elder family who just moved in."

Jason's uncle.

"You knew all this the night we met at Leti's Lounge."

"They'd told me some of it. I suspected the rest. But I didn't have proof."

"I wasn't ready to hear it then. It was too unbelievable, too much for me to acknowledge. Can you imagine learning you might be a victim but not remembering?"

He shook his head.

"I can't put it into words. But when I spoke to Lilliana yesterday, I knew the truth of what you were saying. She couldn't even remember why she didn't like the Champion. All she knew was she didn't feel good around him. Her parents are frustrated with her, so she's just trying to forget anything bad ever happened." Tears poured down my face. "All these years I've been nervous and skittish and compliant. When I was around Maureen, I'd wonder, why wasn't I more like her? Why could she be okay with being disliked by the others? I didn't want to consider being a victim because it hurt too much. But seeing Lilliana, at such a young age, already stuffing down her feelings, burying anything that isn't tidy or acceptable..." I shook my head. "She's repressing these horrors because that's all she knows! This is all I've known!"

Micah handed me a white rag.

"I always knew something was wrong with me. I'd have these bad thoughts and hate myself for it. I thought I was a bad person if I didn't want to hug this person or give something to that person. I didn't understand why I had to pretend it was fine to be inconvenienced, then I berated myself for feeling that way. All these years, pretending, lying, suffering in silence. I don't want another little girl to grow up believing she's bad or broken. Not when the truth is she just needs someone to love her and tell her it's okay to be herself."

I blew my nose.

"And I'll do whatever I need to do this Saturday. For Lilliana. For all the other girls in this damned Community. For Maureen and her family being ostracized, and for the ones who escaped."

"What about you?" he asked.

"What about me?"

"Do it for you. You deserve justice too."

I nodded. I would do this for me too.

"I found something today too. In my mom's closet. Inside a shoebox." I pulled a folded photo from my pocket then handed it to Micah.

He looked at it, closed his eyes, then refolded it. His pained expression hurt me as much as finding the picture did.

It was the missing photo of me. The photo my mom wrote about in her journal. She must have taken it but left the rest.

He returned it to me. I stuffed it in my pocket, unwilling to include it with the rest. After Saturday, I would burn it. Until then, I'd keep it in case the need for more evidence arose.

"Did you look through all the photos? Was Maureen in there?"

"I didn't look through them all, but her name wasn't on the list of the girls who complained. I think somehow Mr. Johnson protected her."

That made me happy. Happy for my friend. Happy that someone was protecting her then and now.

"I probably won't see you until Saturday." This time, he did reach out to touch me.

And I let him.

I sighed. "Jason is back. He introduced me to his uncle. I think he's the doctor who prescribed that medicine, Dr. Scott Tucker. He and Malachi went through Training together. They've been close friends ever since."

"Be careful around him. I don't trust him."

"No one can be trusted. I wish we could leave right now. I don't know if I can make it until Saturday, Micah. This is all too much. We should call the police. We have all the evidence now."

"Now that we have everything, we can call them. We can go to the police station in the city first thing tomorrow morning. But until we show this to the members, they won't believe it. And I won't be able to take my mom out of here."

He was right. People like Mr. Tucker would be sure to spin a very convincing tale, and the way most people revered the Champion, they would think the police set him up. Without them seeing the proof and hearing what we had to say, this abuse would continue. Maybe under new management, but it would continue.

But I'd reached my limit.

Micah took my hand, and I didn't pull away this time. "Tomorrow is Thursday. I'll check on you in the morning and at night. You have to let me know if you're okay and if you can or can't wait one more day. I'll do that again on Friday and Saturday morning, before Service. If we make it to Saturday."

I nodded. I could do that. Knowing the decision was mine helped me breathe a little easier. Didn't feel like I was holding the weight of the world on my shoulders anymore. At least not alone.

THIRTY-EIGHT

ICAII WALKED ME through the orchard until the path appeared for us to go in our separate directions.

This would be the last time we'd see each other until Saturday. Even though that was only three days away, it felt like another loss. Another thing ripped away from me by this community, these people. I could still feel the press of his lips upon mine and despite myself and the gravity of the situation, the corners of my mouth turned upward. He brought that out of me. Only he, and maybe Reen, could make me smile in the midst of the most horrible time of my life.

I'd thought my mom's death would be my low point, but all I'd recently discovered was a stark reminder that life could always get worse. Better times were in reach, and that was enough to smile about. I wouldn't let the Elders, Pillars, or Champion take away this tiny bit of happiness. Or the oceans of it I'd have later. For now, I'd acknowledge what joy I had and hold onto it. It was the only thing getting me through the gruesome confrontations.

When I rounded the block leading home, I found Jason's truck parked in front of my house. My heart leapt in my throat. I checked my phone. Oh no! He'd texted to say he was coming over. I tried to think of an excuse for not being there. Had I seen his message, I'd have replied that I had a headache.

He probably would have come over anyway.

I peeked through the driver's side window, but he wasn't in there. Had he gone inside my house? I raced to my front door—it stood slightly ajar, Before I entered, I heard voices. Who else was with him?

I'd had enough. I flung open the door but remained on the threshold.

Jason and his Dr. Scott turned toward me.

My heart raced, my mind blanked. This was the monster who'd drugged me and countless other poor girls. He might not have administered the drug, but he'd provided them. I couldn't be near that man. Couldn't stand the sight of him. I wanted nothing to do with either of them.

"Nikki, where have you been? Are you okay?" Jason looked extremely worried. In a few easy steps, he was at my side and had grabbed my hands. He was going to pull me inside!

"What are you doing here? How did you get inside my house?"

"Nicolette, dear. Hello again." Dr. Scott approached. "Your fiancé was worried since you missed Service tonight. Are you feeling all right?"

"I'm fine."

"Ahh, well, that is good news. Do come inside. We wouldn't want the neighbors to think something was wrong."

Something *was* wrong. But I couldn't think of a reason to stay outside.

"How did you…? This is—"

"What's the big deal?" Jason asked. "Why are you standing there like that?"

He was right. I was making myself look suspicious. It was better to just go inside. Now that he saw me, there was no reason for either of them to stay.

"I was just surprised to see both of you in here." I stepped into my living room.

"Where were you just now?" Jason closed the door behind me.

"I took a walk. Needed some fresh air. I feel better now. Sorry to make you worry, but as you can see, I'm perfectly fine."

"Yes, you are perfectly fine. Would you mind telling us why your suitcase is packed?" Dr. Scott narrowed his gaze upon me.

Chills raced up my spine.

Jason stepped in front of me. "Nikki, someone stole something from the Champion's—"

Dr. Scott interrupted him, his voice even, professional, aloof. "Some disturbing events occurred this evening. Would you happen to know anything that could shed some light on the situation?"

Bright Lord, save me. Of course they were worried, but not about my well-being. Of course they'd come here, but not to check on me. They were searching for Malachi's secret stash.

"I have no idea what you're talking about." I glared at them both. "Is that why you're here? Why you came inside my house without permission?"

"From what I understand, this isn't your house. Not really."

Dr. Scott stepped closer to me. "The gracious leadership of Bright Lakes is *allowing* you to stay until you and my nephew are wed. In times of emergencies, like tonight, we Elders can take such liberties for the good of the community."

"Nikki, if you know anything, please tell my uncle. He can help." Jason pleaded, now standing at his uncle's side. Both men stared at me.

"I don't know what you're talking about. What emergency? I was packing all night until I took a walk, and I wasn't gone very long." Good. That was a good reply. I willed my face to look as innocent and concerned as I could. I needed them to believe me.

"Then why did your neighbor say they saw you leave more than two hours ago? And why is your suitcase packed?" He picked up my journal, already open to a page of his choosing, and waved it at me. "And why are you spending so much time with Micah Fox?" He tilted his head and took a step toward me. I retreated, backing into the hard front door. I couldn't create any more distance between us, and he continued to move closer.

Jason just stood there. He looked at his uncle in disbelief. Did he really not know what his uncle was doing while they were here in my house? "You went through her diary?"

Dr. Scott turned toward his nephew. "Looks like you're going to have to learn the hard way how to deal with women like her."

I reached for the doorknob. I shouldn't have come inside. I shouldn't have let them close the door. I shouldn't have let that odious man step so close.

Dr. Scott raised his hand. I recoiled, expecting a slap. Instead, something soft covered my face. I screamed, but it was muffled.

Then everything went dark.

ഇരജ

NOISES SOUNDED IN the distance, like voices in a tunnel far away. The ruckus woke me.

Pain shot through my head. I lay on my back on a soft surface. As my eyes fluttered open, I groaned. The light was too bright. I closed them again and tried to hear what the people were saying. Why did my head hurt so much? Why were people around me while I slept? Had I suffered an accident?

Who was speaking? I didn't recognize the voices. Who would— Wait! That was Jason! Oh, Bright Lord, Jason! Memories flooded back. Jason and his uncle had been waiting for me at my house. Then what? Dr. Scott approached, then… I didn't know what happened after that.

"We can't do this. She's my fiancée!" Jason sounded angry.

"She knows something, and we're going to find out whether you like it or not." Was that his uncle?

"You're next in line to be Champion. Do you want the office tainted before you take over? It'll ruin you." A different man.

Who all was here, and what were they going to do to me?

Was that comment directed to Jason? Was he going to be the next Champion? Was that why he was meeting with Grand Elder Butler? My breath came in short spurts, but I didn't want to open my eyes, didn't want to draw attention to myself. From the sound of it, they weren't nearby, and I wanted to keep it that way. But without opening my eyes, I couldn't tell who was present. I patted the pocket of my dress, hoping they didn't take the folded photo of me.

A firm hand gripped my wrist. "She's awake."

I opened my eyes to find Jeremy, Malachi's fish-eyed assistant, leaning over me. He sat in a chair beside the bed, staring at me with venom in his eyes. I didn't dare try to free myself of his grip. I'd heard rumors about how he hurt people—men and women—in the past. I was so naive I didn't believe it when I heard them.

Mr. Tucker entered the room first, grim faced. Determined. Dr. Scott came next, then Malachi, followed by the Grand Elder, then at last Jason. His eyes were red-rimmed, face puffy. All those men were here for me. To hurt me. To find out what I'd been hiding. They had my journal and had no doubt read it all—explicit descriptions of Micah kissing me, bumping into him at the bar, our plans to expose them all. There was no way I could deny anything now. I wanted to scream, wanted to yell, wanted to kick and punch and spit.

Our plan was ruined. I was caught. And what happened to Micah?

Absent any other recourse, I prayed they didn't capture him. Prayed he got away. Prayed he'd gone to the police and a whole SWAT team was coming to my rescue.

"You've caused a lot of trouble, young lady." Malachi pointed a finger at Jeremy, who rose so the Champion could sit beside the bed. Beside me.

I sat up. My heart pounded. Each man looked at me with contempt and disgust. All of them hated me. Except Jason. He'd cried over this situation. Over me. And now he looked at me with an expression of… guilt?

"Look at me when I'm speaking to you." Malachi gripped my chin then yanked my face toward him. His fingers squeezed into my jaw, his nails puncturing my skin. "Tell us where you and my nephew hid the items you stole."

I clamped my lips closed.

He leaned close to my face. His breath smelled like mint, his cologne citrus musk. His deep-set eyes, normally resembling the bluest of skies, looked wrong. Out of place. Shadowed by his furrowed brow and burning with anger. He didn't look like a mad man. He looked like a demon.

And I knew he was going to kill me.

But my mouth wouldn't form words. My tongue felt thick and dry. Even if I did speak, I couldn't deny anything. And there was no chance I'd give up Micah. No way I'd further ruin our plan. I saw the photos. I saw what they did to me, to those girls, to sweet Lilliana and Clarissa. How many victims had there been over the years? How many Elders had, over the years, used the Sacred Text to their own twisted benefit? How many belonged to this ring of monsters?

So many girls of all ages had suffered at their hands, but we weren't the only ones. Many men fell under their wicked thumbs. The men who were bribed with good things, men who were threatened with bad. Men who were simply misled, taught that abusing and subjugating women meant they were doing the respectable thing.

But unlike the girls, these men had a choice in what they did.

We didn't. I didn't. My mom didn't.

"Did you murder my mom?"

He released my face, sat back, then clasped his hands in his lap. His lips curved into a smirk, then a sneer, then a macabre smile. He looked proud. Of me for figuring it out? Or of himself for being so cruel?

"I always knew you were a smart girl, Nicolette." He nodded at Jason. "That's why I knew you'd be perfect for our Jason. He's a good boy. So good, in fact, he still calls you his fiancée even though he's read your cute little diary. You want to know a secret?" He pulled a pack of Juicy Fruit gum from his pocket, chose a stick, then offered me one.

I glared at him. I hated him and everything he stood for.

He tilted his head as if to say, "suit yourself" and unwrapped the gum, then began to chew. After pocketing the pack, he leaned close again. "Jason had no idea about any of this." He spread his hands in acknowledgement of the room and the other men standing aside him. "The last person I had in line to become Champion couldn't handle it, so now I wait a little while longer to introduce them to this aspect of our Faith. Waiting for them to mature helps eliminate disappointment." He balled up the tiny silver wrapper then placed it neatly on the dresser.

"Did you murder my mom?" I yelled.

He punched me in the face before I ever saw his fist. My head whipped to the side before the *crack* of the impact rang out. Fire radiated through my skull and teeth.

My jaw. I think he broke my jaw.

Jason struggled to get to me, but Jeremy and someone else pulled him away from the foot of my bed and shoved him out of the room. I was lucky to have seen it through the stars winking in my field of vision.

"Don't. Interrupt. Me." Malachi said calmly.

I held my face in the palm of my hand, but he grabbed my chin and forced me to look at him again. "I liked Regina, I really did. She was smart like you, and beautiful. That's why I hired her to be my bookkeeper. She was discreet and kept to the Faith. The life of a single mother, a widow, isn't easy, but she was as honorable as any of our Matrons. I respected her. I would have never granted her so much if I didn't hold her in such high regard. And that was my mistake."

One Mama paid the ultimate price for.

His face went fully sinister. "A bitch will always bark. Thanks to you, Jason has now learned this lesson, and I'm confident he won't make the same mistake I did." He buffed his nails on his shirt like he hadn't a care in the world. "Where did you hide my belongings, Nicolette? I assure you, you don't want me to ask again."

I couldn't speak. Blood dripped from my nose over my lips. My head pounded, my ears buzzed. My mouth was… not right. I couldn't open it. Speaking was impossible.

He squeezed my face. White hot pain shot through my head and neck, then I felt weightless. Detached. Out of my body, but not. The agony shorted my pain receptors, numbing my body and clearing my mind. I had awareness of self like I'd never experienced. Nothing he could do to me, nothing he could take from me, would ever change that. I had no fear. If this was my last moment, I would die with dignity.

Hatred spewed off the Champion. The man I'd revered and feared for as long as I could remember was nothing but a petulant, spoiled child. A bully who used violence to get what he wanted. Up until a moment ago, that would have terrified me. Now, calm washed over me. I was content. I had no chance of saving myself, and that liberated me.

Who knew impending death ushered in peace?

There is nothing to fear but fear itself

The Sacred Text resounded through my heart. Like its own heartbeat and I knew no matter what happened next, I would be okay. This man took so much from so many. He violated countless victims. He robbed me of my mother, my innocence, my sense of self. There was no way I would give him Micah too.

"Don't… have… them." I forced the words through my teeth.

"We know you don't have them, girl," Grand Elder Brown said. "Where did you *put* them?"

I shook my head and immediately regretted the motion. "Don't… know."

Malachi dug his fingers into my chin, turned my head, shoved the broken side of my face into the mattress.

As I screeched, everything went dark.

THIRTY-NINE

MICAH

O N MY WAY home, I agonized over leaving Nikki. She was more worried than usual but in just a few days it'd all be over anyway. I slung the bag over my shoulder but as I neared the end of the path. Before exiting the orange orchards, I heard voices. Sticking to the shadows, I inched forward. Several people milled about, huddled in groups. Far from normal.

I checked my watch. 10:40 p.m. Way too late for socializing. Or anything else.

I backtracked to Torrence Avenue instead of taking Chestnut, staying a few trees deep inside the orchards so no one could see me. Finding Torrence empty, I broke into a light jog. As soon as I crossed the street, I retreated into the shadows again. I made it to my block without incident, but as I passed the Richters' house, I heard a voice through their opened window—Elder Chris.

"They found something at Nicolette Simms's place. They'll question her there."

Silence.

He must be on the phone. I crouched beside a bush under his window.

"They didn't say."

Silence.

"If the items aren't at her place, they'll bring her back to the Threshing Floor. I'm sure she'll tell them anything they want to know."

The Threshing Floor? Damn it! I tiptoed away from the window then jogged toward my house. I came to a halt when I spotted my dad talking with Elder Hamilton and Elder Brooks on the sidewalk.

They must know I had something to do with this. I needed my truck but couldn't get to it while they stood there. I ducked behind the large trash bin at the end of the block and pulled out my phone to text Shawn.

We won't make it to Saturday. We go now. Ask Mr. Johnson where's the Threshing Floor.

I waited behind that trash bin until Hamilton and Brooks left. My dad looked up and down the block before going inside. It'd been just over twenty minutes. The stench from the trash can had embedded itself in my clothes. I checked my phone. The display lit up. I'd missed a call—from Jason fucking Tucker. I was going to kill him and anyone else who touched her.

I smashed the call back button. He picked up before the first ring ended.

"What did you do to her, you fucking prick?" I tried to whisper but didn't quite manage to stay quiet.

"Fuck you, Micah. You think I'd call you of all people if I wasn't trying to help?" His voice was low. I could barely hear him.

"What did you do to her, and where is she right now?"

"The room behind Malachi's office at his house."

"I'm coming."

"No, there's—"

I pressed the disconnect button before he could continue. I didn't want to hear his weasley voice for another second.

I ran to the front door of my house, debating for less than a second about going inside. There wasn't another way into the garage, and I needed my truck. I opened the door.

My dad, the asshole, sat at his desk. He was looking at his phone but dropped it when I entered. "What have you gotten yourself mixed up in?" He walked toward me.

I didn't have time to answer him. I walked down the hallway to the door leading to the garage. His footsteps sounded behind me, but I paid them no mind—until he pushed me. I stumbled, nearly fell. After regaining my balance, I wheeled around then shoved him as hard as I could. He staggered back a few steps.

"Micah! You get yourself mixed up with that stupid girl, and I will disown you!"

Did he think that was a threat? Like he hadn't disowned me when I dropped out of that filthy Examination? When I told him I didn't want to be next in line for Champion designation? After I out, they chose Tucker, and other than Community business, he hadn't spoken to me since.

"Tommy? Micah?" Mom appeared at the back of the hallway. She walked out of her room? "Why do I hear yelling?" She was hunched over, leaning against the wall to hold herself up.

I raced toward her and stood her upright.

"What's going on, Micah?"

"Everything's fine. I'm just leaving for a bit." I'd have to leave her here with him if I were going to make it to Nikki in time. Given what

I'd discovered, I didn't trust them with her for any length of time, and I'd wasted too much of it already.

"You're not going anywhere." Dad was on me fast, pulling at the bag on my left shoulder. He was going to rip it. I let my right hand off of Mom and threw a solid punch to his temple.

Mom screamed and swatted at me.

His eyes went wide. He limped to the side, then fell onto the hardwood floor with a thud.

Mom screamed and shook her head "Micah, what are you doing? What have you done to your father?"

Her small frame slid down the wall. She crawled beside her unconscious husband then patted his cheeks.

I hated for her to see me like this—see us like this—but I couldn't keep pretending. Not even for her sake. Too much had happened, and Nikki was in danger. I would get them both out, but Nikki was in more danger. I had to help her first.

I bent down to her, but she swatted me away. "What have you done?" She shrieked. "What have you done?"

"Mom, listen." I grabbed her by the shoulders, careful not to press too tight. Her bones felt brittle in my hands, and her skin was sickly pale. I couldn't remember the last time she'd had a breath of fresh air. Dad wouldn't allow her outside. It was as if he wanted to speed her end.

"Dad has done some really bad things, and there's a girl I need to help, right now."

She just wailed. I don't know if she heard a word I said. She was patting my dad on his shoulder and calling his name.

"Mom, he'll be okay. He's just knocked out. Please, let me put you in bed."

"No, you have to help your dad. You can't leave him like—"

"Mom, I have to go. I'll be back."

I stood, looked at her, pleaded with her to let me put her to bed. But she wouldn't listen. As much as it hurt me to see her like that, I left.

She would be fine. Even her lying, cheating husband would be fine. Nikki wouldn't.

∞ Q

THE GRILL OF my truck crashed through the golden gates leading to Malachi's estate.

I'd dreamed of doing that a thousand times and a twinge of satisfaction came over me at the dent I'd left behind.

The despicable man lived on a ten-acre plot. I sped past the tennis courts, past a rose garden past an ornate fountain. Finally, I reached his ostentatious circular driveway.

Jeremy stood at the front door, thick arms folded across his chest. Guess he heard the crash.

I parked, grabbed the baseball bat I kept on the floor of the backseat, then hopped out of the truck.

He glared at me. "What's wrong, little Micah? Mama didn't read you a bedtime story tonight?"

I climbed the steps two at a time.

"You're a big man with your little bat. You gonna use that on your sweet girlfriend?"

I growled and prepared to swing.

He pulled a gun, pointed it at my face.

I froze. My breath caught in my lungs. I knew he'd put up a fight, but I hadn't considered him having a weapon. I couldn't die like this.

"You really thought I was going to let you hit me? Stupid boy." He chuckled and stepped closer to me. "That's your problem—you think you're smarter than everybody. But you're the dumbest one here, little Micah. You could've had all of this, but now you're staring death in the face. You and your girlfriend, as soon as we get the documents back. Where are they? In your truck?"

I stared at him but wouldn't say a word and he didn't know what I knew.

"Of course they're in the truck. You're the only person dumb enough to bring the evidence—"

Tucker slammed a 2x4 into the side of his head. Twice.

Jeremy fell hard on the stairs.

I grabbed his gun then patted him down to see if he had any other weapons. He didn't. I took a set of keys—just in case.

"He's not dead, is he?" Tucker looked shocked. Fucking wimp.

I didn't even look at him. "He's napping. Where is she?"

"I just saved your life. You could at least thank me."

"Thank you. Where is she?" I didn't have time to exchange pleasantries with a fool.

"I don't know about you, but I don't go around beating people or shooting people."

"You just molest little girls?"

"I had no idea—"

"I'm not here for you. Where is she?"

"There are others in there with her." Jason stalled.

"We need to go. Now. Are you going to show me where they have her, or do I need to find her myself?" I walked past him toward the front doors.

Malachi's office was in the back of the mansion. The room was supposed to be behind that.

Tucker went ahead of me. We passed a theatre room, an indoor swimming pool, and a large den before reaching his office. The Bright Lord's Faith symbol was engraved on both doors. The handles were as thick as my bat and ran the length of the door, floor to ceiling.

He swallowed. "I'll go in first to see where everyone is, then I'll come back for you."

I hated his plan, and I hated listening to him, but it made sense. I dipped my head once in agreement.

He pulled the handle then stepped inside. The door opened and closed without a sound.

I waited in silence for him to come back. And waited. And waited.

After ten minutes, I yanked on the door. It was lighter than it looked and slid open with ease. I peeked inside before entering—no one was in the immediate area. The carpet was a deep purple and very plush. It absorbed my steps, but I still advanced cautiously. At the back of the office sat a mahogany stained desk. On the wall behind it was a framed word in bold black print upon a sparkling golden backdrop.

CHAMPION.

Paintings of himself, his wife, and two daughters hung on one wall, and I wondered where they were tonight. Why didn't we see them as we made our way through the house?

I put that thought out of mind, circled around his high-backed brown leather chair, then pressed my ear to the wall—no, not wall. A camouflaged door. I couldn't hear anything. No voices, no scuffles. No sounds at all.

The gun felt slick in my hand, so I gripped it tight. I'd never used one before. Never had a reason to. If necessary tonight, I'd figure it out. As soon as I opened that door, I didn't know what I'd find. Saving Nikki was worth it.

She'd been so scared. I should have taken her to the police station right then. We had all the evidence we needed, but I'd been worried about the innocent people in the community. I'd been worried about my mom. And what did we get for our troubles? Nikki had been abducted—and Lord knew what else. I knocked my dad out in front of my mom. And now I was breaking and entering the Champion's home with a gun in my hand. Jeremy wasn't completely wrong. I did think I was smarter than them, but this was a stupid way to show it.

I opened the door to find Jason unconscious and sagging in a chair. Someone pulled my arm, knocking the gun from my hand. I took the brunt of a tackle, and crashed down to the floor. My elbow cracked on the marble tile. I tried to rise, but someone's foot pressed on my chest, holding me down.

Elder Tucker.

My uncle stepped beside him, shaking his head. "I should've kicked you out when you dropped out of Examination, Nephew. Such a disappointment."

This wasn't the way things were supposed to go down. I had a plan—a good plan—but it had fallen apart. Nikki had been taken. Even from the floor, I could see her splayed on the mattress behind them. What had the bastards done to her?

"I hope you burn in hell," I spat.

Elder Tucker stomped on my chest, and I heaved.

"Oh no, nephew, that's where you're going." He pushed Elder Tucker away from me then raised his foot.

A loud boom sounded.

"Fresno Police Department! Put your hands up, now!"

FORTY

MY EYES OPENED to broken beams of sunlight streaming through white window blinds.

White window blinds? I didn't have blinds in my room. I sprang to a seated position then immediately fell back. A pounding, deep and sharp, tore through my head, forcing my eyes shut. I placed the palm of my hand at my temple as if that would stop the pain.

"Nikki!" The familiar voice set me at ease. At least partially.

Then a hand gripped my left shoulder.

Oh no! They took me! I screamed.

No, I didn't. I tried, but my mouth wouldn't open. The only sound that broke through were whimpers, then my racing pulse drowned those out. I thrashed and kicked. They might kill me, but I wouldn't go easy.

The woman who'd called my name demanded I calm down.

I wouldn't calm down! I'd been calm for years and horrible things happened. Not just to me, but my mom and other girls.

"Open your eyes! Nikki, it's me. Reen. It's me, Maureen." She repeated.

Reen?

I fell still and opened my eyes. Leaning over me and looking exactly as she did the last time I saw her, other than the frighteningly worried expression. Even so, she was beautiful. And she was here! Golden dreadlocks fell along the sides of her face, glowing in the sunlight that streamed into the room. She looked like an angel.

"It's me, Nikki. It's me." Her worried eyes softened, and a smile tugged at the corner of her mouth as recognition calmed my defenses.

I didn't know when the tears started, but my face was soaked.

She wrapped me in an embrace, and I sobbed into her arms. She was safe, and she was here. I was safe, and I was here.

"How are you feeling this morning, Nicolette?" A man in a white coat entered my room and introduced himself as Dr. Schwartz.

Reen released me and stepped back.

"On a scale of one to ten, what's your pain level? Raise your fingers to tell me."

My fingers? Why not just—I couldn't speak. Couldn't open my mouth!

I straightened up, looked around. Reen sat in a chair next to my *hospital* bed. So, I was in a hospital. There was an IV in my arm and a machine displayed my vital signs.

I held up six fingers. If I didn't talk or attempt to move my mouth, I felt a little better.

"Okay. I'll get the nurse in here to increase your pain medication. In the meantime, there are two police officers who wish to interview you about the events that occurred last night. Is it okay if I send them in now?"

So that's why I couldn't open my mouth. My jaw was fractured.

The memory of Malachi hitting me flashed through my mind. I looked at Reen and attempted to speak through clenched teeth. "Micah? What happened to Micah?"

"Are you referring to Micah Fox?" Dr. Schwartz answered. "He's being treated one floor down. I believe he's scheduled to be discharged later this afternoon."

I sighed with relief. He was alive. We were both alive! And the police were here. We got out. We actually got out. We actually got out! And the tears resumed.

"Can you give her a moment before sending in the police?" Reen asked the doctor.

I assume he agreed because I heard the door shut.

Reen told me everything that happened after I blacked out in what Leadership called the Threshing Floor. Micah reached out to Shawn, and Shawn brought Mr. Johnson and the police. Though Dr. Scott and Jason had taken me, the Champion had done the most damage. And Jason… he played a role in rescuing me.

The officers took my full statement, starting with what happened to me when I was young, going through Mama finding out, them killing her to keep her quiet, Micah and me working together to gather evidence, and ending with what happened last night. They wouldn't let Reen remain in the room during the interview, but as soon as they left, she returned, and she stayed with me overnight. When I wasn't resting, she'd give me sips of ice water and share updates of what she'd been up to since her family was evicted.

I'd overexerted myself while giving my statement, and Reen struggled to understand my grunts, so I started texting.

Why didn't you reach out to me after you were evicted?

I could tell she was carefully choosing her words before speaking. Finally, she said, "When I was braiding your hair a couple days before your bridal retreat, you were nervous. Rightly so, but you'd just had a good conversation with Jason about your concerns and decided you would continue with the wedding. By then, Shawn and I had already decided to leave Bright Lakes after we married. There was no way we would raise any children of ours there."

I understood, though it still hurt to hear she made those decisions without telling me.

"I wanted to tell you but figured I should wait until after your wedding or sometime later but not right before you left on your retreat. It would've been selfish of me to put a damper on your happiness. Of course, I didn't know they would evict us. But once they did, I realized if you wanted to stay there with Jason, you would end up… just like them." Her voice shook.

"I didn't want to try to convince you why your decision was bad or why me leaving was good. You're my best friend, and we'd already argued about Jason. I knew you weren't ready to accept the truth of all that was happening in the community."

She placed her hand on my arm. "And I'm not saying that to be mean, Nikki. Please don't think I'm being a jerk right now. You'd made your decision, and there was no way they'd let you visit me or me visit you after you married into the Tucker family. So, I figured I'd let this be a clean break. I never expected any of this, though." Silent tears streamed down her face.

"Had I known you were ready to seek the truth, I would've done all I could to help." She reached for a tissue. "I also didn't know Shawn, Micah, and my dad had a plan this whole time. Remember when I told you Micah and Shawn wanted to start a business together?"

I remembered it hadn't made sense to me then.

"Well, they weren't just talking about business. They'd been working together for some time to expose Malachi and the other Elders.

Apparently, it wasn't until you told Micah about your mom's journal that they had what they needed to move forward. Last night, when Micah texted Shawn…" She took a few deep breaths and wiped tears from her face. "We were so scared. That's when he told me everything." She blew her nose. "I really hope you can forgive me."

I didn't need to think about forgiving her. Maureen always told me the truth. Even when I didn't want to believe or receive it. Living in that place was a constant, internal battle to live a truly honest life. But it wasn't impossible. Reen was proof of that.

She was also proof that sometimes living an honest life meant being punished for it.

Of course, Friend. I love you. Thank you for telling me.

Her phone rang. She read my text then wrapped me in a hug.

ଯର

After an X-ray of my jaw the next morning, and receiving instructions for managing a wire-sealed mouth, the doctor discharged me.

I DIDN'T KNOW where to go or what to do, but the Johnson family made my decisions for me. Mrs. Johnson insisted I stay with them until I got on my feet. Mr. Johnson's friend was renting them a two-story townhouse until they secured a home of their own. She insisted there was plenty of room and wouldn't hear any argument from me.

Of course she wouldn't. I couldn't speak. Nor did I have anywhere else to go.

She drove me and Reen to the townhouse. Thomas waited for us in front of the carport.

He opened my door, helped me out, thanked the Bright Lord I was safe, then told me to let him know if I needed anything. When I stepped out of the car, and around the lawn, there was Micah standing in their doorway.

Like the true pillar of strength he was, Micah waited patiently for me.

I sobbed as I walked toward him. He looked weary. Mrs. Johnson had said his ribs were badly bruised in a fight with Mr. Tucker, so his movement was limited. As much as I wanted to throw myself into his arms, I resisted.

He touched the side of my face, scanning me head to toe as if searching for additional injuries. I placed my hand atop his and leaned into the warmth of his skin. He was safe. I was safe. That's all I needed.

He laced his fingers through mine.

"I can show you where you'll be sleeping, Nikki, then you and Micah can catch up." Mrs. Johnson said as she approached and Micah backed out of the doorway, allowing us to follow him inside.

A flight of stairs stood to the right of the entrance, and a small living room sat to the left. It opened to a dining room, and beyond was a medium-sized kitchen.

"I'll wait for you down here."

Those were the first words I heard him speak since we parted at the orchard. It felt like a lifetime ago. A nightmare ago.

"Micah isn't able to climb stairs just yet." Reen began climbing the carpeted steps.

I reluctantly unlaced my fingers from his, already saddened by the loss of his touch, then I followed my friend up the narrow staircase.

"My dad got extra beds yesterday. One for Micah downstairs in the room with Shawn, and one for you in my room."

At the top of the stairs was the door to a bathroom. On either side of it was one bedroom.

"That's my parent's room." Reen said pointing to the left. "We're on the right." Carpets lined the hallway and the walls were bare, but it was clean and safe and everyone I loved was here. I couldn't have been happier.

The bedroom was small but more than enough for us to share. Two twin-sized beds sat on opposite ends of the carpeted room, the headboards separated by a central window. A decent-sized closet stretched along the wall near the footboards.

"My dad and Micah had your things brought here this morning." The suitcases I'd packed a few days earlier stood next to my new bed. The suitcases which caused a domino effect leading to my and Micah's injuries.

"Did your doctor give you a list of things you can eat and medication you need, Nikki?" Mrs. Johnson asked.

I'd forgotten she was behind us.

"If so, I can make a run to the store and pick them up while you get comfortable."

I nodded, handed her the list, then followed Reen around as she showed me the rest of the house. There wasn't much to it, but it was perfect.

We had dinner together at their small dining table. It was made for six, but we scooted in folding chairs and made it work. While everyone talked and dined on asada tacos, refried beans, and Spanish rice, I sipped a protein shake through a straw and occasionally sent messages to our newly created group text. Other than our injuries, I couldn't have been happier.

"We were really worried about you for a while, Nikki." Mr. Johnson's expression showed his grief and relief. "We knew once these two got engaged"—he pointed at Shawn and Reen— "we'd have to make some quick decisions. Tucker and Malachi go way back, so there was no way you would have been able to remain connected to Maureen."

"We prayed you'd see through the facade and make the right choice, honey," Mrs. Johnson added. "But things like this can be really confusing. Unless you can accept the ugly truth, no one can help."

Mr. Johnson nodded. "Bright Lakes wasn't corrupt. It really was a great place for believers. But once Malachi won the position of Champion…"

"That was over twenty years ago," Mrs. Johnson said.

He sighed. "It doesn't matter when. Just that it happened. Malachi started adding a bunch of new rules and guidelines—all kinds of restrictions to keep strong-willed people out and punish good people who stayed. Then other Communities followed his example and implemented the same standards. People easily fall for his charms before realizing what they're doing."

"I never agreed with it. Didn't want nothing to do with it. I tried to tell you." Mrs. Johnson folded her arms and rocked in her chair.

"I know, I know." He swatted at his wife like a pesky fly. "I realized too late. Anyway, Nikki, we're glad you and Micah got out. All that's left is for the people to find out for themselves."

"Dad, do you think he'll go to prison?" Timothy asked.

"He's got good attorneys and some people high up who support him, but the evidence against him is strong. All we can do is hope and pray justice is served."

"I wish we could do something more," Reen said.

After dinner, Shawn and Reen went for an evening stroll, giving Micah and me some privacy, though I'm sure they wanted some alone time too. I lay facing him on his narrow bed, careful not to get too close or put pressure on his chest. But he pulled me as close as he could manage and draped an arm around my waist.

"I'm sorry I didn't realize what was happening until it was too late."

I leaned away from him far enough to make eye contact and shook my head. None of this was his fault. How could he blame himself?

"You told me to call the cops, and I didn't. I was so focused on exposing them to the whole community that I didn't consider they would move so quickly after I took his stash. I didn't even know they'd realize I had it so fast. I should have thought of that and moved to the next step right then." A tear fell from his eyes. "I thought you were dead."

The sight of it ripped my heart. Knowing how he fought for me, put himself in danger to save me... not to mention all those girls. He was my living, breathing hero.

"Before the police came into that room, I saw you on that mattress." His voice was husky, and he didn't finish his thought.

I wiped the tears now streaming down his handsome face then reached for my phone.

I might be hurt, but I'll be just fine. We'll both fully recover from this.

I raised the phone up so he could see what I wrote.

He nodded. "Everyone was arrested. My dad, Malachi... all of them."

I hated to ask, but I needed to know. So, I texted again.

"What happened to Jason?"

"Turns out Tucker really didn't know about the Elders' extracurricular activities. He didn't know about the girls or your mom or what they planned to do with you. In the end, he did what he could to help. And if it wasn't for him, I'd be dead."

He told me about what happened with his dad, and Jeremy, and the events that ultimately led to my rescue. I recounted the events that followed my return home after our meeting that night.

Somewhere in between talking and texting, I fell asleep knowing I was safe and free. And my sleep was sweet.

The End

AUTHOR'S NOTE

Did you enjoy this book? If so, indie authors like me need all the help we can get. Please review this book on Amazon and/or Goodreads so other readers can more easily find it.

ACKNOWLEDGMENTS

This story flew out of me! In five months, it transformed from thought to completed draft. But not without help!

I am more than grateful for my vivacious team of beta readers. You ladies did not hold back and the debates amongst yourselves steered me true. Thank you for your helpful feedback and your encouragement along the way.

Elise Ayres, Grace Berg, Sara Bosse, Latasha McCoy, Andrea Hurst, Andi Lambert, Laqusha Locke, Lynette McIntosh-Madrigal, Jamilah Moore, Amie Penning, Jenny Plumb, and Marcy Pusey.

To my patient editor, Staci Troilo. Your kindness helped me understand the labor of love editing really is, and I thank you for polishing my rocky story.

Angie Zapata and Katelyn Marotta. You believed in this story from day one and read all of my horrible first and second drafts. I am humbled by your faith in me and in this story. Thank you from the bottom of my heart.

My children, who let me sit at the kitchen table for months on end and not cook dinner. Thank you for bringing me snacks and making sure I went to sleep on time!

To you reader, for choosing to pick up this book or click the ebook link. Thank you for reading this story to the end, and I hope you saw parts of yourself, or someone else you know, within the characters.

Thank you all for supporting my book! More to come...

ABOUT THE AUTHOR

Joyce's debut novel, *A Truth That Whispers Lies*, is a testament to her belief in every woman's ability to find true liberation from societal, cultural, or religious limitations. She is a fan of wild dandelions and uses them as a metaphor throughout her bodies of work.

Joyce lives in central California where the summers are long and the fruit is abundant!